THE COLDEST TRAIL

A LONE MCGANTRY WESTERN

WAYNE D. DUNDEE

WOLFPACK
PUBLISHING
— EST 2013 —

Paperback Edition
Copyright © 2021 Wayne D. Dundee

Wolfpack Publishing
6032 Wheat Penny Avenue
Las Vegas, NV 89122

wolfpackpublishing.com

This book is a work of fiction. Any references to historical events, real people or real places are used fictitiously. Other names, characters, places and events are products of the author's imagination, and any resemblance to actual events, places or persons, living or dead, is entirely coincidental.

Paperback ISBN 978-1-64734-352-1
Kindle ISBN 978-1-64734-351-4

THE COLDEST TRAIL

PART ONE

CHAPTER 1

——

Lone McGantry cursed himself for allowing his anticipation over what lay ahead to make him neglectful about his back trail. Avoiding those kind of mistakes was what had kept him alive this long on the frontier of the American West. What was more, given the guaranteed risk of his current venture, now was especially no time to start getting sloppy.

It was dusk of a mid-May day in the heart of Nebraska's fabled Sandhills. Thanks to heavy snowmelt and plentiful spring rains, the surrounding landscape of treeless, endlessly rising and falling grassy hills was painted a rich green, now tinted bluish in the twilight. The air was still, cooling rapidly after the afternoon's heat. Lone had stopped for night camp on a gentle western slope with a thin stream, lined by a few scraggly bushes running along its base.

After watering his horses—mount and pack animal—he'd staked them to graze and then carried his saddle gear to a patch of flattened grass a few yards away where he intended to cook some supper and eventually spread his bedroll. It was as he was turning away from the stream, freshly filled coffee pot in one hand and some brushy twigs for kindling in the other, that he spotted the brief, telltale reflection of something on a hilltop back to the east and a bit south. It came and went in the span of an eyeblink but it was long enough to heighten Lone's awareness and provide what might prove to be a welcome warning. Whatever it was, it wasn't something natural to the terrain. Glass or gun barrel, was Lone's guess, catching a leftover streak of sunlight up there on that crest of higher ground.

Having noted and registered the brief flash for what he suspected it might be, Lone didn't let it outwardly alter his movements. If the glint had come from binoculars or a spyglass trained on him, he didn't want to give any sign that he now knew someone was there. Returning to the spot where he intended to make his cook fire, he knelt down and proceeded to strip the leaves off the twigs he'd carried from the stream and then broke the dry stems into smaller pieces for kindling. As he worked at getting a fire going, his mind raced.

The route he was taking wasn't a commonly traveled one. Except for the remote trading post he'd visited earlier in the day, there were no towns or accommodations of any kind for two or three days in any direction. Maybe a few scattered cattle ranches—but all afternoon there'd been no sign of cattle to warrant any wranglers having business this far out, especially so late in the day.

No, Lone decided, either he was being followed or somebody just happened to be taking the same route he was. One seemed as unlikely as the other. But then, on further reflection, he remembered the two drifters who had shown up back at the trading post just as he was concluding his business there with Ansel Clement. He hadn't paid the pair much attention other than to make them for a couple of shiftless types looking to land somewhere long enough to make some getting-by money before they would move on once more. They hadn't struck him as being particularly dangerous or menacing yet, again, he'd barely taken time to notice them. At the moment, his mind had been churning too excitedly on something else—the unexpected bit of luck Clement had provided and the desire to follow through on it by getting on the trail again as soon as possible.

So now here he was. On the trail. And wishing he *had* paid more attention to the two drifters. Not only that, but also wishing he'd paid more attention to his back trail throughout the afternoon. Had he done so, he would have recognized long before this that somebody was moving up behind him.

Lone cursed himself again. For many years (until recent times when hostilities with the Red Man had faded to the point of forcing him to do some drifting of his own between odd jobs), he had been one of the most renowned Indian scouts on the plains. Survival meant staying alert to your surroundings at all times. Doing so had become as natural and automatic to him as breathing. This lapse today, even if turned out to be something minor, was unforgivable and something he damn well couldn't start making a habit of.

When the fire was crackling good, Lone dumped a handful of coffee beans that he'd mashed that morning into the pot and set it on the edge of the flames to start brewing. He dismissed his original intent to also fry up some bacon. All things considered, he would keep his supper meal simple. The coffee would wash down some beef jerky and a couple of the biscuits he'd purchased back at the trading post. That would suffice.

Lone squatted on his haunches before the fire, slowly chewing a bite of jerky, waiting for the coffee to boil. With darkness deepening around him, in the flickering light of the flames he was revealed to be a tall, solidly built man nearing forty. Beneath a shock of thick brown hair in need of trimming was a square, ruggedly featured face anchored by a prominent nose extending from between restless, deep set blue eyes. He moved with deceptively powerful grace for a big man and though at the moment he appeared outwardly quite relaxed, calm even, on the inside every muscle was poised and ready to hurl him into motion if need be.

The next hour would paint a pretty clear picture as far as the intent of whoever was back there to the southeast. If it was an innocent fellow traveler who just happened to be coming along in Lone's wake, then there was every reason to expect the fire would draw him on ahead, seeking to share the camp. On the other hand, if whoever was back there continued to hold off, then that would signal he (or they) were waiting for darkness to thicken even more before moving in … and not for a friendly visit.

By the time Lone was done eating and had had enough coffee, it was full dark. No one had come forward requesting to share his camp. Though the moon was being lazy about making an appearance, the first early stars were starting to glitter weakly in the sky. If he'd had his 'druthers, Lone would have wished for some cloud cover this night. But it wasn't to be, there wasn't the slightest wisp of a cloud anywhere in sight. What was more—if he'd been paying closer attention, damn it—he would have chosen a campsite with some kind of cover close by. As it was, this slope was wide open on all sides. The only hope was the low, puny clumps of brush down along the edge of the stream.

But Lone had fought against Comanches and Apaches who seemingly could find concealment behind a pebble or a stunted weed. From them he learned to use what the land gave you. So, the puny clumps of brush would have to do.

After the fire had died to a thin curl of smoke rising out of gray ashes, Lone stretched out in his bedroll. He pulled his saddlebags and possibles pack close in beside him, settled back against his upturned saddle for a pillow, tipped his Stetson down over his eyes. Around him, the sounds of a Sandhills night, complete with the lonesome wail of a faraway coyote, floated on the cooling air. Lone listened to these but, more importantly, he listened for any sound that didn't belong.

*****

Two and a half hours later, Lone still lay motionless and keenly alert in the darkness. Only he was no longer in his bedroll. Instead, he was a dozen yards away, bellied down tight to the damp ground amidst the scraggly brush beside the stream. Under the cover of darkness, he had slowly, silently extracted himself from the bedroll, leaving a lump meant to be his sleeping form by shoving the saddlebags and possibles pack beneath the blankets in his place. Then he'd wormed his way down slope to find concealment and wait.

Patience in situations like this was something Lone had acquired during his scouting days. He'd learned it from hostile braves who were capable of displaying the patience of a stone until it was time to strike with full ferocity—making it a lesson to be absorbed quickly and held tight by anyone meaning to survive against them.

If all of tonight's precaution turned to be for naught, then he might end up feeling a little silly come morning. But he would still be alive. More to the point, if the steps he was taking proved to be warranted, then he'd be giving himself a chance to remain alive under those circumstances as well.

It wasn't much longer before Lone got the answer as to whether his instincts were accurate. His big gray gelding, Ironsides, gave the first indication—a warning chuff that said he'd caught wind of something or someone he didn't like coming too close. The former scout smiled wolfishly, glad the waiting was over and that it was time to find out what his stalkers were going to try.

CHAPTER 2

The way Lone had it figured, the men closing in on his camp had one of two things in mind—either they would settle for the minimal risk of trying to spirit away his horses; or they would go for the whole works, take everything and leave only his carcass behind.

For a pair of lowlifes like he'd seen back at the trading post, the resale price for a couple of stolen horses would make an acceptable payday. And, as stated, at a lesser risk. But the rest of what was also available—the supply packs, the saddle gear and guns, his boots, and especially the money he had revealed when dealing with Clement—would be hard to resist, especially at two to one odds.

Shortly after Ironsides' chuff, Lone heard another sound he took as a sufficient sign of the intruders' full intent. One of the clumsy fools stepped in the water a few yards down stream. So, they were closing pincer-like on his campsite. If they'd only meant to take the horses, there'd be no reason for one of them to be down here at the bottom of the slope.

Lone hugged the ground tighter and at the same time tightened his grip on the already drawn Colt .44 he held wrapped in one fist. He wished he also had his Winchester Yellowboy rifle, but he'd opted to leave it in its saddle scabbard up at the campsite so as not to have its absence look suspicious. With his night vision long since adjusted, he could see the camp fairly clearly in the muted illumination of the stars and the now risen half moon. So, he had to reckon his stalkers could discern the same. But that was okay, Lone told himself; if there was only two of them and lead started flying at these close quarters, his six-gun ought to be sufficient to handle the job.

As if bidden by that thought, the answer to if or when there would be gunplay was abruptly provided. From a short way up the slope, a nasally voice shouted down, "I got hold of the horses, Everett—go ahead and give him what fer!"

An instant later, the man standing in the water cut loose with a repeating rifle of his own and began pouring round after round into the lumpy bedroll Lone had abandoned. The quietness of the night was shattered. Horses shrieked in alarm, gunfire rolled out over the grassy dunes.

Up to that point having been forced to remain totally still in order to maintain his cover, Lone now tossed those restraints aside with an angry snarl. He twisted onto one hip and then jackknifed to a half-sitting position, head and shoulders thrusting suddenly up out of the rustling, shuddering brush. The rifleman, who until then had only been a sound in the water, now loomed very distinct before Lone. The murky outline of his shape was discernible on its own but made even more so by the muzzle flashes of his rifle. Lone extended his arm and took almost casual aim. The Colt bucked twice in his fist, spitting flame and lead.

The rifleman jerked and spun under the double impact of bullets striking only a second apart. The rifle dropped from his grasp and he toppled away and down, emitting a dying, gurgling whimper before hitting the shallow water flat, throwing a silvery splash in the moon- and starlight.

Knowing that his shots had made their own telltale flash that would show his position to the other ambusher up on the slope, Lone immediately crabbed half a dozen feet away and came to a crouch behind another puny clump of brush. He was facing up the slope, focused on the spot where he knew he had staked his horses. But visibility was too poor at that distance, even under the clear sky, for him to be able to clearly make out either the animals or the nasally-voiced man who'd called down claiming he had hold of them. If the man started shooting from that spot, Lone would have to hold off returning fire—even with a muzzle flash to aim at—for fear of hitting one of his horses. If it came to trading more lead, he'd have to try and figure out a way to flush the bastard and put him on the run before he could finish him.

And then came the revelation that the man on the slope seemed hesitant to join in more shooting. "Everett?" he called down in a tentative, slightly quavering voice. "What happened? Why'd you stop … are you sure you got him blasted to hell and gone?"

"The only thing Everett is sure about," Lone hollered back, "is that his blastin' days are over. And the only thing that's hell and gone is him—I figure he's passin' through Satan's fiery front gate right about now."

"Everett! Why you letting him say those thing?" The second ambusher's voice turned strident with a mixture of fear and disbelief. "Call him out for the dirty lyin' dog that he is!"

Lone chuckled tauntingly. "You ain't very quick on the uptake, are you pal? Everett's days of tellin' anybody anything are past … less'n you want to pay a visit to him

down in the hot place and talk it over with him there."
Lone paused, his voice turning raspy when he added, "I'd
be plumb happy to arrange transportation for you—unless
you throw your guns down right now and step forward with
your hands in the air."

Now the man on the slope bridled. "No damn way that's
happenin'! Why ain't you dead, you sneaky bastard?"

"Because of exactly that—I'm sneaky," Lone told him.
"Plus, I got a brain instead of the dried up little peas rattlin'
around inside the skulls of a couple clumsy backshooters
like you and ol' Everett here. Though I reckon his is too
waterlogged by now to do any rattlin', even if he could still
wobble his stupid head."

"Shut up! Ain't it enough you killed him—there's no
call to run him down even more now that he's dead!"

"The real shame," Lone said, "would be if he ain't all the
way dead and we're wastin' time just talkin' about him."

"What do you mean he ain't dead?" wailed the man on
the slope. "You said you killed him!"

"I said I shot him," Lone countered. "I can't say for
positive he's dead because I ain't had no chance to check.
He's layin' over there in the water. The way this creek sorta
naturally burbles along, I can't tell but what he might be
blowin' bubbles, fightin' to try and keep breathin'."

"Well for God's sake go find out—don't let him drown!
What kind of cold-blooded monster are you?"

His anguish and concern for his fallen partner was
enough to cause the second ambusher to lower his guard
and step forward, moving away from the horses, as if
he wanted to rush to the creek and check on Everett
himself. This small bit of movement toward Lone was
enough to bring the man adequately into focus. The
former scout could now distinguish the pale blob of his

face, the murky outline of his body.

And he could also make out a long-barreled revolver held down alongside one hip. That made too much of a risk to take.

In answer to the question posed, Lone once more rasped, "The kind who don't cut slack to backshootin', ambushin' bastards like you." And, with those words, he again raised his Colt and triggered a .44 slug straight to the center of the pale blob.

CHAPTER 3

——

Although Lone had been pretty sure, even in the dark, the light of a new day revealed for certain that his two would-be ambushers were indeed the pair of drifters he'd encountered briefly back at Clement's trading post.

The whole reason for Lone traveling to the remote trading post to begin with, was that he'd learned widower Clement and his two sons had added a horse trading operation to their business a couple years back. The boys rounded up wild horses, broke them, then put them up for sale to the growing number of cattle ranches spreading into the area as well as to army buyers for the forts still functioning in the region. Sometimes the Clements also bought small herds for resale.

It was hearing about the latter practice that had drawn Lone's interest. He was looking neither to buy nor sell horses, not in this instance. But what he *was* looking for was a particular batch of horses—about twenty in number—that had been stolen from a small ranch down near North Platte a little over three months prior. More to the point, he was looking to catch up with the murdering polecats who had taken them and killed one of the ranchers they rightfully belonged to.

"The man they shot up was called Peg O'Malley. Me and him was partners in that little horse ranch, just gettin' it off the ground," Lone had explained to Clement. "He was an old mountain man who'd lost one leg years back to a grizzly. From then on he got by on a wooden pin from the knee down—hence how he came to be called Peg."

"Sounds like he must have been a pretty tough old bird," Clement remarked with an admiring smile.

"He was. Tough enough to hang on for several days after those skunks left him for dead. Hung on past all reason or expectation." Lone's expression had been grim as he related this. "You see, I was away for a spell on a job of work aimed at bringin' in some extra money for the ranch. So, I was at the far end of the state when the thieves hit. Waitin' for me to get back is what kept Peg clingin' to life. Clingin' to ask me a favor and to give me the one whisker of information I've got to go on about who waylaid him. They caught him by surprise, though, meanin' he had very little to give."

"So, the favor he asked was to avenge him. Right?" Clement asked.

Lone had responded with a single shake of his head. "No. He didn't have to ask that, he knew I would see to it. The favor was a personal matter—a specific request on where he wanted to be buried. Fulfillin' that obligation got a little complicated, took me away for a while longer. But now I'm back and I'm workin' on an obligation I set for myself ... trackin' down the scum who killed my partner and took our horses—and makin' 'em pay."

"Sounds like you have every right," Clement allowed. "But you sure got a mighty cold trail to try and follow."

"Maybe so. But it got a site warmer," Lone told him, "when I rode up and spotted that steeldust stallion you got in your corral yonder."

Clement's gaze had followed Lone's to the horse in question. "Me and my boys bought him several weeks back as part of ..." he started to say. But then he stopped short and his eyes darted back to Lone. "Hold on a minute. You ain't saying that horse came out of your herd that got stolen, are you?"

"Not part of the herd, no. But he got stole right along with rest. You see, that steeldust happened to be the personal mount of my partner."

"You sure it's the same one? I mean, steeldusts are a common enough breed."

"It's him. Rascal is his name." Lone pointed. "I can't see it from here, but the brand on his rump is a backward C with three prongs stickin' out of the curve. The Busted Spur brand. Mine and Peg's ... am I wrong?"

Clement shook his head, looking dismayed. "No, you ain't wrong." And then the rest of it, each man relating his side, had gotten pieced together from there.

Lone told how, since he had such little to go on—not knowing how many were in the gang of thieves, which way they had gone, not even exactly how many horses they'd taken—he began making wide, arcing sweeps to the north and slightly west, inquiring about a group of men pushing approximately twenty horses. He'd concentrated especially on some of the larger cattle operations who might have been in the market to add to their remudas. A wrangler at one of those had mentioned Clement.

Clement recounted that, yes, a little over two months earlier five men had shown up at his place with a string of twenty-two horses they were looking to sell. Their story was that they were former wranglers from a ranch off to the south that had gone belly up and the horses were part of their pay-off, in lieu of wages the ranch owner wasn't able to fully meet. The men said they wanted to get the best price they could get for the animals and then use that money to travel on to the gold fields up around Deadwood in the Dakotas. Since Clement had heard of a handful of small and medium-sized ranches struggling to survive after a particularly harsh winter, the story hadn't sounded unreasonable. So, he offered a lot price that he figured he could make a profit on later by selling the string piecemeal when mounts would be needed for the spring roundup on still-operating spreads, and the deal was struck.

"That steeldust is the last of the bunch," Clement had summed up. "As good as his lines are, he'd've been among the first to go if he hadn't pulled up lame and it took a long time to get it healed proper. He's sound now, though. Reckon him bein' left behind, so's you could spot him right away when you rode up, turned out to be a kind of cockeyed piece of luck for your search. Though, if you'd asked, I still would've told you what I could about those fellas who passed through. No reason not to—especially after hearin' the truth about what a lowdown bunch they was."

Lone had a hunch Clement wasn't being entirely honest when it came to having no suspicions about the men who'd brought in the horses, that they were honest wranglers who had accepted the animals in place of owed wages. More like he'd seen it as only a thinly plausible story. But with no strong evidence to contradict it, it nevertheless provided a chance to buy some good stock he could turn around and make an easy profit on.

If Lone had wanted, he could have made an issue about

the twenty-two stolen horses rightfully belonging to him. But he had little interest in trying to press that matter now, and even less time to waste with it. What interested him far more was getting Clement to live up to what he'd said about being willing to spill on "the lowdown bunch" who'd shown up with the string.

"I hadn't ever seen any of 'em around before, I can say that pretty certain. I've got a good memory for faces," Clement claimed, "and all of that bunch were strangers to me."

"What about names?" Lone asked.

"The only full name I caught was the one who signed the bill of sale. Henry Plow, was what he put down. He did it as sort of the representative for all of 'em, on account of some of the others not being able to write I don't think. I can show you that bill of sale inside, by the way. As to any other names, there was a couple more they tossed back and forth, familiar-like, amongst themselves. Elroy and, if I heard right, another one they called Scorch."

Lone's eyes bored into the trading post proprietor with increased intensity. "Scorch?"

"Uh-huh. Kinda odd, ain't it? But that's the way I heard it."

"How about descriptions?"

"Oh, they were a memorable bunch right enough. Quite a mix," Clement said. "Henry Plow, the one who did the signing, he was kind of a dandy. His clothes were dusty and showed some hard miles, but you could still tell they was of fine quality and it seemed a safe bet he liked to do some struttin' in 'em when they were brushed and fresh. The one called Elroy, he was an older fella. Sorta worn and tired and lookin', but still with some stringy toughness to him I'd bet, then there was a big brute of a Negra. Didn't say nothing, just sorta loomed over everybody, eyes all the time sweepin' on lookout. Another silent one was barely past a kid. Tall and slender, with wide eyes that just stared off into space most of the time. He was kinda spooky, a little tetched in the head I'm thinkin' and finally there was the one called Scorch. He was spooky too, but in a more straight-ahead way. Had an air of danger about him, like a coiled rattler ready to strike. Like he'd be *happy* for the chance. Made me think he was pissed off at the world for that scar he has to carry around on his face and was anxious to lash out and do some scarrin' of his own."

"What kind of scar on his face?" Lone's voice was barely above a whisper.

"A burn mark of some kind," came the answer. "Runs from the corner of his left eye down over his cheekbone, almost to the hinge of his jaw. All sickly pink and puckered, not at all pleasant to look at." Clement paused and then his eyebrows lifted in sudden realization. "Hey, now I get it. Scorch—that must be why they call him that."

Still in a raspy whisper, Lone said, "Yeah. Must be."

*****

It was the information gleaned from Clement that had spurred Lone away from the remote trading post in such an excited state that he'd failed to properly keep an eye on his back trail and subsequently almost paid a heavy price for his inattention.

After he and Clement finished their discussion out by the corral, they'd gone inside for a brief time. Clement made a production of showing his bill of sale for the twenty-two horses, even though Lone didn't ask for it. While inside, Lone had accepted the offer to take a noon meal of venison stew and fresh biscuits. Before leaving, he'd also purchased some extra cartridges, a few other items to replenish his supplies, and a sackful of the biscuits. It was during this time that the two drifters had wandered in. Clement's son had seen to their needs but it was obvious now, in hindsight, that the pair had been paying attention to more than just their own business. In Lone, they'd seen what represented a chance to acquire more than anything they could afford to purchase over the counter.

When Lone and Clement went back outside, there was one final matter Lone went ahead and took care of. He traded the pack horse he had arrived with for Rascal, Peg's steeldust from the corral. The latter was a superior animal, so under most circumstances it shouldn't have been an even-up trade. But the look in Lone's eye when he made his offer—a look that said, without words, *"you know damn well that animal is mine anyway"*—left Clement with no objection to the swap.

Thinking back on it now this morning, as he shoveled dirt over the shallow hole in which he'd planted his two would-be ambushers, Lone wondered fleetingly if Clement had anything to do with their coming after him. But no, he decided, the man wasn't cut from that kind of cloth. He might not be above leaning far enough toward the shady side to take in some stock of questionable ownership, but he didn't lean so far as to want any part of flat-out robbery and killing. The two drifters—Everett and whatever the other one was named—had acted on their own.

Considering the information Clement had given him— invaluable details Lone had been so sadly lacking before— the former scout was more than willing to forgive the man his trace of larceny. As to how trustworthy the information he'd provided might be, Lone believed it accurate to the best of Clement's recollection. The key had been his mention of the curly wolf called Scorch. That matched the one thing Peg had been able to tell Lone—apart from his burial wishes—as he lay dying. The handful of words Lone had never shared with another soul … *"Look for the man with the burned face!"*

That was all Lone had had to go on at the start. But now, thanks to Clement, he had considerably more. The number of men involved, a handful of names, and a possible destination.

It was still a mighty cold trail, but the signs to watch for along the way had become a whole lot plainer.

CHAPTER 4

———

The town of Crawford, on the edge of the Pine Ridge region up near the top of the state, had changed significantly since the last time Lone passed through. Originally a small, quiet settlement starting as a tree farm that attracted a handful of residents and basic businesses to serve homesteaders and small ranchers arriving in the area, the coming of railroads to the region and an increase in the size of the garrison assigned to nearby Fort Robinson to help protect them, brought about the transition.

First it was the Fremont, Elkhorn, and Missouri Valley Railroad reaching the fort and then continuing on up into Wyoming. Now tracks for a second railroad—the Chicago, Burlington, and Quincy—were fast approaching from the south. Along with the tracks had come a vastly different element, rapidly and in considerable quantity. In short, Crawford became a boisterous boom town. Serving the needs of hard-working farmers and ranchers was these days very much secondary to meeting the entertainment requirements—saloons, gambling joints, and brothels, in other words—of the railroad laborers and the soldiers from

Fort Robinson, one or the other or both swarming in pretty much round the clock. The older business section, consisting mostly of tidy, well-maintained wood frame structures, was all but swallowed by rows of newer operations housed within a hodgepodge of hastily-erected, various-sized tents.

Lone arrived just short of noon, three days practically to the hour from when he'd ridden up to Clement's trading post. Astride Ironsides, leading Rascal, now serving as his pack animal, as well as the two horses formerly owned by his recent ambushers, he threaded his way slowly, steadily between the rows of tents, aiming for the older business district. Along the way, he was hailed several times by barkers planted in front of some of the tents, urging him to try his luck at the gaming tables inside or perhaps satisfy his wildest fantasies of the flesh from a selection of the most exotic and beautiful females anywhere on the frontier. Lone took in this colorful, noisy display and thought wryly of days past when he was younger and wilder and might have been tempted by the lure of such promises.

Reaching what might be called the downtown, a two block stretch of older stores and businesses, Lone found it appeared mostly as he remembered. The buildings a littler grayer and more weathered it was true, a trace of weariness hanging over them. The one he wanted was a sturdy, boxlike log structure on the far end of the second block. A faded sign nailed above the front door read TOWN MARSHAL.

A long-limbed young man slouched in a wooden chair tipped back against the outer wall of the marshal's office sat eyeing Lone as he came up the street. Nothing about him moved except his eyes. This remained true until Lone reined Ironsides up at the hitch rail directly before his perch.

Tipping his chair down flat, the young man squinted up

at Lone and said, "Something I can do for you, stranger?"

"I'm lookin' to have some words with Marshal Woolsey," Lone told him, taking note of the deputy's badge pinned on the front of his shirt.

One half of the deputy's mouth curled up in a halfway smug smile that Lone didn't find particularly appealing. "Well now. That's gonna be sorta hard to do. On account of Marshal Woolsey has, er, passed on."

"Passed on, as in left town … or you sayin' he's dead?" Lone wanted to know.

"Dead."

Lone glared at the young man. "You ought not beat around the bush about something like that. You ought to say it plain and show some respect when you do. Chet Woolsey deserved no less."

The deputy rose up out of the chair. He was tall and beanstalk thin, barely past twenty, all sharp angles and knobby elbows with a nose and an Adams's apple vying for which protruded the farthest. He was wearing brand new, still-stiff Levis that made whisking noises when he moved. And the gunbelt worn around his bony waist surely must have required some extra holes punched in its tongue in order to get it cinched tight enough to stay up.

In response to Lone's chiding tone, he started to say, "Now see hear, mister …" But then, when the full heat of Lone's glare registered, he let the words trail off. Scowling, he resorted to a question instead. "Was Woolsey a friend of yours?"

"I knew him well enough to know he was a good man," Lone answered. "When did he die?"

"Near a year ago. And he, uh, didn't just 'die' … he got killed. Shot down at Calamity Jane's Place."

Lone cocked an eyebrow. "*The* Calamity Jane?"

The deputy's head bobbed. "That's right. She opened up one of the first businesses over on Tent Row. When she heard how the railroad was causing a boom hereabouts so she brung a string of dancing girls down from Deadwood and right from the first commenced packing in crowds every night to near bursting the seams of the tent. Calamity herself has since left town—gone off to join Buffalo Bill's Wild West they say—but her place is still going strong."

Before anything more could be said, the door of the building opened and a stocky, bleary-eyed, middle-aged man filled it. He wasted no time cutting a disapproving glance in the direction of the deputy, "Jesus Christ, Alvin, if you're gonna take up spoutin' long-winded lectures on the seedier history of our town, you think maybe you could do it somewhere besides right outside the window where you know I'm tryin' to get some shuteye?"

Deputy Alvin blushed a bright red and looked like he wanted to crawl off and hide somewhere. "Wow, Marshal, I sure never meant to disturb you. I guess I wasn't thinking, I – I just—"

The marshal quieted him with a dismissive wave of one hand. "Never mind, I wasn't sleepin' all that great anyway. Startin' to get too hot for daytime sleepin', and only gonna turn worse before summer's over. And, at the same time, you can bet the blasted nighttime shenanigans on Tent Row that keep me up to all hours ain't gonna ease up neither."

Alvin looked uncertain as to whether he was supposed to try and do something about one or the other—or maybe both—of the problem conditions.

The marshal put him at ease by relaxing his disapproving look and then saying, "I'm up now, at least for a while, and it's near noon. You might as well go catch some lunch at the Irishman's. Don't take too long and bring me back a corned beef sandwich and some iced tea."

"Yessir!" Alvin hastened off to do as bid, practically at a run.

Once he was gone, the marshal swung his attention to Lone. "I hear you say you were a friend of Chet Woolsey?"

"I knew him some," Lone allowed. "Acquaintance, is probably a better word. I had dealings with him a few years back when I was doin' some scoutin' out of Fort Robinson at a time when there was an uptick of Indian trouble in the area. Whenever I came to town, me and the marshal hit it off well enough."

The man in the doorway let his gaze travel past Lone and make a sweep over the horses strung out behind him. Bringing his eyes back, he said, "So you came by again now to say hi for old times' sake or some such?"

Lone tipped his head in a faint nod. "Reckon that would've been part of it, yeah. More to the point, I had some questions I wanted to ask and some information I wanted to give in return."

"Uh-huh. Information like maybe about those spare horses with empty saddles you're leadin' around?"

"You recognize those horses?" Lone asked.

"Nope. Far as I can tell I never saw 'em before in my life. But that don't keep me from sorta automatically wonderin' about the health and well-bein' of whoever used to be in those saddles."

"If you can spare a few minutes of your time," Lone told him, "I'll be happy to explain. That's part of my reason for comin' here."

The marshal regarded him some more before saying, "Come on inside, then. We'll talk."

CHAPTER 5

———

"So, it was a couple days south and east of here—where the two owlhoots belongin' to those horses jumped you. I got that straight?"

The marshal had introduced himself as Stu Karlsen. He was fiftyish, average height, thick through the gut but also through the chest and shoulders. He had a clean-shaven bulldog face, wary eyes, and a thatch of iron gray hair that poked out in places, still rumpled from the nap he'd been taking.

The jail office was small and cramped, though tidily kept, with an L-shaped pattern of heavily-barred cells running along part of one wall and across the back. All were empty at the moment. A pot-bellied stove and the marshal's desk occupied the middle of the room. There was a gun rack mounted on the wall at one end of the desk, a pair of straight-backed wooden chairs hitched up in front of it. A rumpled cot was jammed into a corner against the front wall, just off to one side of the door.

From where he sat in one of the wooden chairs, Lone responded to Karlsen's statement, saying, "Uh-huh, that's

how it went. All their possibles and everything I took off
their bodies is right here," he added, reaching out to slap
one hand down on the saddlebags he'd carried in with him
and placed on the chair next to his. "Nothing in the way
of identification, nothing in the way of anything, really.
You're welcome to go through it, too, if you want. Even
for a couple of ambushin' rats, it's a pretty pitiful collection
representin' all the worldly possessions of two sorry lives."

Karlsen was half-leaning, half-sitting on the front edge
of his desk, arms folded across his chest, facing out at Lone.
"You said one of them was named Everett. How do you
know that if you didn't find any identification?"

"It's what one of 'em called out to the other in the midst
of the shooting."

"I see." The marshal pooched his lips thoughtfully
for a moment. Then: "But what I don't quite see is why
you're going out of your way to tell me all of this. If it
happened the way you say, them jumpin' you and all,
then you did what you had to and you're lucky to be here
tellin' the tale. Even if it was otherwise, though, you got
to realize it happened way the hell out of my jurisdiction.
Meanin' that no matter if I thought something might
be fishy—which I don't, mind you—there wouldn't be
nothing I could do about it."

"I understand," said Lone. "But, first of all, you got to
remember I thought I was comin' here to tell my story to
Chet Woolsey. I figured I owed it to him, to make sure he
heard it from me first in case any questions arose."

"What kind of questions?"

Lone spread his hands. "Since I had no idea where
those jaspers were from or where they were headed outside of tryin' to drygulch me, for all I knew they might've
been from somewhere hereabouts. Was that the case, me

showin' up lookin' to sell off their animals and gear—but without no sign of them—could have earned me some suspicion. As it was, just havin' empty saddles on those nags caught your eye."

"I'm paid to notice things like that," Karlsen reminded him.

"All the more reason I'm glad I came here straight-away then. Though I'm sorry—and I don't mean this as no offense to you—that Chet ain't here to be the one I'm reportin' to." Lone jabbed his thumb in the general direction of the rowdy part of town he had ridden in through, what he'd now heard referred to as Tent Row. "Judgin' by the way things appear to be bustin' at the seams around here nowadays, I'd guess that Chet gettin' gunned down ain't the last shooting the town has seen."

"That's what some folks call progress."

"So I've heard. But don't count me as one of 'em."

Karlsen grunted. "Shootin's have got so common most nights on Tent Row that death by anything less than three bullet holes is considered natural causes."

"And it's up to you—and Chet before you—to try and keep a lid on it?"

"Yeah ... 'try'. Tryin' is what keeps me up nights and attemptin' to catch up on my sleep in the daytime." It was if the marshal felt he owed some further explanation for why he'd been caught napping. Then, his mouth pulling down at the corners, he added, "Far as your friend Woolsey, I never really met him. Between me, you see, there were two other marshals. One of 'em only lasted a week."

"Jesus. Not that I don't admire most men who pin on a lawman's badge, but how many city fathers did it take to hold you down and nail that one on you?"

Some sort of dark memory appeared to pass through

Karlsen's eyes. "Long story," he said vaguely. "But what's done is done and I'm doin' my damnedest to ride it out. I make sure to keep the riff-raff out of the good heart of the town and do what I can to hold back the bloodletting on Tent Row, not let it turn into a full-out flood."

"Again not meanin' no offense to nobody," Lone said, "but I hope you got more than that skinny young deputy backin' you. He might be willing, but he sure don't look to be packin' much sand in those stiff new britches."

Karlsen gave a short chuckle. "Don't sell Alvin all the way short. He's what you might call a work in progress. He does what I ask of him, which is mainly to keep an eye on things around this part of town in the daytime … Come night is usually when the curliest of the wolves start to howl over among the tents. For that, I got a couple rough ol' cobbs sidin' me. They ain't no spring chickens and they ain't always dug their own heels real firm on the right side of the law. But that's where they're dug in these days and that's good enough for me. They owe me some big favors from way back, so they're payin' up."

"Whatever works," Lone said.

The marshal unfolded his arms. "You said you came here to give some information and then ask some questions. I take it the information was squarin' things about those horses you led in, how you came by 'em and all. That it?"

"That's right. Now that we got that squared away, I plan on sellin' 'em off for whatever the lot—nags and gear—will bring. That's why I hung on to 'em. I ain't some flat broke drifter, but neither am I so flush I'll pass up the chance to rake in some extra jingle when it practically lands in my lap—especially if it comes courtesy of a couple snakes who tried to kill me."

A wry smile briefly touched Karlsen's mouth. "Sensible."

Lone puffed out his cheeks and expelled a breath. "Okay. So that takes care of that. Now, what I was hoping to find out from Chet—or now you—concerns a whole different pack of vermin. Five of 'em, to be exact."

As succinctly as possible, Lone went on to relate the story of the cold trail he was on. He told of the initial theft and killing, why the delay in him only now showing up in pursuit, and the new details about the five men he had only recently learned from Ansel Clement. While he talked, Karlsen listened without interruption; his eyes showed interest, his facial expression revealed nothing.

When Lone was done, the marshal said, "So what you're wantin' to know is if I can add anything about anybody matchin' those descriptions or that partial list of names."

"That's my hope," Lone conceded. "If there was any truth in what they told Clement about headin' for Deadwood after they left his place, it seems a good possibility they might make a stop here. At least long enough to top off their supplies, maybe lay over a day or two. Based on the Crawford I remembered from before, I figured five like them stood a fair chance of bein' remembered. Considerin' all your growth and 'progress', though, I see where they might not stand out so much after all."

"If you catch up with these men—"

"*When* I catch up with 'em," Lone cut him off. "Ain't no stop in me until I do."

Karlsen gave it a beat, then nodded. "Okay. When you catch up with them, what is your intent?"

"Justice. Seein' to it they pay for what they done."

"Uhmm. And how will that justice and the proper payment be determined?"

"By circumstances at the time," Lone answered.

When Karlsen looked caught off guard, puzzled, Lone

gave it to him in more detail. "Look, I'm out for vengeance. You'd be a fool not to see that. And I'd be a fool if I didn't understand how, you wearin' a badge and all, you ain't likely to be comfortable aimin' me after somebody you figure I'm gonna go and simply gun down. But consider this … men like them—and I hate to even call such scum 'men'—ain't the type to have *only* killed my partner and stole our horses. I'm bettin' that, if their full identities was known, each of those mangy curs can lay claim to a string of crimes as long as your arm."

"That's what I meant by 'circumstances at the time'— circumstances at the time I catch up to 'em, I'm sayin'. In other words, if I happen on one or more of 'em and they've already been planted for some other piece of wrong-doin'— or maybe behind bars scheduled to swing—well, I'd have to accept it and ride away satisfied. Not near as satisfied as if I'd personally and directly stopped their clocks for what they did to me and mine, but as long as I knew they'd been sent to bark in Hell, I could live with it."

Karlsen regarded him silently, intently.

"On the other hand," Lone went on, "was I to run down one or more of the critters, just me myself, somewhere out in the big lonely—you know, outside the reach of any proper legal jurisdiction—ain't no sense pretendin' I'd hesitate to try and handle it on my own. Under those circumstances, I'd do my damnedest to personally and directly send 'em to bark in Hell."

The marshal let that hang in the air for a minute before he replied, "Well. You lay it out straight, I've got to give you that. Which makes me inclined to be straight with you in return. And the straight of it is that, yeah, the five you're describin' did pass through here a while back. Unfortunately, they hardly came and went without doin' some things to make themselves 'stand out', as you put it."

Lone hitched up a little straighter in his chair. He didn't want to appear over eager, but this sounded possibly more promising than he'd dared hope.

"The one called Scorch, in particular, had a way of gettin' himself noticed," Karlsen went on. "And I don't mean just on account of his scarred face. In fact, there were times he seemed to use that—pushin' it in people's faces, practically darin' 'em to make some comment or even just ask about it—so he could lash out and make trouble. And trouble is what he got, in half a dozen different joints on Tent Row. To the tune of two knifings and a shooting, all in the span of little more than a week."

"You arrest him?"

The marshal wagged his head. "Couldn't drum up no charges I could make stick. Nobody died and, in the end, the victims and witnesses all claimed it was self defense—that Scorch agitated it but the other fellas all made the first move. I knew damn well it was intimidation, that everybody was too scared to say otherwise, but I couldn't prove it."

"The other four—they do the intimidatin'?" Lone asked.

"Mainly only one. The big black one they call Barge. Barge Kanelly is what he full goes by I found out later. And Scorch is Lester 'Scorch' Bannon. I found that out afterwards, too." Karlsen made a sour face. "If I'd known that and the rest sooner, I'd've had enough to go on and I could have taken a lot stronger action when I had the chance."

"You said you found out most of this later, 'afterwards'. Did something more happen besides the trouble they caused on Tent Row?"

Karlsen's expression turned even more sour. "Plenty more happened. Just under six weeks back, a train carrying the payroll for the soldiers at Fort Robinson got robbed passin' through the Pine Ridge only a few miles over. Half-way between here and the fort. Five men hittin' fast and hard and mean, shootin' and killin' like mad dogs, then gettin' clean away before any survivors from the crippled train could make it on through the rough country and get word to the fort."

A frown pulling down the sides of his mouth, Lone said, "Let me guess. Right about that same time, Scorch and his boys lit out of town."

CHAPTER 6

———

"The day before," Karlsen said, confirming Lone's guess. "Announced they was goin' on to Deadwood, just like they told your tradin' post fella. But in addition to the suspicious timing, came descriptions from more than one survivor that, even though all the robbers wore masks, one of them was clearly a black man of above average size. What was more, a wounded guard heard one of the robbers call another one what he thought sounded like 'Torch'. When the army investigators came asking questions around town and I heard those details, it wasn't hard to add it up as the work of Scorch's bunch."

"Like I said," Lone bit out through clenched teeth, "I knew the killin' and thievin' they did at our piss-ant little horse ranch was neither the beginnin' nor the end for that pack of mongrels."

"You called it right, no doubt about it," said Karlsen. "Once the army investigators went to work, it didn't take 'em long to turn up a pretty nasty history for Scorch and Barge in particular. Seems they started workin' as a team back on the Mississippi not long after the war—pirating, robbing, gun running, transportin' slaves even after the darkies were all supposed to be freed. It caught up with 'em, though, and they ended up in prison. A real Louisiana swamp hellhole. But it wasn't long before they managed to bust out. After that, reports of 'em started showin' up in different places as they made their way into Texas and then points north. Our bad luck, they've now ended up hereabouts."

"The other three joining 'em along the way, I take it?"

Karlsen nodded. "Seems to be the picture. Last I heard, not even the army had managed to dredge up much information on either the oldster called Elroy or the spooky kid as described by Clement, the tradin' post man. I'll pass what he told you about them on to the army as soon as I can, though, to see if it helps 'em pin down anything more."

"What about the fifth gang member—the dandy who signed the bill of sale for my horses as Henry Plow?" Lone asked.

Karlsen pushed away from the desk and paced a few steps over toward the stove, pressing the heels of his hands to the small of his back. Then, turning to face Lone again, he said, "Henry Plow. Believe me, nobody's forgetting him. He's too much of a damnably annoying piece to the whole stinkin' mess."

Lone said nothing, just waited for him to go on.

"Backin' up a bit, it seems this Plow was a riverboat gambler on the Mississippi about the same time as Scorch and Barge were involved in their various schemes. There's suspicion, but no proof, their paths likely crossed and Plow probably participated in some of the other two's dealings. But, because of that lackin' proof, he didn't go to prison with 'em. Which led to more suspicion—but, again, no proof—that he likely had a hand in their escape." The marshal returned to his desk and hitched a leg up on one corner before continuing. "What *is* known, is that Plow disappeared from the river shortly after said prison break and before long started showin' up in Texas at some of the same places as Scorch and Barge. The curious thing is that he'd often be seen in their company—but then, a good share of the time, he'd hang around a town all on his own after the other two moved on. Seems the gambler in his blood, flat wouldn't allow him to walk away if he was ridin' a winnin' streak. So, he'd stick around until the cards started to turn and only then take his leave, to show up again in the company of the others at some point later on."

"Not sure what you're drivin' at. But the fact he was with 'em when they sold my stolen horses at Clement's place," said Lone, "don't leave much question he was part of the stealin' and killin' of my partner. That's all I need to know."

"I can appreciate that. But if you'll just take it easy," Karlsen responded somewhat irritably, "there's a point to me goin' into so much detail about him."

Scowling, Lone held his tongue and waited for the rest.

The marshal pinned him with a hard stare as he said, "What I'm fixin' to tell you now comes with a warnin'. You need to keep it in mind on account of it falls within my jurisdiction. What's more, there's army investigators swarmin' all over this thing so you'd best take them into consideration as well."

Lone's scowl stayed tight. "Up to now, Marshal, we've been levelin' with each other. Now, all of a sudden, you sound on the verge of crawfishin' around to *not* tell me something."

"I'm going to finish tellin' you," Karlsen countered. "You'd poke around and find out anyway. But heed my warning when you hear the rest. This is a dicey situation and you bullin' in half-cocked won't help it work out for the better."

"Just spill it."

Karlsen took a breath, let out part of it, then said, "Henry Plow … he's still in town."

"And you and the army are just … what? Lettin' him stroll around free as the breeze?" There was a sharp edge of incredulity in Lone's tone.

"It's like I explained about his behavior in other places," Karlsen replied. "Plow rode in with Scorch and the others but he didn't leave with 'em. He's been havin' a run of good luck at two or three different tables on Tent Row and ain't ready to give up on it. The army immediately hauled him in for questioning once Scorch and Barge were identified as two of the train robbers. He not only denied knowin' anything about the robbery but he put on a mighty good show of bein' shocked over hearing it. He admitted that, yes, he'd rode in with the others and had been figurin' to rejoin them again in Deadwood after his luck cooled here. But he claimed no specific meeting place had been set, just that he'd be on the lookout for the rest once he got there. And now that he'd been made aware what a bunch of villains they were, he swore, he would do just the opposite and steer as far away from them as possible."

"What a pack of lies! And the army couldn't crack him?"

"No, and they leaned plenty hard. I know, I was there for most of it. Ploy's a lying weasel, but he's so good at it he knows how to stay damned cool, even under pressure."

"You said five robbers hit the train. Where'd the fifth one come from if it wasn't Plow?"

"Hell, everybody figures it *was* Plow. But believin' it and provin' it are two different things. Nobody sits at a card table round the clock, especially when Plow was known, like I said, to drift back and forth between a couple, three different establishments. Wouldn't have been too hard for him to slip away long enough to help with the robbery and then return to one of the games without anybody thinkin' much of it. On top of that, to back up his silver tongue, he made sure he also had an alibi for the time when the robbery was takin' place."

"What kind of alibi?"

"Seems 'Handsome' Henry Plow, as some call him, has one other passion that rivals his card playin'. This got displayed at the time of the robbery when he took a break from the gaming tables for a spell and slipped off to play some other kinds of games with a certain soiled dove who had caught his fancy. Since keepin' track of how much time she spends with a customer is one of this gal's specialties, she was real positive about how long Plow was with her."

"And it never occurred to anybody that a whore can be paid to lie?"

"She got leaned on just as hard as Plow but still stuck to her story. Plus there were other witnesses in the saloon, Calamity Jane's Place, who remembered seeing the two of them leave the gambling floor together at around the time in question."

"Which could have been set up exactly for that purpose—to make sure they were seen together. After that, it all hinges on the girl's word as far as how long Plow actually stayed with her. So, he paid her well enough to hold up under one round of tough questionin', but how much more can she take? What if you lean on her even harder and lay it on thick about how much trouble she could be in as an accomplice not only to the robbery but to the killin' that was part of it, too?"

"We were plannin' exactly that. But then the whole thing got taken out of our hands."

"What is that supposed to mean?"

"It means," the marshal said, his tone turning grim, "that before we could set her down for another round of questioning, the girl—Suzie Belle, she called herself—ended up dead."

"That's awfully goddamned convenient for Plow, wouldn't you say?" growled Lone.

"I say yeah, it sure as hell is. But that don't change the fact the girl is dead and we can't pin anything about it on him. What's more, it makes Suzie Belle's testimony giving Plow an alibi for the train robbery damn near as solid as a deathbed confession."

"That stinks worse than buffalo droppin's under a hot sun."

"Tell me about it," Karlsen said sourly. "The girl was stabbed in a back alley behind Tent Row. The knife was still in her. Several folks recognized it as one usually carried by a fella called Squirrely, a half-retard who gets by doin' scutwork all along Tent Row. He was known to have been particularly attracted to Suzie Belle and was always pesterin' her for a poke, though she wouldn't have nothing to do with him. Bein's how Squirrely ain't been seen since the body was found, there's those who believe that's proof he must have cracked when Suzie turned him down one too many times. So, he knifed her and then, out of fear and terror over what he'd done, he fled off into the wild and uncut."

"Yeah, he's out in the wild somewhere," Lone grunted. "Not very far, though—shallow-buried in some gully where Plow left him, then took his knife and brought it into town to pay a visit to Suzie Belle for the sake of makin' sure she'd never change her story about where he was at the time of the train robbery."

"'Bout the way I figure it, too," agreed the marshal. "But figurin' and provin' are two frustratingly different things."

Lone's eyes turned brittle. "I learned a few tricks from the Injuns back in my scoutin' days. Let me have a few minutes, just me and cool Mr. Plow, I bet I can thaw the truth out of him, alibi or no alibi."

"No. That's exactly what you *can't* do!" Kalsen told him. "Number one, I won't allow it in my jurisdiction—not even on Tent Row. Number two, there are federal under-cover men watching Plow around the clock. They would intervene even if me or my deputies didn't. Don't you see? Everybody knows Plow is lyin' his ass off. It's just a matter of time before the cards start fallin' against him here an then he'll move on."

"If that train robbery took place near six weeks ago, he sure is bidin' his sweet time!"

"Under different circumstances he likely would have moved on before this," Karlsen explained, working at remaining patient. "But he knows damn well he's bein' watched, and so far his luck at cards has been holdin' fairly steady. Still, the federal boys are bettin' it won't be much longer before he decides to make his move and head off to join Scorch and the others again, thinkin' enough time has passed for nobody to remain interested in him or, if they are, that he's slick enough to shed 'em out on the trail. Even if he does, there are other federals already in Deadwood, scourin' for some sign of the other four. They'll be there to pick up Plow when he rides in. One way or the other, when the pack re-forms there'll be a force ready to close on 'em like pincers."

"I still say my way would be quicker and surer," Lone

said stubbornly.

Karlsen regarded him. "I hope you're more sensible than that. When you came in here and started tellin' your story, I thought you were—else I wouldn't have been so open with you. But if you prove me wrong now, it'll go hard on you and I'll do my part to see it does. The federal boys are on top of this, let them handle Plow."

"And me just ignore him when he's right here in my reach? That's a damned hard thing to ask of me!"

"In your place, I can understand that," the marshal allowed. "But letting the federals handle Plow is the safest way. They're locked on him and they've got the patience and the manpower to make it pay off. The pressure to reclaim that payroll is too strong and comin' from too high up."

"I don't give a damn about the payroll," Lone seethed. "I've got my own score to settle!"

"If you mean that, then why not head for Deadwood—continue after the other four? If you have luck trackin' them down, the federals might even welcome it. But let their surveillance here on Plow play out instead of takin' the risk of queering the whole scheme and sendin' a signal for the rest to scatter even wider."

A still fuming Lone didn't have a ready response for that. Before he could come up with anything, the front door opened and Alvin came in with the marshal's sandwich and iced tea. The interruption was enough to break up the tension that had built in the room.

Lone rose from his chair. "Thanks for your time, Marshal. I'll be goin' now, I got some horses to get shed of."

"You do that," Karlsen said, his tone neutral. Then, hardening it slightly, he added, "Just keep in mind what we talked about."

CHAPTER 7

Lone left the marshal's office with conflicting feelings churning inside him. On the one hand he had learned some worthwhile added information about his quarry—some more complete names and backgrounds, along with further verification (to whatever extent the claims of the gang could be believed) of Deadwood being their ultimate destination. All details that could prove useful as Lone continued to close in on them. But then came the revelation that could be immediately useful—the fact that gang member Henry Plow was still right here in Crawford, practically within arms' reach. Only he was designated *Off Limits* for the sake of allowing the army's surveillance of him to play out in accordance with their plan for him to eventually lead them to the rest of the train robbers.

Eventually. Lone swore under his breath. *Give me fifteen minutes—half hour, tops—alone with that card-shufflin', horse-thievin' killer and I'll have him spillin' everything he's got to give on the rest of the pack he runs with.*

But following quickly on the heels of those thoughts— thoughts admittedly fueled by rage and a craving for revenge—came the echo of Karlsen's warning about *"queering the whole scheme and sendin' a signal for the rest to scatter even wider."*

Lone cursed again. The notion of leaving Plow to the army and in the meantime going on to Deadwood to continue his pursuit of Scorch and the others wasn't without a certain amount of appeal. No matter by what means Plow ended up providing a lead to the rest of the gang, it was still going to come down to that: Confronting them wherever they'd gone to ground and then taking necessary measures from there.

Lone told himself he could stand leaving Plow under the army's watch if it meant a chance for him to get the jump on beating them to the others somewhere in the Deadwood vicinity. Then he'd be willing to trust the army to sufficiently punish Plow in due course. Like the former scout had told Karlsen, he would *prefer* to personally settle up with each gang member individually but if Plow paid by swinging at the end of a federal rope, well, that might have to do.

As he mounted Ironsides again, Lone's insides were still in turmoil, undecided on exactly what course of action he was going to take. The only thing he knew for sure was that he needed more time to chew on it and, while he was doing that, there were some other matters to get out of the way. First, he wanted to unload the ambushers' horses he'd been leading around. Next, he'd see to accommodations for Ironsides and Rascal—a good rubdown, a bed of fresh straw, a feast of grain and hay. Then he'd tend to himself with a hot meal followed by getting checked into a hotel. No matter what else, he'd be staying at least tonight in Crawford. Come morning, he'd have his mind made up on how he planned to proceed.

*****

At a livery stable on the edge of Crawford's older business district, just short of where the sprawl of Tent Row began, Lone got a decent price for the spare horses and saddles he'd acquired. He probably could have pressed for more but wasn't in the mood for a lot of haggling and he welcomed that the liveryman also made an offer on the gunbelts and rifles, saving the bother of trying to find another buyer for them. Additionally, the operation looked suitable for also leaving Ironsides and Rascal in its care.

So it was that, after some satisfactory horse dealing and having a very tasty late lunch at a restaurant called O'Leary's, Lone's mood had settled considerably as he emerged from the eating establishment with the intent to head for a hotel he had spotted further up the street where he would secure a room for the night. Since it was only the middle of the afternoon, he planned on at first occupying the room just long enough to leave off his saddlebags and possibles pack, get cleaned up a bit, maybe shave and switch to a clean shirt. Then he figured on hitting the town some more. Lone wasn't adverse to sitting in on a few hands of poker if the company looked right, throwing down a few beers and a shot or two of redeye if so inclined. The fact he'd been warned to lay off Plow didn't prohibit him from having a first-hand look at the culprit and asking a few questions elsewhere.

The two men slouching out front of O'Leary's—one leaning against a support post of the boardwalk's shingled overhang, the other standing on the inside of the hitch rail with his elbows propped on the cross bar—looked sullen and edgy. Anxious for something to happen, willing to help it along if they had to.

Some might have glanced at the pair and not given them much thought. But Lone sensed something more. For one thing, they looked out of place here in the older part of town. Scruffy, heavily whiskered, bleary-eyed; clad in soiled work shirts, baggy trousers held up by suspenders, slouch hats on their heads. No weapons on display. Possibly railroad laborers, Lone guessed, or maybe just bored out-of-work saloon toughs on the prod for trouble. They were a loose match for a number of other men he'd noted milling about on Tent Row when he'd passed through. These observations, heightened by the way the pair's gazes cut immediately to him when he stepped out onto the boardwalk, sent warning bells tingling through the former scout.

The one leaning against the post straightened up. He was a lean number, thirtyish, average height, a ledge of shaggy, pale brows hanging heavy above eyes that glinted with a spark of petty meanness. Taking a cigarette from the corner of his mouth, he flung it away and said, "Your name McGanty?"

Lone looked him up and down slowly before pinning him with a straight, flat gaze. "Could be, who wants to know?"

"I'm the one who asked it, ain't I?" came the reply.

The one at the hitch rail pushed off his elbows and said, "Never mind names. Ain't *who* you are that interests us, stranger—it's *what* you are."

Lone turned his head slowly and gave this one the same unhurried once over. What he saw was an hombre about the same age, a little more muscular through the shoulders, with washed-out blue eyes, stringy hair trailing down the sides of his face, and a pronounced jut to his jaw.

"What I am," Lone said, a trace of annoyance entering his voice, "is a fella goin' about his business. None of which concerns you two. So, let's leave it at that."

He gave it a beat, hoping that would be the end of it but

suspecting it wouldn't. His suspicion proved right quick enough when Stringy Hair said, "Oh no. We ain't of a mind to let this be until you do some explaining."

To which Shaggy Brows added, "And some mighty quick and fancy explaining is what it's gonna take satisfy us."

Lone took a second to look past this pair of fools, his eyes sweeping up and down the street. Everything seemed to be in a post noon lull, with very little activity taking place. There were people moving around inside some of the stores, visible through the glass, and a creaking, heavily loaded freight wagon had just rolled past. But otherwise the boardwalks appeared empty. The only other person in sight on the outside was the stick figure shape of Deputy Alvin once again on his perch in front of the marshal's office way down the line.

"I suppose," Lone sighed, "I ain't gonna be able to swat away you two fleas until you at least get off your chests tellin' me what this is supposed to be about."

"You don't watch your smart mouth," snarled Stringy Hair, jutting his jaw out farther yet, "you're gonna hear what this is about and you're apt to get a hell of a lot more."

"And we'll see who swats who," added Shaggy Brows.

Lone heaved another sigh, this one heavier and more ragged. "Listen, you two peckerwoods, I'm in a lousy mood with a lot crowdin' my mind already—I'm warnin' you not to crowd me no more or it won't work out good for you."

The pair looked at one another as if astonished anybody would speak so boldly to therm.

"Do you believe this piece of trail trash?" Shaggy Brows said.

"What I believe is that we're gonna have to by-Go show him—" Stringy Hair only got out that much of a response before Lone cut him off.

Having heard enough and had enough, Lone decided to go ahead and take this confrontation where it was clearly going to end up. Reaching suddenly across his chest with his right arm, he grabbed the saddlebags draped over his left shoulder and yanked them off in a slashing, backhand motion that slammed them hard to the side of Shaggy Brows' face. The *whap!* of leather against flesh and bone sounded like the crack of a whip. Shaggy Brows was knocked away from his post, sent spinning off balance, and pitched out onto the dusty street.

Lone followed all the way through with his swing, extending his arm full to the right. Then, hesitating only the half second it took to roll his wrist and shift the weight of the saddlebags, he dropped his shoulder and swung again, this time lunging into a swooping uppercut that crashed the heavy satchels to the underside of Stringy Hair's obligingly jutted chin. Again, there was a satisfyingly loud smack of impact. The blow lifted Stringy Hair up on his toes and propelled him backward until he flipped over the cross bar of the hitch rail and was also deposited out into the street.

A minute or so later, when Shaggy Brows and Stringy Hair lifted their stunned, battered faces and looked around, the first sight their blurred eyes came to focus on was Lone. He was leaning casually against the post formerly occupied by Shaggy Brows. His saddlebags were again draped over his left shoulder and gripped in his right fist, leveled to generally cover both sprawled men, was his Frontier Colt. The gaping bore of its muzzle was the second thing the pair of blurred eyes came to focus on.

"Now then, boys," Lone drawled. "You got a taste of what comes from annoying me. You want to try for really pissin' me off?"

CHAPTER 8

——

The street that had been so deserted only a few minutes earlier was now stirring with a dozen or more people all gathering in front of O'Leary's restaurant. The fracas between Lone and the pair who'd braced him, brief as it was, had been enough to attract the attention of clerks and customers from surrounding businesses, as well as from inside the restaurant itself.

It had also drawn the attention of a frantic, wide-eyed Deputy Alvin, summoning him to come galloping down the street, gangly limbs pumping wildly. He'd covered the distance with admirable speed but now, as he crowded to the front of the onlookers spread in a loose semi-circle before Lone, he was puffing so hard from exertion and excitement he could barely get any words out. Glancing past him, Lone was reassured to see the stocky form of Marshal Karlsen—evidently alerted by Alvin before his took off—following at a more lumbering pace.

But, in the meantime, the young deputy seemed to feel obligated to try and take charge of the situation. Still puffing hard, he demanded, "What's going on here? … What's the cause for this disturbance?"

Shaggy Brows and Stringy Hair had each risen partly from their sprawls but were still on the ground in sitting positions. Though not ordered to do so in actual words, a cold stare from Lone and an even colder one from the muzzle of his Colt had made it advisable to just hold that way.

But the presence of the townsfolk clustered around and now the arrival of the deputy began to restore some of their earlier pluck. "What's going on here," Shaggy Brows blurted out in response to Alvin's question, "is all the cause of that maniac comin' out of the restaurant and commencin' to whale on me and my pal for no reason."

"And now, as you can see," joined in Stringy Hair, "he's threatenin' us with a gun!"

Alvin's eyes cut to Lone. He tried to look hard and determined but, more than anything, he looked uncertain and suddenly somewhat remorseful for what he'd barged into the middle of. "How about it, mister?" he asked. "What's your side of the story?"

"Well, I reckon I agree with about half of what they said," Lone drawled. "I *did* whale on 'em some, and I *am* standin' here holdin' this hogleg."

"Which needs to get put away, pronto-like!" This came from Marshal Karlsen, arriving on the scene and shoving his way through a handful of gawkers. He came to a halt beside Deputy Alvin and stood there breathing a little heavy too.

Lone held his eyes a moment before tipping his chin in a faint nod. "Alright. I'll leather my iron. But I'd appreciate it if you and your deputy keep an eye on that pair. They got no hardware showin', but they seemed mighty confident about bracin' me in spite of me plainly bein' heeled."

"How about it, you two? You carryin' any weapons?"

Stringy Hair scowled. "We been spendin' time on Tent Row, Marshal. Body'd have to be loco to hang around there without some kind of self protection."

"I don't want a speech," Karlsen said impatiently. "What I want is you on your feet and a show of what you're carryin'. Bring it out slow and easy."

A minor ripple passed through the crowd, a sign of anticipation—or maybe hope, in some cases—this might generate some more excitement. To show his readiness, Deputy Alvin decided to rest the heel of his gun hand on the butt of the short-barreled Remington holstered too high on his hip.

The pair sitting in the street pushed to their feet and slapped dust from their britches, glowering at the townsfolk looking on as if daring any one of them to make some remark. Then, slowly, they reached in their pockets and held out their hands to show the marshal what they unearthed. For Shaggy Brows it was a lead-weighted leather sap and a lock-blade folding knife; for Wild Hair it was a two-shot, over-under derringer.

As he dropped his Colt back into its holster, Lone couldn't resist remarking sarcastically, "I guess I was in more danger than I thought. If I'd've got a pea shooter like that aimed it at me, I might have cracked a rib laughin' at the sight of it."

This time the ripple that passed through the gaggle of onlookers was one of wry amusement. It drew a sweep of hateful glares from both Stringy Hair and Shaggy Brows.

Stringy Hair brought his to bear strictly on Lone, saying, "Messin' with us would've got you more than a cracked rib if you hadn't sucker-punched us the way you did!"

"That's enough," Karlsen barked. "Put your hardware

away, like McGantry leathered his Colt. Keep it that way. Then the only thing I want out of any of you is to hear what this is all about."

"I was working on getting 'em to tell me that when you showed up, Sir," Alvin spoke up. Lone couldn't tell if he was being petulant or just wanting to make sure the marshal knew he was on the job.

Karlsen gave his deputy a sidelong glance and then said, "All right then, Alvin. Go ahead and finish gettin' 'em to tell you. If I can make a suggestion, though—since we've already met McGantry here, start by findin' out the names of the ones who just picked themselves up off the ground."

Before Alvin had a chance to echo the marshal's request, Shaggy Brows responded, saying, "My name's Howie Brown, my pal is Vern Garber. We work for the Chicago, Burlington, and Quincy Railroad, bringin' up tracks from the south. We're part of a terrier crew punchin' through the Belmont Tunnel. Our foreman is Big Jim McGann, he'll vouch for us."

"I know McGann. He ain't one to put up with slackers on his crew," said Karlsen.

"Maybe not on his crew. But this is pretty far off course from that tunnel," Alvin noted.

"Even terriers get a day off now and again," Brown came back. "And when we do, we don't waste it by re-mainin' out there on the Pine Ridge."

"So, you waste it by instead coming into town and getting into trouble?"

"We ain't the ones who brought no trouble to your town," protested Garber, still scowling at Lone for his remark about the derringer. "If you want to worry about that, then you ought to be worryin' about this horse thief you got standin' here in front of you."

Lone cocked an eyebrow. "You start throwin' around words like that, mister, you better have more than that pea shooter to back 'em up."

"Just hold easy," Karlsen was quick to say. He aimed that mainly at Lone, then cut his gaze to Garber. "That's a mighty serious claim, bub. What *have* you got to back it up?"

"What I got is a horse and saddle yonder at the livery stable—took there and sold off by this McGantry fella only a handful of minutes ago," said Garber. "Only trouble is, I know for a fact—and Howie can back me up on it—that the horse I'm talkin' about, a little paint filly, couldn't have ever properly belonged to this hombre. Not for sellin' or for anything else."

"That's right," agreed Brown. "The fella that paint rightfully belongs to, a friend of ours name of Everett Tanner, would have sooner parted with his right arm than that horse. Ain't no way nobody could have got her away from him legal-like."

"Once again, you two chowderheads are half right," grated Lone. "You see, in a manner of speakin' your friend Everett did give up his right arm to grant me possession of that filly. He gave up his arm and everything else—because I killed the sonofabitch after him and another skunk tried ambushin' me back down the trail!"

This drew the sharpest reaction yet from the onlookers, a collective gasp followed by a buzz of shocked utterances. Out of the crowd stepped a lanky man of forty or so, jug ears and a long, weathered face under a wide brimmed Plains Boss hat that had seen better days. Lone recognized him as the liveryman he had dealt with earlier.

"That's the same story McGantry told me when I bought them horses off him, Marshal," announced the liveryman.

"I believed him on account of I seen how he came down from your office just before, and he said he'd already explained it all to you."

"That's right, Fred, he did. And I believed his story too."

"I tried to tell these other fellas. But they didn't want to listen."

Garber's scowl intensified as he turned his head from side to side, raking it over everybody. "Seems to me there's an awful lot of obligin' goin' on when it comes to listenin' to whatever McGantry has to say. What makes him so special? What about what me and Howie have to say?"

The marshal pounced on those words. "It's real interestin' that you all of a sudden want somebody to listen to what you have to say. The reason McGantry got listened to was that he came straightaway to my office and explained how he came into possession of that paint and the other horse he led in. He did so to make sure there'd be no questions or misunderstandin' that might cause trouble over him showin' up with 'em. That didn't strike me then—nor does it now—as the act of somebody with something to hide."

"How about," sneered Brown, "the act of a connivin' horse thief exactly *with* something to hide but tryin' to cover his ass in case somebody called him on it?"

"That still brings us back to you two, and your partner's lament about nobody listenin' to what you have to say." Between narrowed slits, Karlsen's eyes danced back and forth from Brown to Garber and back again. "The trouble with that, you see, is that neither of you ever came forward to give anybody a chance to listen. Why is that? If you were so sure a horse thief and possible murderer had just ridden into town, why didn't you bring it to the attention of me or one of my deputies instead of tryin' to take the law into your own hands?"

Much of the color drained from Brown's face and he averted his eyes. But Garber, he of the naturally defiant chin, wasn't so easily cowed. "Okay," he allowed through gritted teeth, "I reckon you got a right to wonder about that. All I can say is that me and Howie, knowin' our place as only just rowdy track-layin' tunnel rats and strangers in town … well, past experiences where that was the case in other places has made us, er, what you might call reluctant to purposely plant ourselves in front of anybody wearin' a badge."

"If you work for Jim McGann," Karlsen growled, "he can tell you that railroad workers—same as anybody else, even on Tent Row—get a fair shake in my town as long as they don't ask for otherwise."

Garber hung his head a bit. "It's true enough we never heard nothing to the contrary about things here in Crawford."

"Then you should have kept that in mind when it came to handlin' this matter," Karlsen told him.

Curiously, Lone felt an easing of his bitterness toward the two terriers who'd brought all this on. They were showing blind loyalty to a friend and having trouble accepting said friend was capable of taking a bad turn. Up to a point, that was understandable. He said, "Where did you know that Everett fella from?"

Brown frowned at the question, then replied, "We worked with him on a crew layin' a spur line down south of Denver last winter."

"So, the last time you saw him was when?"

Brown and Garber exchanged looks before Brown said, "A day or two into February, it was. That job down there finished up and right afterwards me and Howie signed on to come up here and start on the tunnel goin' through the

Pine Ridge. Everett and Fred said they reckoned they would be comin' up to join us but first they had to go pay a visit to a dyin' aunt over by Kearney, Nebraska."

"It was Fred's ma, Everett's aunt," interjected Garber. "They was cousins, remember?"

"Yeah, that's right," Brown acknowledged. "Anyway" —now directing his words back to Karlsen and Lone— "that's why me and Howie have been on the lookout, ex- pectin' 'em to be showin' up here any day now. So, when I spotted McGantry paradin' down Tent Row, leadin' their horses, I knew it wasn't a good sign. I straight off went to fetch Howie. By the time we got to this part of town, we saw McGantry leavin' the livery stable and goin' into the restaurant. It was from the liveryman we first heard the pack of lies about the ambush and the rest."

Lone let the "lies" remark slide and said, "This cousin. Fred, you say his name was? You figure he was the second ambusher who tried for me?"

Garber gave him a hard look. "If that's the way it went, I reckon so. If anybody was ridin' with Everett, it would've been Fred. His full name was Fred Kelper … You oughta at least know the name of a man if you're gonna kill him."

Lone felt his anger flare again. "If he'd've come around handin' out introductions instead of lead, maybe I wouldn't have had to kill him at all."

"Everybody just keep cool heads," the marshal warned. He swept his gaze over Lone, Garber, and Brown, letting it linger on each one for a measured beat before he continued. "It seems clear enough to me that Brown and Garber here worked for a spell down in Colorado with this Everett and his cousin and they all hit it off real good. When you're doin' hard work like layin' rails, it's mighty important if you can build up some camaraderie to offset the bone achin' drudgery. But how well do you really get to know somebody under those circumstances?"

"If you're talkin' about Everett," Brown said stubbornly, "you'd get to know him good enough to understand plenty damned quick how much he loved that little pinto filly!"

Karlsen heaved an exasperated sigh. "Damn it all! Ain't nobody disputin' the man wouldn't have willingly gave up his horse. That's the whole point. He *didn't* willingly give it up—he got killed playin' a bad hand and the horse was left up for grabs. Once a man is dead, it don't matter no more how he felt about much of anything. And if he dies in a way that's violent and dishonorable, then it matters even less."

"You're bein' awful quick to convict and condemn Everett and Fred, ain't you?" protested Garber. "All on the say-so of some stranger ridin' in out of nowhere!"

"I already told you why McGantry's story rings true to me. I ain't gonna explain it again," Karlsen snarled, "especially when I ain't heard nothing to make me think otherwise. What's more, whatever happened between him and those other two happened somewhere back on the trail—out of my legal jurisdiction, even if I did have any suspicions."

"So, I'm sorry you lost a couple of friends and sorry, too, you have to consider they appear to have had a side to 'em not worthy of your friendship in the first place. But that's the way it is, and that's the way I'm sayin' this is gonna end."

Nobody said anything for a minute. A quiet murmur of what sounded like assent, agreeing with the marshal's judgment on the matter, rippled through the crowd of onlookers.

Karlsen once again let his gaze settle for a moment on Lone, Brown, and Garber, each in turn. Then he said, "One more thing: The boundaries of this town are *very much* within my jurisdiction. Any further disturbance over this matter—from any one of you—will be met hard by me and my deputies. Is that understood?"

Again, nobody said anything. The message was clear.

"All right. This is over. Get on about your business," declared the marshal. Then, spreading his arms and turning to address all those gathered to watch, he said, "Same for the rest of you. Show's over. Get on back to doin' what you're supposed to be doin'. Clear the street!"

Deputy Alvin was quick to join in. Spreading his long, matchstick-thin arms in the same manner as Karlsen, he ordered, "Shoo! You heard the marshal. Show's over— clear the street!"

CHAPTER 9

———

When he finally got checked into the hotel, Lone decided to remain in his room longer than he'd originally intended. For starters, he had a tub of hot water drawn and took himself a good long soak. Then he shaved, dressed in clean duds from the skin out, and arranged with the front desk clerk to have his dirty clothes sent out for laundering. After that, he pulled the flask from his saddlebags and stretched out fully clothed on the bed where he rolled things slowly over in his head between occasional nips.

For a time, his thoughts drifted away from the grim business directly at hand and lingered instead on the somewhat bittersweet memory of a lovely Oriental gal named Tru Min Chang whom he had met in the course of fulfilling Peg O'Malley's dying wish. Tru was the victim of her own series of misfortunes and was struggling to reach her only remaining relative, an uncle, in Fort Collins, Colorado. Since the mountains above Fort Collins was where Peg had requested he be buried, it only made sense for Lone and Tru to journey there together from North Platte. Some unexpected complications and difficulties were encountered along the way, yet they nevertheless succeeded in reaching their destinations. But one particularly unexpected complication remained: The shared romantic feelings that had built up between Tru and Lone. What made this development bittersweet was the unfinished business of the vengeance Lone had vowed to deliver on the curs who had killed Peg O'Malley. Given the time already lost, it wasn't something he could delay addressing—not even to pursue his feelings for Tru. And so, after burying Peg on what he called his Forever Mountain, Lone had left Tru behind in Fort Collins and rode away with a promise to return one day, if the fates allowed, and if she was still waiting.

Bringing his thoughts back to the present, it didn't take Lone long to decide he might as well cooperate with not directly confronting Henry Plow. Though a big part of him still badly wanted to, he nevertheless saw the wisdom in letting the disputing army surveillance team, work their plan. It would serve as a sort of backup insurance, was how Lone convinced himself to accept it, aimed at eventually leading to the rest of the gang in case they couldn't otherwise be ferreted out. But, at the same time, Lone's willingness to hold off on Plow meant he would have the freedom to continue full bore after the others and do his damnedest to run them to ground before any more interference cropped up.

He'd head out again early tomorrow, he concluded lying there on the bed, but for tonight he would cruise the saloons and gambling joints along Tent Row on the chance he might pick up a few more tidbits of information from the time Scorch and his pack of curs had spent here.

And Lone wanted to at least lay eyes on Henry Plow while he had the chance. Get a sense of the dandy who had signed the bill of sale for his and Peg's horses, fill his nostrils with the putrid scent of the bastard in hope the day might yet come when he'd have an opportunity to breathe in that stink again when nobody was standing in the way of him eliminating its source.

And so it was, some hours later, well after full dark, Lone was occupying a bar stool in Calamity Jane's Place and unobtrusively watching Henry Plow play poker at a nearby table. Calamity Jane's, not unlike the handful of other joints Lone had already visited along Tent Row, was crowded, smoky, and raucous. The fact it was only the middle of the week did not seem to restrain its patrons in the slightest; Lone could only wonder what it was like on a Friday or Saturday night. Said patrons, on this night, were a colorful mix of soldiers, railroad workers, gamblers, businessmen and drummers, some shifty-eyed nondescripts, a few wrangler types, and of course a generous scattering of scantily clad bar girls.

The distinction here, at least as far as Lone had seen in any of the other places he'd been, was the wide stage erected in one corner of the main room. Every hour or so, a line of eight dancing girls—dressed even scantier than the bar girls circulating around out on the floor—would come and go through a high-kicking routine to the accompaniment of a piano player, a drummer, and a banjo man. Then a voluptuous brunette in a clinging gown with a daringly scooped neckline would appear to sing a couple of songs. Her voice was nothing special but the way she looked and moved more than compensated for missing a key now and then. When the singer finished, the dancing girls would do another round of high-kicking to finish the show until next time.

"When the original Calamity Jane opened this place," explained the talkative bar tender who kept pushing foamy beers in front of Lone, "she had a string of dancin' girls right from the start. After she moved on, the new owner decided to keep up the tradition. Nobody seems to mind."

"Yeah, I can see why," allowed Lone. After taking a pull, he frowned in puzzlement and said, "Wait a minute, you said the *original* Calamity Jane. You mean there's more than one?"

The barkeep chuckled. "Oh no. Everybody knows there's only one Calamity Jane. Lord help the world if there was another. But after she left, the new owner was shrewd enough to know he'd do better by continuin' to trade off her name as much as he could. That's why he kept her name on the place. Then the other thing he dreamed up was to start introducin' his top gal—that was the songbird you saw perform a bit ago—as Calamity Jane Jr. He claims she's some kind of shirt-tail relative, though it really ain't true. But the way she looks, especially in those tight show-off dresses she wears, nobody minds that neither. She can call herself whatever she wants."

The young lady in question happened to be standing by a card table only a few yards away where a rather intense poker game was in progress. She'd been there earlier, when Lone first came in, then had left to perform her songs only to return to the table after the set was done. She stood at the shoulder of a man dressed in a cream white suit with a red string tie. He looked to be about fifty or so, silver gray hair combed straight back from a widow's peak and reaching down either side of his face in precisely trimmed sideburns. He had very even, exceptionally white teeth that were frequently on display though often without conveying any true humor. The familiar way in which the singer's hand rested lightly on his shoulder and sometimes brushed across the back of his neck implied their relationship was something more than just employer-employee.

Noting Lone's appraisal of the pair, the barkeep said, "That fella she's standin' by is Cliff Breeson. He's the boss, the owner of the joint. Every once in a while he'll sit in at one of the tables if he sees a high stakes game buildin' up. When he does, he likes to have Janie standin' close by. He says she brings him luck."

"I can think of all sorts of reasons for a fella wantin' to keep her close by," Lone said with a crooked grin.

"Doubt there's anybody with workin' equipment who ain't got that reaction to Janie. But it's a good idea not to speak of it too loud," advised the barkeep. "Breeson's powerful jealous. He's got Janie branded strictly for his own … even though the louse ain't above havin' himself a poke with one of the other gals if the mood strikes him."

Lone drank some of his beer. As far as he was concerned, there was only one thing that made Breeson worth paying any attention to … okay, having the luscious Calamity Jane Jr. hovering close by maybe made two. But mainly it was the identity of one of the other players sitting in on the game with the saloon owner—Henry Plow. The descriptions supplied by Ansel Clement and Marshal Karlsen likely would have been enough for Lone to identify the skunk. But something more also factored in—a primitive, gut-level thing, like a predator's instinct for knowing when its natural prey was near and vulnerable. When, upon first entering, Lone had paused for a moment to survey the room, a jolt like a streak of lightning had run through him the instant he laid eyes on the handsome, dark-haired man sitting across the poker table from Breeson. He knew with ice cold certainty, no matter any other input, he was looking at the hated Plow.

Using every ounce of restraint he could muster, Lone

had walked on past the card-playing horse thief and killer and found himself an empty stool at the bar. It took a couple quick shots of redeye to get his tightly coiled muscles relaxed enough to stop his clawed hands from trembling. After that he switched to beer and slowed to nursing the foamy brew while he began his own surveillance of sorts.

Amidst all the surrounding boisterous activity, it would have been easy for Lone to drag out his covert observation for as long as he wanted. It helped even more that the game in progress seemed to be drawing the interest and attention of a number of others besides just the former scout. Some were gathered around the table, watching steadily; others seemed to be keeping tabs more intermittently. Whatever the case, it was quickly evident this particular game seemed to amount to something significantly bigger than the typical contests taking place all up and down Tent Row.

It didn't take long for the talkative barkeep to get around to explaining what was going on. "That Plow fella," he said, tossing out another unnecessary confirmation of identity, "has been hangin' around town for quite a spell now. Month or so. He first showed up with a pack of real hardcases, the kind Plow and his dandified ways hardly seemed to fit with. To the relief of all, those other hombres took off after a few days—robbin' an army payroll train on their way out, mind you. But Plow had made his break with them before that and so he stayed behind, playin' cards in different places and managin' to win more than he loses."

To which Lone had noted, "I can see he's kind of a dandy, like you say. But he don't look so flush that I'd take him for havin' won overly big."

Lone was referring mainly to Plow's attire. He saw what Clement had meant by the way he'd described the man—like somebody striving to cut a finer appearance without quite having all the tools. His chiseled facial features were perfectly groomed, from slicked-back, precisely combed hair with a few strands purposely out of place to form a dashing comma above one eyebrow to a smooth, strong, clean-shaven jawline that swept forward to a cleft chin. Below this, however, his clothing, while of good quality, had definitely seen enough miles to be beyond prime condition. A sheen in places where the material had worn thin, traces of fraying at the cuffs of his coat sleeves, more of the same on the tails of his string tie. These things stood out all the more in comparison to Breeson's crisp apparel, yet Plow seemed totally oblivious even a bit cocky, despite the contrast.

"Maybe he ain't won overly big so far," the bar tender said in response to Lone's observation, "but it could be he's on his way to changin' that. This past week the cards have been particularly kind to him here at Calamity's, see. To the point where Breeson decided to start sittin' in on his games to try and win back some of the house's money. This is their third night of goin' head to head. The other players at the table are nibblin' around the edges some, but they drop out early on all the big pots and those come down to either Plow or Breeson. From what I can tell, Plow has been edgin' ahead slow but steady—and that ain't sayin' nothing about what he'd already won before Breeson started sittin' in."

"That's got to be rubbin' the boss kinda raw."

"You ain't wrong. *Real* raw," the barkeep affirmed.

Lone continued to watch the game and nurse his beer. Now that he knew more details about what was going on, he could sense the tension hanging over the table— like a steel bar suspended within the cloud of cigar and cigarette smoke hovering under the ceiling. Those at the table showed varying degrees of awareness for what they were involved in.

The three players other than Plow and Breeson—a pair of plump businessmen and an out-of-place looking gent in a cowhide vest—appeared edgy but at the same time too caught up to walk away. Breeson wore a mask of grim determination except for flashes of a wide smile whenever he took a big pot. Plow held his mouth faintly curved in a half smirk at all times. The small audience gathered close around the table stayed relatively quiet and intently focused on how the cards fell; none more so than the curvaceous Calamity Jane Jr., planted firmly at Breeson's shoulder. The one exception as far as outward displays of emotion was the statuesque blonde bar girl plastered to Plow's shoulder—a direct counterpoint to Breeson's songstress—who squealed with delight and pressed against Plow with even greater abandon when he raked in a pile of chips.

The swirl of other activity elsewhere inside the saloon went on loudly and energetically while the contest taking place between Plow and Breeson almost seemed like it was happening in its own little world, an isolated bubble apart from everything else.

Until, suddenly, invaders threatened to crash through that isolation.

CHAPTER 10

———

It started at a table about a dozen feet from where the intense poker battle was being waged. A pair of bearded, rugged-looking, buckskin clad men—meat hunters for the railroad crews had been Lone's guess when he first scanned them (an assessment that would later be confirmed)—were seated at this table with one of the plainer bar girls wedged between them. An angry low rumble began to issue from the pair, growing louder and louder until it became noticeable even above the din that filled the rest of the room. And then the curses and accusations that became decipherable out of the rumble revealed that an increasingly heated argument was in progress—and the mousy bar girl, who looked frozen in terror between the two, seemed to be the source of the disagreement.

"I'm the one who spotted her and invited her to sit down with us!" bellowed the shorter of the hunters, a bull-necked, thick-shouldered specimen with wiry copper hair.

"But I'm the one who's been buyin' her drinks and who she clearly favors the most!" came back the other man, taller and sandy-haired, more leanly muscled though still solid and formidable-looking.

"Yeah, and that's the only way you can get any woman interested in you and your ugly-ass ape face—pump 'em full of booze until they can't see straight!" declared the shorter man.

"Well what you better get straight on seein'," replied the tall hunter, "is me and little Zarita here takin' a trip to her place out back and spendin' some special private time together."

"Now lookee here, Salty. Been times we shared the last drops in a canteen and the last bites from a plug of tobaccy. Hell, we even shared the same woman a time or two in the past." As he said this, the short man with the bulging shoulders wrapped one meaty hand around the bar girl's slender arm where it rested on the tabletop. "But this ain't one of those times. I'll be the one takin' Zarita out back and you can wait your damned turn!"

The tall hunter addressed as Salty rose to his full height and grated out through clenched teeth. "Take your paws off her, Buster. I mean it—I'm warnin' you. Do it and do it quick, else I'll rip that arm off and wallop the tar out of you with it!"

Buster complied by letting go of Zarita's arm. But at the same time, he also thrust to his feet, in the process sweeping one thick arm outward and upending the table where all three had been sitting. As the table fell away and the glasses and bottle of redeye skidded off and crashed to the dirt floor, Zarita clapped both hands to the side of her face and let loose a piercing scream. Other patrons closest by, who'd already begun taking notice of the escalating disturbance, now shifted farther back in alarm. A couple other bar girls in the mix also saw fit to scream. Across the room, the derby-hatted mountain of a man Lone had long since pegged as the bouncer, hopped down off his high stool beside the front door and started toward the two buckskinned belligerents. But the swell of patrons retreating away from the trouble inadvertently blocked his path and slowed his forward progress.

But there was nothing slowing what seemed to be the inevitable clash between Buster and Salty. Having knocked the table in one direction and shoved Zarita back the opposite way, Buster now made another sweeping motion with his arm and this time from his fist jutted ten inches of gleaming, menacing Bowie blade. The sneer on his lips and the whiskey-fueled rage in his eyes were equally menacing. "You always had a notion your height and your spider-long reach was enough to take me, didn't you, Salty? But you never had the guts to actually try. So now I'm forcin' your hand. Bring it on, you gutless pile of hot air, and we'll find out together."

In response, Salty produced a savage knife of his own. The two men immediately dropped into half crouches and began circling one another. This brought forth more frightened squeals and gasps of alarm. It also brought owner-proprietor Breeson to his feet with an angry command. "Stop this, you fools! Put those knives away!"

The only thing this accomplished was to make Salty toss a quick glance in Breeson's direction. In the end, this proved to propel the fight rather than halt it because Buster saw Salty's momentary distraction as an opening to try and take advantage of. With an angry roar, the compact, muscular hunter lunged at the taller man, his knife thrusting viciously ahead of him.

At the last second, Salty managed to twist out of the way and avoid the thrust. At the same time, his free hand clamped a grip on the wrist of Buster's knife hand as the arm extended past him. Maintaining this grip, Salty was able to use Buster's momentum, as the charging man continued bulling forward, to complete his twisting motion and swing Buster around with him. This threw both men off balance and sent them lurching and staggering, barely able to stay upright and locked together now as Buster's free hand closed around the wrist of Salty's knife hand. This unsteady entanglement rammed directly into the table where the high stakes showdown between Plow and Breeson was taking place.

Plow's blonde girlfriend leaped out of the way, releasing a scream of her own that was the loudest and shrillest so far. Plow was knocked out of his chair and spilled to the floor, as were the two plump businessmen and the fellow in the cowhide vest. The table got slammed violently to one side, chips and cards sent rattling and fluttering. Breeson, only because he was already on his feet, didn't get knocked down. Nor did Calamity Jane Jr. The brunette songstress backed agilely away. But Breeson, though not knocked down, nevertheless received a hard enough bump from the jolted table to be sent staggering back almost into the arms of Lone on his bar stool.

An instant latter, tripped by the feet and legs of the men who had been spilled from their chairs, the two hunters—continuing to strain and struggle in attempts to make use of their blades—toppled heavily, awkwardly to the ground. This jarred loose the grips each had on the knife hand of the other and they scrambled frantically to pull apart and rise up with blades slashing blindly, wildly.

This caused Lone to draw his .44 for the bizarre purpose of thinking he might have to shoot Buster because the enraged fool was slashing so recklessly it looked like a stunned Henry Plow was at risk of not being able to get out of the way of his blade! Saving Plow's life was the last thing Lone gave a damn about—but now wasn't the right time for him to die. Not before the wretch had given up, one way or another, what he knew about Scorch and the rest of the gang.

As Lone was preparing to gun down Buster if he had to, a foolishly bold Breeson was advancing on the knife-brandishing Salty. As he took a long stride toward the half-risen hunter, Breeson withdrew from under the lapel of his suit coat a short-barreled Manhattan Tip-up revolver, saying, "Drop it, I tell you!"

But the overly pompous saloon owner badly miscalculated on three counts—one, Salty was angered beyond good sense; two, the gun wasn't intimidating enough; and three, Breeson stepped too close. The latter was the most costly mistake of all because before he even had the Tip-up leveled and aimed, Salty reacted by uncoiling his long, powerful legs and a thrusting up and forward to drive the full length of his blade into Breeson's gut. The saloon owner stopped short in mid stride, bent slightly forward uttering a sound like "huh!", and then reflexively squeezed the trigger of the gun. As bright scarlet blood bubbled out of his wound and down over Salty's wrist, flame and smoke and lead spat from the half-raised muzzle of the Tip-up.

More screams and curses filled the air, whipped to a greater frenzy by the report of the little revolver. Into the mix, Lone added the roar of his Colt as he re-adjusted his aim away from Buster and planted a slug into the chest of Salty before he could do any more harm. The punch of the Colt's .44 slug knocked the tall man back and down, his lifeless hand releasing the knife and leaving its handle protruding out from Breeson's stomach. Seeing this, Buster immediately stopped his own thrashing about and wild slashing and, eyes bulging with horror, wailed, "Salteeee! My God, you ain't gone and got yourself killed, have you?"

This caused Lone to adjust his aim back again, thinking that now it might be himself he'd need to protect from the newly anguished Buster. But before anything came of that, the mountainous bouncer—finally having broken through the clog of backing-away patrons—immediately pounced on Buster from behind and wrestled him to the ground. Buster put up hardly any resistance. His Bowie slipped from his fist and clattered to the ground. Once again, the compact, muscular hunter wailed, "Oh God, Salty … they done killed you!"

It was only then that Lone saw the rest of it. Saw where Breeson's spasming trigger finger had discharged the errant round from his gun.

Henry Plow still lay where he'd first been spilled from his chair. Only now he seemed to be sprawled flatter and more completely motionless than the last time Lone glanced his way and it was certain that neither the red-rimmed hole just ahead of his right ear nor the thick worm of blood crawling slowly out of it had been there before.

CHAPTER 11

———

"All these days and weeks of damnable patience! Watching, waiting … *Knowing* the sonofabitch was part of it yet holding off on the gamble he would eventually lead us to something bigger. Now all wasted and gone in a single, wholly unrelated pull of a trigger! Of all the filthy, rotten luck!"

For the second or third time, Colonel Myron Hassett slammed his right fist into the palm of his left hand as he paced back and forth. He had plenty of room to pace in the spacious main room of Calamity Jane's Place, now emptied of all patrons and staff. The select handful of men gathered around the captain were here on his orders and there were guards posted outside to keep anyone else out.

Lone was among those present. Also on hand was Marshal Karlsen. There were four others—three soldiers in uniform whom Lone did not know, and a short, rusty-haired man dressed in the clothes of a common laborer. The latter Lone was familiar with from some years past. His name was Red Trimball. Back in his scouting days, Lone had worked with Trimball out of Fort Kearney. Trimball had been a lieutenant in the cavalry then. As had been revealed to Lone amidst a rush of other details he was made privy to over the past few hours, Trimball was still in the army—a captain now—but operating undercover and thus out of uniform as part of the surveillance team shadowing Henry Plow. Col. Hassett was his commanding officer and in overall charge of the detail assigned to recover the stolen payroll. Needless to say, the untimely death of Plow was a setback to the recovery operation and pressure for results from higher up the chain of command was bound to increase all the more.

"As rotten a turn as it was," said Trimball, bitterness evident in his own tone, "we can't let it defeat us. If we still think the rest of Plow's gang is holed up somewhere around Deadwood—and I *do* believe that, otherwise I would have argued harder against this wait and watch game we committed to here—then we'll have to increase our concentration on finding them. After all, they're where the payroll money is and that's the whole aim, right?"

"What makes you so sure the money is with them?" Karlsen asked.

Trimball spread his hands. "Come on, Marshal. Five men pull a robbery, four ride away and one stays behind— you think the four are gonna trust the one to hold the take and bring it along at his leisure? Especially a gambler like Plow?" Trimball shook his head. "No. From all reports, Plow has—or had, I guess I have to say now—some kind of special allowance to be a little free with his coming and going. But it wasn't *that* special. And there's no doubt Scorch is the leader of the bunch. Where he is, is where the money is going to be."

"What if," Lone said, "this time Plow was plannin' to break his pattern of always joinin' back up with rest? From what I understand, he's stuck around here quite a bit longer than he usually does when he separates from the others. Might he have taken his cut and been figurin' to drift on his own for a while?"

Trimball shook his head again. "Not likely. No reason to think he was on the verge of making that change. He's hanging back longer than usual simply because he knew he was under scrutiny due to suspicion he was part of the robbery. Plus—having gone through his personal items with a fine tooth comb since his death—I can state firmly that a total of the money we found was a long way from what he would have got from his cut of that payroll."

Karlsen said, "And he didn't blow it gamblin' because—from what me and my deputies saw, as well as your surveillance—he won more than he lost."

"And that was born out by what was in the money belt he wore," affirmed Trimball. "But even that wasn't overly much, which fit the high spending ways all of us also observed."

Lone shifted on the chair where he'd parked himself at the start of this. It had turned into a very long night. He decided to try and move things along by saying, "It probably ain't the best time to mention this, but since I haven't yet been told exactly why I was invited to this pow-wow—not that I'm ungrateful, mind you—I reckon I'll point out that if I'd been allowed to have my way and could've spent a few minutes with Plow while he was still alive, then all this blasted guessing wouldn't be necessary."

Col. Hassett's brows pinched together disapprovingly. "I assure you, Mr. McGantry, this is the first I am hearing of such an offer. Not that it would have made any difference as far as accepting it, I further assure you. What's more, if I interpret your suggestion correctly, I doubt I would have agreed to making you part of this 'pow-wow', as you put it."

"Fine by me," said Lone, rising to his feet. "I laid out good money for a hotel room I'm claimin' mighty poor use of. So, if I ain't needed here, I'll be more than happy to go take a stab at still tryin' to get some of my money's worth."

"Take it easy, Lone. Don't be so hasty." Trimball held up one hand, at the same time pinning Lone with an imploring gaze. When he had the former scout halted, he turned to the captain. "With all due respect, sir, I ask the same of you. Over the years, both in and out of uniform, McGantry has many times proven a valuable asset and I think he can be again in this matter. As far as his remark about Plow, yes, that may have sounded harsh—but I would remind the captain that Plow and the others we're dealing with are a mighty harsh lot themselves. They proved that by the ruthlessness with which they attacked the train crew and our payroll guards."

"I'm well aware of the traits shown by the vermin we're after, Captain. But that in no way means I will condone the same from men under my command," Hassett declared haughtily.

That was enough for Lone to again get ready to depart.

This time it was a throat-clearing growl and a sharp look coming from the colonel himself that stopped him. "However … since it was only a remark and no direct action was taken, I'm willing to overlook it as an incident we now have a clear understanding there will be no repeat of."

"To be sure. That's understood, sir," Trimball assured him.

Lone didn't say anything, which, as far as he was concerned, meant he gave no such assurance. Nobody seemed to notice enough to call him on it.

The colonel gestured. "In that case, Lieutenant, go

ahead and explain what you have in mind for how you intend to proceed—now minus Plow, but instead utilizing Mr. McGantry."

"Yeah. This 'asset' would kinda like to hear that, too," said Lone.

"Naturally you have the right to refuse," Trimball told him. "But given your own interest in Scorch and the rest and assuming you'll be headed for Deadwood where they're believed to be, I've got a hunch you won't."

Lone glanced over at the marshal. "I take it you filled 'em in on me?"

Karlsen nodded. "I did."

Lone cut his eyes back to Trimball. "Just to make sure you got told straight—my interest in that pack of thieves and killers is to deliver a kind of justice some would call payback. I want 'em all dead, preferably puttin' up a fight that gives me just cause to kill 'em myself. If it works out that they instead swing as the result of a trial, I can live with that if I have to. But I don't know that I'm willin' to be Haslett's slowed or distracted by worryin' about the recovery of your payroll money."

"All you have to do is flush 'em out. We'll take care of recovering the money," Trimball responded.

"Don't you have men already in and around Deadwood who've been workin' on flushin' 'em out for some time now?"

"Yes we do. So far they've had no luck."

A corner of Lone's mouth curled up. "Nice to know you got faith in me after all these years, Red. But what makes you think I'll have any better luck stirrin' those skunks out of their hidey hole?"

"Because I want to make you a stalking horse," Trimball answered. "By the time you get to Deadwood—if you're willing—I aim to have you painted as somebody those curs will come after and save you the trouble of needing to search too hard for them."

"A stalkin' horse, ain't that just a fancy term for *bait*?" said Lone. "Whatever you call it, anybody it gets applied to ends up in a mighty unhealthy position. And you're askin' me to be *willing* to go along with the idea?"

Trimball shrugged. "You said you wanted to get this bunch in your sights, wanted your chance at payback justice. This will give you that. All I ask is that you leave at least one of them alive long enough to tell us where the money is."

"Now just a minute, Captain," protested Hassett. "You make it sound like you're setting up an execution. I certainly can't—"

Trimball cut him off. "Not an execution, sir—a confrontation. A fight maybe, if that's what the gang decides to make of it. We'll have our people on the scene, hidden, when they come for McGantry. Once we spring our trap … well, like I said, it will be up to them to see how it goes from there."

"Keep in mind I might have a little something to say somewhere in there, too," Lone reminded him. "Situation like that, there may come a point where the stalkin' horse won't find it advisable to wait for some other hombre to make the first move."

"Long as everybody remembers we need one left alive long enough to tell us what we need to know," Trimball repeated grimly.

"There you go again." The colonel groaned with dismay. "As long as you keep phrasing part of your plan in that manner, it makes it difficult for me to be agreeable. Besides, what magic charm do you intend to bestow on McGantry that will make him so irresistible to the pack of vermin we've been unable to ferret out otherwise?"

Trimball smiled. "Simple. We'll give them reason to want to kill him as badly as he wants to kill them. I can't think of a way for them to accomplish that without revealing themselves."

"I hope," Lone drawled, "you're figurin' on them revealin' themselves while only just *trying* to accomplish the killin' me part."

"That would be the general idea, yes."

"You still haven't explained what's going to create all this incentive for the gang to go after McGantry," pointed out Marshal Karlsen.

Trimball pursed his lips a moment before replying, "There's an old saying that goes something like: A lie will travel halfway around the world before the truth ever makes it out of town. I plan on testing that notion by spreading a lie that will reach Deadwood well ahead of Lone and give the Scorch gang cause to be laying for him as soon as he gets there."

Trimball gave that a minute to sink in, then continued, "The lie I propose spreading to Deadwood is that it was Lone who shot and killed Henry Plow. The fight that broke out here in the barroom caused enough chaos and confusion to make that a reasonable fabrication—especially considering Lone *did* draw and fire his gun. Then, adding to that twist of the facts, we could build on the actual truth of a revenge-minded Lone being on his way to Deadwood to deal with the rest of the owlhoots who killed his partner and stole his horses. We could maybe even work in a hint that Plow spilled some useful piece of information about the others before Lone gunned him. Give them all the more reason to want to intercept and deal with him as soon as possible."

"What about the stolen payroll money? No mention of that?" Karlsen asked.

"No. We leave that totally out of this. The gang already knows there are army investigators combing the Deadwood area trying to get a line on them as a result of the robbery," Trimball said. "I'm hoping that will add to their wanting to deal with Lone quick—so he can't draw any added attention, especially in case he did get some kind of lead from Plow."

Lone frowned. "What I don't get is what makes everybody so sure Scorch and the rest are still stickin' around Deadwood. Don't get me wrong, I *hope* that's the case. I understand it's where they let on they were headed, and I'd even believe they probably went there. But if they know the army is sniffin' around close, why not light a shuck for parts unknown? Ain't like they don't have the robbery money to live large wherever they decide to go. And I can't buy a bunch like them havin' the loyalty to hang back overly long, puttin' their necks on the line just waitin' for Plow to catch up."

"Agreed they wouldn't risk four necks for the sake of one," allowed Trimball. "But the thing about the payroll, see, is that the biggest share of it was made up of newly minted gold and silver pieces. The gang couldn't have known that until they actually got their hands on the haul. But once they did, they'd have to figure word would spread plenty fast and wide following the robbery to be on the lookout for anybody spending new coins too freely. So, they won't be doing any 'living large' off the take unless they get a powerful long way off before they try."

"Which brings me right back to why you think they haven't done exactly that—made dust for somewhere far removed from Deadwood?"

"For starters," Trimball explained, "we know they *did* show up there. We had men in the area almost immediately. Scorch and the others showed and then disappeared, but there've been no reports of them leaving out through any of the surrounding area. Let's face it, Scorch and Barge both cut pretty memorable figures yet we haven't had any luck turning up a single sighting of anybody matching their descriptions beyond their original arrival in town. That's what makes us believe they're still there, holed up somewhere in the hills close by. Laying low, waiting for things to cool down and Plow to re-join them. The kid or the old man are indistinct enough to slip in and out of town for supplies as they need them, and to catch wind of any new developments."

Lone said, "Which is how you figure they'll hear about me—my supposed shootin' of Plow and the rest."

"Tha's right, that' what I'm counting on." Trimball eyed him. "But can I count on you? How about it, Lone? You willing to throw in together on this?"

CHAPTER 12

———

When the girl who called herself Calamity Jane Jr. entered her private chambers and turned up the lantern just inside the doorway, she gasped at the sight of Lone sitting there, reverse-melting out of the shadows as the lamp's glow filled the room.

"Best not to scream," he advised in an easy drawl. "If I meant you harm, I could have throttled you before you ever turned up the light."

She stood very rigid, watching him with wide eyes, trying hard not to appear frightened. "That's supposed to put me at ease—hearing that you thought about throttling me but didn't?"

"Never said I thought about throttlin' you, said I *could* have if I'd wanted to."

"And that's supposed to somehow be more reassuring?" Up close, under the heavy makeup and face powder, Lone saw she was a little older than he'd first guessed; closer to thirty than twenty. Still quite pretty, though, with a perfect oval of a face highlighted by luminous dark eyes and a wide, expressive mouth all framed by a foamy spill of rich brown curls. Features adding nicely to the package of ample curves so proudly displayed by the performance gown she still had on, though now with a thin shawl slipped over her bare shoulders in deference to the night chill.

"If I do decide to scream," she said, those luminous eyes now narrowing some, "there are men very close by who are trained to deal with intruders like you."

"I know. I saw 'em returnin' from the doctor's with you."

This brought a flash of suspicion and anger to the eyes. "You've been stalking me!?"

"Not like you mean. I've been waitin' for the chance to catch you alone. To talk."

"Yeah, like I haven't heard that line before. What makes you think I'd be any more interested in talking to you than I would—"

"Because," Lone cut her off, "you're a gal with some things to hide and right about now you're wonderin' what it is I might know that you don't want to get out. That's why you're willin' to listen instead of callin' for help."

"Wait a minute. Now I recognize you," the brunette said suddenly. "You're the one who shot that maniac with the knife!"

"That's right," Lone allowed. "Sorry I was too late puttin' him down to do your friend Breeson much good."

"Breeson." The way the girl echoed the name sounded to Lone like it carried a hint of disdain. "He didn't do himself much good, either, with that silly little gun he pulled."

Lone said, "It's for sure that silly little gun, as you put it, didn't do Henry Plow any good. A bullet to the temple—even a .22 caliber dealt by accident—is a lousy card to draw."

As he said this, Lone watched her face closely for a reaction. He saw a trace of what he was looking for, but she hid it well.

He gave it a beat before adding, "But at least he got it quick and clean. That's more than can be said for Breeson. You just came from the doctor—how bad a shape is he in?"

The girl gave a faint shake of her head. "The knife sliced through some important things on his insides. The doc had to open him up even more to get in there and try to sew them back together, get the internal bleeding stopped. But he'd already lost a lot of blood and the injuries were awfully severe. Doc says if he makes it through the night, he might have a chance. But he didn't sound like he was holding out much hope."

Lone's mouth pulled briefly into a grimace. "Tough way to go. Comes my time, like I said, I'll hope for the quick and clean route."

"Which would also include the man you shot."

The statement seemed to contain an accusatory tone that Lone didn't much care for. Frowning, he said, "Am I supposed to feel bad about that? The way him and the other drunken rowdy was swingin' their knives around, it looked like a good chance somebody else was gonna get sliced if they hadn't been stopped."

"Two men are dead and one is close to it. But why should you feel remorse for any of them—you're just a stranger passing through, right?"

"Not quite," Lone grated. "Maybe I simply can't afford to get tore up over the dead men left lyin' in my wake. But I favor survival over reachin' the end of my string, thanks, and none of that means I haven't still known remorse."

"I bet."

"In fact, it might surprise you to know that right at the moment I'm feelin' particularly remorseful—or maybe regretful is a better word—for one of the very men you just mentioned, the gambler, Henry Plow."

This time the girl was unable to control her startled reaction. "You knew Henry?" she blurted.

"Not near as good as I wanted to," Lone responded. Then, hardening the gaze he fixed on the pretty songstress, he added, "That's why I showed up to have this little chat with you. I want to learn more about him."

The girl quickly resorted to feigned confusion and irritation in an attempt to cover her slip-up from moments ago. "What are you talking about? You're not making any sense! What could you possibly hope to learn about Plow from me? He'd only been in town for a few days and I only ever saw him the times he sat in at one of our gambling tables."

"In that case," Lone said, "why were you sending Plow signals earlier tonight about what cards Breeson was drawing against him?"

The girl's mouth dropped open but nothing came out.

Lone continued, "I was watching the game from the bar for quite a while. Meanin' to size up Plow. But in the course of looking on, I started to see a very sly but unmistakable pattern to your little quirks and movements whenever you were standing close to Breeson—supposedly for the sake of bringing him luck. Only it was plain to me that any luck you were bringing was all aimed Plow's way."

"That's preposterous! Why should I do anything to aid some shiftless gambler who'd only been in town a handful of days? And what chance did either of us have to develop what you describe as this set of sly little quirks and signals that no one else was able to notice?"

"The answers to those questions," Lone told her, "are exactly what I came here to find out. And if you won't tell me, then maybe Breeson—or whoever's next in line to take over this joint—will be interested in hearin' your explanation for why you were helpin' some outsider siphon off the house's money."

At that point there came an insistent slapping against the canvas flap that served as a front door to the room, one of half a dozen private chambers sectioned off at the rear of the large tent structure that housed the saloon and dance hall. "Jane! Are you all right in there?" came a man's voice in concert with the slapping. "It sounded like you're arguing with someone."

Once again, a startled look crossed the girl's face. Recovering quickly, she called back, "Everything's okay, Cal. I'm visiting with an old friend."

"What old friend?"

"He stopped by the saloon earlier, just before the trouble broke out. He's been waiting to, uhm, see that I'm okay."

The voice identified as "Cal" said in a disapproving tone. "You've got a man in there with you? Christ, Jane, that's awfully bold, don't you think? I mean, Cliff is across town practically at death's door."

His tone didn't sit at all well with Jane. "What are you implying, Cal? For your information, I have the right to entertain any visitor I choose. Cliff doesn't own me, no matter what shape he's in. And *you* sure as hell have no say in my business!"

The response came back as a snarl. "Don't be so sure about that. I think something damn fishy is going on here. I'm coming in!"

Before Jane could protest, the canvas flap—which had no means of being locked such as a conventional door—was thrown open and a tall, trim man in a business suit stepped through. Immediately behind him, ducking and twisting his body awkwardly to fit through the opening, came a second man. This one Lone recognized as the derby-hatted human mountain who earlier had been functioning as the saloon's bouncer.

As they entered, Jane backed away from them and moved closer to Lone. At the same time, Lone rose revealing from the chair he'd been sitting in and nonchalantly laid the heel of his hand to rest on the grip of the Colt riding on his hip.

Once inside, the pair of newcomers halted and surveyed what was before them. The gent in the suit—fiftyish, classically handsome and well groomed but with an unhealthy pallor and a subtle deterioration to his features that spoke of too many years in too many dim, smoky saloons—appraised the scene with quick sweeps of bright, suspicious eyes. While he was doing this, his oversized companion— "Orson" Lone had heard him called in the aftermath of the saloon fight—looked on more blankly, as if waiting for someone to tell him something to do.

Though his gaze came to rest on Lone, Cal's words were for Jane, saying, "Well. Aren't you going to introduce us to your old friend, Janie?"

"I don't make a habit of introducing intruders," the songstress snapped back. "You have no business barging in here uninvited, Cal. I demand you turn around and get out."

Before the suspicious-eyed man could respond, Lone spoke. "The name's McGantry. Lone McGantry. There's your introduction. With that out of the way, I'd be obliged if you respected the lady's privacy and left now, as she requested."

Cal blinked a couple of times, as if uncertain what he'd just heard.

Once again beating him to a response, this time it was Orson who spoke first. "Hold on a minute, Mr. Drummond. I recognize this jasper now. He's the fella who shot that buckskinner what knifed Mr. Breeson!"

CHAPTER 13

————

Cal Drummond's mouth had opened to say something but now he clapped it shut and just scowled at Lone for a long moment. Then he opened it again and said in a measured tone, "Is that right? Are you the one who shot Cliff's attacker?"

"I am," Lone allowed. "Like I explained to Miss Jane here, for the sake of your friend Breeson I regret I didn't get my shot off faster."

"Yes, that was unfortunate. But at least you were able to prevent any further injury," Drummond said.

"I'd've been there in another second," Orson huffed defensively. "I'd've got that 'skinner, too, and cracked his skull just like I did his partner's. If the doggone crowd hadn't blocked my way, I could have got to 'em both before Mr. Breeson was stuck so bad."

"Nobody's blaming you, Orson," Drummond told him. "Like I said, the whole thing was very unfortunate."

"Anything like that happens again," Orson grumbled, "I ain't gonna be so gentle on anybody gets in the way of me and the trouble spot. I'll bust however many heads I have to get me a path cleared pronto-like!"

"That's very charming and reassuring to know," said Jane somewhat tartly. "So, since we all can rest easier knowing that, I think it's time we get back to you uninvited gentlemen taking your leave."

Drummond's scowl returned. "Now just a minute, Jane. Why so unreasonably rude? In addition to being an old friend of yours, the fact it was Mr. McGantry's brave intervention that provided our dear Cliff the slim chance he's fighting to hang on to. That rates recognition, a celebration. You have no right to keep such a hero all to yourself."

Lone didn't know for sure what game Drummond was playing, but he knew he was in no mood to participate in it. Moving forward a step to stand beside Jane, he said, "I appreciate the flattery, Drummond. But there's no need to lay it on any thicker. The only thing there's a need for is you to do what's been plainly and politely asked of you. So, I'll say it once more—you and your pal need to beat it."

First, what little color there was in Drummond's face faded away. Then, in a rush, it was replaced by a crimson flush. Towering behind him, Orson's broad, fleshy face bunched into a fierce scowl that put to shame Drummnd's version.

Seeing these reactions, Jane was quick to say, "Everybody take it easy. Haven't we had enough trouble for one night?"

"Not necessarily," Drummond replied. "Not if some saddle tramp thinks he can come galloping in here and start ordering me around in my own establishment!"

"It's not your establishment yet," Jane came back acidly. "The last we saw of Cliff, in case you forget, he was still breathing."

"I'm still a partner. And that gives me all the say I need," Drummond insisted.

"You want I should make it so this McGantry is the one who leaves, Mr. Drummond?" asked Orson. "And I can break him up a little on the way out, teach him a lesson about mindin' his manners."

Lone heaved a loud, exasperated sigh. "You know, one of these days—just once—I keep hoping to run into a musclebound ape like you who has a morsel of a brain to go with all that brawn."

Orson held up two pumpkin-sized fists. "I got all the brains I need right here, Mr. Smart Mouth. Say the word, boss. Let me take care of this annoying flea and teach him an overdue lesson while I'm at it."

In an eyeblink, Lone's Colt was in his fist. Aiming it casually in the direction of the two men, he drawled, "Go ahead, Drummond. Say the magic word you think might move that fool fast enough to beat a couple .44 slugs. And if you have one of those slippery little hideaway poppers under your coat like your partner had, I guarantee that trying to reach for it would be a real bad idea."

Everything froze for a long, raggedly tense moment.

Until Jane threw up her hands and said, "This is nonsense! It isn't worth it. You should go, McGantry. I can handle this if you'll just—"

But Drummond didn't let her finish. Suddenly bending at the waist and pitching himself low and to one side, he shouted, "Take him, Orson!"

While only intending to get out of the big man's way, Drummond's desperate move to do so inadvertently hooked the toe of one highly polished boot on a leg of the stand in the middle of the room upon which the glowing lantern sat. This resulted in not only tripping Drummond and sending him toppling to the ground, but it also jarred the stand so sharply that the lantern tipped over and rolled off to smash between the fallen man's flailing legs. And from there holy chaotic hell erupted!

To his bitter chagrin, Lone was caught off guard. He hadn't been prepared for such a reaction from Drummond, not with a gun trained on him at such close quarters. And once everything was plunged into darkness by the shattered lantern, it was too late to do any blind trigger pulling.

The blackness was instantly filled with the sounds of frantic movement. Lone heard Jane emit a frightened gasp and then stumble uncertainly. On the ground, Drummond was cursing and thrashing about, apparently trying to clamber to his feet. And above all there was the rush and heavy footfalls of a large mass hurtling closer—Orson making a bull-like charge even in the smothering dark. The conditions were close enough so that the man mountain had a good chance of plowing into Lone despite not being able to clearly see him. Yet Lone dared not risk a shot because he was unsure where Jane had stumbled to. All he could do was grip the Colt tightly and brace himself.

When it came, the thudding impact of Orson slamming into him was akin to being caught in the path of a stampeding longhorn. But big as Orson was, Lone was no small man himself and he had set himself squarely to meet the charge. Still, getting rammed by Orson's weight and momentum drove him back. The chair Lone had vacated only a short time earlier was turned to splinters and his back was shoved hard against the canvas wall of the room. Had he not withstood a portion of the giant's force, the canvas may have torn open.

It held, though, and the two men became locked in

a struggle up against it. Lone dug his boots in deep and surged with all his weight and strength back against the onslaught of his attacker. The former scout turned his hip just in time to block a savagely thrusting knee meant to hammer into his groin. At the same time, Orson's hard, heavy fists began crashing repeatedly into his ribs and the sides of his face. Each time they landed it was a numbing blast to Lone's nerves and senses.

In the midst of this, Lone managed to get his left arm wedged in between their bodies and used it to deliver two piston-like uppercuts, one just under the point of Orson's chin and the second to his Adam's apple. This caused the big man to gag and falter momentarily but in a matter of seconds his fists resumed their repeated hammering.

Swinging those heavy arms again and again was taking a toll of its own, though. Orson was used to pounding men down quickly, not having them stand up for any length of time to the punishment he dealt out. Finding in Lone McGantry somebody who didn't go down so easy was a big change for him. Sensing this—counting on it, in fact— Lone weathered two or three more blows, gut clenched and chin tucked in tight, before he had the timing he wanted between the slowing sweep of Orson's left arm; and then he brought his right up and around as hard and fast as he could, crashing the barrel of his Colt to the side of Orson's head, just above his ear.

The giant was jolted. His knees sagged momentarily and for an equal beat of time his arms hung loose. Lone took full advantage of this brief lapse. First, he drew his head back and then immediately thrust it forward, slamming the flat of his forehead into Orson's face, mashing his nose to a cartilage-crunching, bloody smear. The big man jerked back, issuing a kind of bubbling wail. Lone cut the sound short by swinging his Colt again and delivering another hard rap to the side of his opponent's head.

This time Orson was clearly stunned. When his knees buckled a second time, they weren't so quick to straighten again and he staggered half a step to one side. Lone lowered a shoulder and drove it into Orson's chest while he was partially off balance, forcing him back even more.

But any satisfaction Lone felt for having tentatively turned the tide of battle was short lived. Not because Orson suddenly mounted a comeback, but rather because of what Lone was able to see once the big man's mass was shifted from the way it had been engulfing him and blocking his view.

What Lone saw—past Orson's bulk, out in the middle of the room—was flickering tongues of flame licking up higher and hungrier. At the same time, he realized that the strange keening sound he had been hearing for the past several seconds, what he thought was ringing in his ears from the clubbing blows he'd absorbed, was actually Cal Drummond screeching in terror as the flames crawled up his coal oil-soaked legs. When he had tripped on the table leg and brought the lamp crashing down after him, the fuel spilled from its ruptured reservoir and the flame from its wick had turned the poor bastard into a human torch.

Throbbing illumination filled the room as more flames followed the puddle of spilled coal oil out toward its edges and spread wider across the floor. From somewhere out of the edge shadows, Jane reappeared wielding a blanket which she began slapping down on Drummond's burning legs. The man continued to screech as he kicked and twisted frantically.

"Fire!" Lone immediately bellowed at the top of his

voice. "Fire! Come a-runnin'!"

He knew that fire in a layout like Tent Row could spread dangerously fast and pose a devastating threat to anyone in earshot. The mere sound of the word would bring assistance scrambling.

Someone who didn't seem to catch on quite so fast, though, was Orson. Lone had barely gotten his warning shouted out, his attention thus diverted, when the bouncer attempted to continue their fight by throwing a looping roundhouse at the side of the former scout's head. Only Orson's still groggy condition from having the Colt bounced off his own head and Lone jerking away after catching a last-second flicker of movement out the corner of his eye prevented the blow from landing. Recoiling with a backhand slap from his left hand that re-focused the giant's attention, Lone stuck his face close and snarled, "Not now, you damn fool! Can't you see what's goin' on? Get over there and help your boss!"

Orson wavered for another moment before full realization finally hit him. Muttering a curse, he lunged away and rushed toward Drummond.

Holstering his Colt, Lone went to Jane and unceremoniously pulled the blanket from her hands, saying, "Give me that. Go get some more if you have any. A basin or pitcher of basin of water, too. And watch where you're stepping—don't let the hem of that long gown get caught by the flames!"

Jane turned without question and hurried to do as he said.

Lone was relieved to hear, outside, a chorus of voices growing in volume and repeating a warning of the dreaded words "Fire! Fire!"

Armed now with Jane's blanket, Lone also moved in

Drummond's direction, swatting down at flames on the floor to clear his way. He reached the fallen man the same time as Orson and immediately threw the blanket down over the saloon partner's smoldering, squirming legs. "Use that to finish smothering any remainin' fire on him and then haul him outta here," he ordered the bouncer. "Help's on the way!"

Orson knelt beside Drummond and began using the blanket to pat down every sign of a flame or glowing ember still visible on his clothes. Then he left the blanket draped over the injured man's waist and legs, shoved his hands in under each armpit in order to lift Drummond's head and shoulders, and began dragging him out the front opening. "Please be careful … Oh God, it hurts," Drummond whimpered repeatedly.

Lone turned back to see Jane emerging from a secondary area that he guessed to be her bedroom. She was carrying two folded blankets in the crook of her left arm and in her right hand she held a tall porcelain pitcher. And that wasn't all. Something far more intriguing—and something Lone would have enjoyed perusing at much greater length under different circumstances—was the fact she had removed the skirt portion of her performance gown and was gliding toward him on very shapely legs encased only in black fishnet stockings.

When Jane caught his gaze lingering in spite of circumstances, she said coolly, "You told me I should take care not to let the hem of my gown get caught on fire, didn't you?"

"Indeed I did," Lone conceded, reaching to take the pitcher and one of the blankets from her.

A moment later, as they were shaking out their respective blankets with the intent of using them to beat back the fire until help could arrive, Jane gave a sharp intake of breath and exclaimed, "McGantry! Look!"

When Lone's eyes followed the line of her alarmed gaze, he saw things had worsened in a matter of seconds. In addition to the blazing puddles on the floor, the legs of table that had previously held the lamp were now on fire and more flames were rapidly climbing one of the side walls. Thick, choking smoke was building up and churning down from the ceiling. Most concerning of all, however, was the result of Orson dragging away Drummond. In so doing, he had inadvertently smeared a track from one of the burning floor puddles over to the front opening and now flames had jumped from the puddle and were licking hungrily up the canvas flap that had fallen closed. Further exit out that way was effectively blocked!

"We're trapped," Jane said, fighting to control the strain in her voice. "We can't beat this fire back long enough for help to get in here!"

"Then we ain't gonna waste any more time tryin'!" Lone declared. He wheeled to face the back wall he and Orson had been jammed against in their struggle. Over his shoulder, he ordered Jane, "Wrap yourself in that blanket!"

While she once again obeyed without question, Lone hurled the contents of the pitcher against the wall, wetting the canvas with a shoulder-high vertical splash that dribbled down to the floor. Tossing away both his own blanket and the pitcher, he reached across his waist and yanked the bone-handled Bowie from its sheath on his left hip. In a long downward sweep, the Bowie's razor sharp ten-inch blade laid open a slit fully through the water-drenched outline on the canvas wall. Chill nighttime air poured in, feeling momentarily refreshing. But, at the same time, the gust of clean oxygen that came with it was like lifeblood to the blaze inside the room. Flames leaped and crackled with new vigor.

Turning once more to a blanket-shrouded Jane, Lone re-sheathed his knife before wrapping one arm around her waist and scooping the other behind her knees. Sweeping her up and pivoting back around, he took a long stride toward the exit slash he'd created, saying through clenched teeth, "If it's all the same to you, Miss Calamity—let's get the hell out of here!"

CHAPTER 14

———

"Jesus Kee-rist, McGantry! We've had tornadoes blow through here that did only slightly more damage than you've managed in not even twenty-four hours!"

From where he stood hovering over Lone, a sweaty, soot-streaked Marshal Stu Karlsen made exasperated gestures with both hands and then let his arms drop wearily back down to his sides. Seated before the ranting lawman on an upturned wooden bucket, the equally smudged and rumpled former scout tipped up the water canteen someone had handed him and took several unhurried gulps.

After lowering the canteen and passing the back of his free hand across his mouth, Lone canted his head and squinted up at Karlsen. "Reckon it's sort of a talent I got," he said, his voice a bit hoarse from smoke inhalation.

"Talent, my foot! A pain in my ass is what you've become and it's a malady I've had about enough of." Karlsen reached out, jerked the canteen from Lone and tipped it up for a long pull of his own.

The sun was up now. The beginning of a bright, clear day that at the moment was dimmed by the smoke haze hanging in the air over this section of the main street that ran through the heart of Tent Row. A dozen yards from where Lone and the marshal were taking a breather after participating in the battle to extinguish the blaze, the main structure of the tent housing Calamity Jane's Place remained standing.

The chamber where the fire had started was in ashes, as were rooms to either side. There was a fair amount of torn canvas walls made to allow access to the swarm of firefighters, along with evidence of some scorching and smoke damage in close proximity to the burnt-out areas. But nothing more serious. The main room of the saloon was basically untouched except for the charred smell that would linger for a while (a welcome counterpoint, some would claim, to the usual stale stink of spilled booze, body odor, and cigar and cigarette smoke).

Beating down the fire and keeping the damage so contained was thanks to the rapid, energetic response from three or four dozen people pouring in from neighboring businesses all up and down Tent Row and even several citizens, including the marshal and his deputies, showing up from the older downtown section. A bucket brigade was formed—drunks, saloon toughs, gamblers, barkeeps, even a few doxies pitching in—and in conjunction with that several men went to work with shovels and pitchforks, flinging heaps of flame-smothering dirt and ripping away flaming sections of canvas. Everybody seemed to instinctively find something useful to do and, in the midst of this roughly controlled chaos, Lone actually caught himself pausing for a moment to marvel at the efficiency of it all.

Apart from Lone and Karlsen, only a dozen or so folks were left milling about now. Several of them, including the two crusty older deputies the marshal had described to Lone earlier, were monitoring the perimeter of heavily burned area to make sure there were no hidden hot spots that might flare up unexpectedly.

"I mean it, McGantry," said Karlsen, handing back the canteen. "I've bent over backward to be fair and reasonable with you yet every time I straighten up you're involved in some new fracas. This one" —he jerked a thumb to indicate where the fire had broken out— "could have turned into a major catastrophe."

Lone's mouth pulled into a grimace. "What the hell, Marshal—you think I sparked that fire just to stir up some excitement? I damn near got my onions fried in it!"

"Why were you in that girl's room so late in the first place?"

"That's my business."

"You're lucky Captain Hassett and his men headed back to the fort right away after our meeting, otherwise he'd be the one asking that question."

"And he'd get the same answer."

"Fine," Karlsen growled. "If you want to keep your business all your own, then I think it's time for you to take it and move on. Especially since you're ..." He let his words trail off and looked quickly around to make sure no one was close enough to overhear. Then, continuing, he said, "Since you're workin' with the army now, ain't you supposed to be makin' for Deadwood anyway?"

"I full intend to do just that," Lone told him. "Army or not, I got my own reasons for headin' that way, remember? But since I ain't had no sleep for near twenty-four hours and this bout of fire-fightin' has frazzled me some extra, I had in mind to grab a smidge of sack time and get cleaned up a mite before I ride out. You gonna allow me that, Marshal, or are you kickin' me out of town straightaway?"

Karlsen considered the question with a hard scowl. Then: "If all you do is sleep and wash up before takin' off, I reckon I can't begrudge you that. But I'm warnin' you … get involved in any more trouble while you're still here, you'll wish you would've lit a shuck when you had the chance."

"Real charitable of you, Marshal." Lone took another drink from the canteen. Lowering it, he asked casually, "What became of that gal after the fire was brought under control?"

"Janie, you mean?" The marshal paused, regarding him for a beat before continuing. "Naturally she lost everything. She went off with some other gals who said they' put her up for a while and see to it she got some necessities. Got a particular reason for askin'?"

Lone shrugged. "Just hopin' she made out okay is all."

"In case you're wonderin'," Karlsen said, "it sounds like Cal Drummond is gonna be okay, too. Bad burns on both legs, but not so deep as to do any permanent muscle damage, the doc says. He'll be gimpy and sore as hell for a while, but eventually should come out of it. Big Orson's stayin' over there at the doc's, keepin' an eye on Drummond and Cliff Breeson both … last I heard, Breeson's outlook ain't near so rosy."

Lone stood up and handed the canteen back to Karlsen. "Rosy outlooks are hard to come by Marshal. But you got one all your own by expectin' to be rid of me a little later today."

*****

Lone slept longer than he' intended. Out on the trail, he always rose before the sun. Other times, he had the ability to somehow "set" his mind for the length of time he wanted to rest and seldom missed the target by more than a few minutes. This seemed to be one of the rare exceptions.

After returning to his hotel room from the scene of the fire, Lone had stripped down, scrubbed the soot and sweat from his face and upper extremities at the room's washstand, then stretched out on the bed meaning to sleep until noon. Opening his eyes now, however, he quickly judged by the angle of sunlight pouring through the curtained window that it was certainly later than that. How much later he moved to find out by pushing up on one elbow and reaching for his pocket watch that he'd left lying on the nightstand.

He didn't complete his reach for the watch, though. What stopped him was the sight that greeted him from across the room.

In a high-backed, padded chair positioned against the wall between the window and washstand, the young woman known as Calamity Jane Jr. sat gazing back at him. She seemed quite calm; taking slow puffs from a thin black cigarillo that she held between two fingers and, apparently, patiently waiting for Lone to wake up.

After quickly scanning the rest of the room to determine no one else was present, and at the same time pressing slightly down with one shoulder for the reassurance that his .44 was still where he'd tucked under a corner of the pillow, Lone brought his gaze back to settle on the brunette songstress. Allowing a side of his mouth to quirk up faintly, he said, "I guess turnabout is fair play. Last time I was the one who showed up unannounced and uninvited in your room."

Cocking one eyebrow, the girl said, "Let's hope the similarities end there."

"I go along with that, especially if it means not including

a visit from your two friends," Lone said. "Do they know you're here now?"

"In the first place, they're not my friends. In the second place, where I am now—or any other time—is none of their business."

"Okay. That sounds reassurin' as far as those two go. But what about Cliff Breeson? I got the impression that you and him are … well, that he would have cause to take exception to you bein' in another fella's hotel room."

Jane took a draw from her cigarillo, exhaled a jet of smoke out the corner of her mouth. "Breeson is dead. The doctor wasn't able to save him."

Lone didn't know what to say except, "You have my sympathy."

Jane eyed him through a curl of smoke, as if she found the remark somewhat surprising, maybe a bit curious. "That's kind of you to say," she responded. "But, to be perfectly candid, things between Cliff and I weren't … the best way to put it, I guess, is that our relationship wasn't really what most folks believed it to be. What he made a point to *let* them believe."

This time Lone held off saying anything.

"I didn't mean for that to sound entirely cold and un-feeling," Jane went on. "Naturally, I never wished Cliff dead—especially not in such a gruesome way. But, at the same time, neither can I pretend to be devastated by his passing. In fact, it gives me the chance to get clear of certain … *complications*, in my life."

Now it was Lone's turn to regard her for a long beat before saying, "Lady, you ain't makin' a lick of sense so far. But I have to admit you got me interested."

"Good. You should be. This could be of benefit to you also."

"Before we go any farther, though, we need to address a certain detail. Last night, you were the one minus part of your clothes—not that I'm complainin', and not that it seemed to bother you overly much at the time. Plus, I see you've since addressed the matter." Lone made a gesture to indicate how Jane was presently attired in a simple white cotton blouse and long maroon skirt. "But now, under these covers," he added, "you caught me in, er, not much more than my socks. I'm all for hearin' the rest of what you got to say, but I'd favor doin' it with my britches on."

"By all means. Go ahead and put them on, then," Jane said coyly.

Lone glowered at her. "Like that's gonna happen with you sittin' there."

"Really, McGantry? I wouldn't have taken you for the shy type. And as far as where I stand when it comes to shyness, the revealing outfits I wear every night at the saloon ought to answer that plainly enough."

"So, you're sayin' you wouldn't bat an eye if I threw back this blanket and came slidin' out in nothing but the bottom half of my long johns?"

"Only maybe if the back flap was down and I had to see your hairy, pale arse." Jane's brows pinched together. "At that disturbing prospect, I change my mind. I'll keep my eyes shut tight, I promise, until you say otherwise. Just get on with it, for God's sake, so we can return to talking about more important stuff."

CHAPTER 15

———

"I first met Henry Plow a number of years back on the Mississippi River," Jane was explaining. "I was working as a hostess in the gaming lounge of a riverboat called the Cairo Queen. Henry was already making his way behind a deck of cards. I was much younger then, still very naive, and he was a dashingly handsome rogue who made my head and heart spin. Way too easily, I hate to admit."

"And once our romance got going strong, I'm also not proud to say, he taught me how to spy on the hands other gamblers were holding against him and to reveal key cards with a clever system of signals he had worked out. I quickly learned how to position myself in order to spot and pass along information at the most opportune times. As Henry already knew and I soon found out, most men—even when involved in a high stakes poker game—seldom have any objection or suspicion when it comes to a pretty gal hovering attentively near."

Lone was dressed now. Jane had another cigarillo going. She remained in her chair; he was seated on the edge of the bed, listening to her work her way up to telling him why she had come here.

"No telling how long it would have gone on like that," she continued. "I never felt good about fleecing others like we were, but I was stupidly in love and making Henry happy was more important than anything else, until Scorch Bannon and Barge Kanelly showed up. For reasons I never understood, Henry immediately fell under Scorch's spell. He changed, practically overnight. Oh, he still liked gambling and having fun—but hearing some of Scorch's ideas excited him in a whole different, darker way. And what was worse, it turned out that Henry had a knack of taking a basic idea Scorch came up with—usually a robbery of some kind—and planning specific details for the best way to pull it off."

Hearing this, Lone had a hunch he now understood the reason Bannon allowed Plow's "special" forays apart from the rest of the gang.

"Cheating at cards was one thing," Jane stated. "But when beatings and killings started being part of the robberies Henry participated in with Scorch and Barge, I couldn't stomach that. Worse, I couldn't stomach the way Scorch started looking at me more and more openly. Most sickening of all was the feeling I had that if Scorch decided he wanted me bad enough, Henry—either out of fear or simply wanting to make Scorch happy the way I always wanted to make Henry happy—might expect me to give in." Jane visibly shuddered at the thought. "That's when I knew without doubt, I had to get away. So, the next time they all went out on a job, I took off. I started putting as much distance as possible between me and the river and never looked back."

"And you never saw or heard from any of them again until they showed up here in Crawford?" Lone prompted.

Jane exhaled a stream of smoke. "I didn't want to believe it, but somehow I always knew they were going to turn up again. I guess it's a sign you can never run away from your past sins."

"So, you jumped right back in by helpin' Plow run a winning streak at cards, even after him and the others pulled a bloody train robbery."

"It wasn't like that!" Jane snapped. "I worked out a deal with Henry before the robbery took place. I had no idea they were going to hit that train until it was too late. I'd been led to believe they were just stopping over to rest for a few days before moving on to Deadwood."

"So, what was your deal with Plow?" Lone wanted to know.

"He was going to be my ticket out of here. In exchange for helping him run a winning streak, he was going to take me along with him to Deadwood. He said he would be leaving separate from the others, as he often did."

"Why was it necessary to make a deal with Plow? If you wanted to go to Deadwood, what did you need him for—why couldn't you have left any time you wanted?"

Jane shook her head. "You don't understand. When I first came here, it was as part of the troupe of girls Calamity Jane brought with her—the *real* Calamity Jane, I'm talking, not this pretend 'Junior' version they ended up saddling me with. She put us under contract, said she would be opening up a grand place exclusive of any male partners and promised she would see to it us girls got a fair shake of the proceeds for a change. And, for a while, that's how it went. She opened her place, it was a big success, everything was good."

"But then she went on one of her benders, drinking harder and harder and not letting up. Started pissing away most of the profits in ways none of us girls ever knew reassuring about. Next thing we *did* know, she'd taken up with Breeson and sold him half interest in the place to keep it afloat. Not long after that, the offer came from Buffalo Bill to join his Wild West Show. She accepted it, sold out the rest of the way to Breeson, and was off like a shot."

"Leaving you and the rest of the girls still under contract—but now to Breeson," Lone summed up.

"Which he wasted no time reminding us of, and also made sure we understood that he intended to see each and every one of us fulfilled our obligation. From there, it didn't take long for him to come up with the idea of re-naming me 'Calamity Jr.', making me the star of the showgirl feature, and claiming me as his." Jane scowled. "I admittedly didn't resist very hard. Not at first. He wasn't physically repulsive, he bought me nice things, he gave me my own private quarters."

"While he was pampering me, he began offering the rest of the girls in the troupe a chance to earn bonuses by entertaining male customers on the side. As far as I know, none of them ever took him up on it. So, then he began bringing in bar girls—young pretty ones, not the usual hard-worn doxies you find working the line in most boom towns—who were more cooperative. It was quickly obvious that Breeson was sampling the merchandise right from the start. But I didn't care, it meant fewer times he'd come 'round looking to paw me."

"Sounds like a pretty lousy set-up, both as a romance as well as working conditions," Lone remarked.

Jane stabbed out the butt of her cigarillo in a glass ashtray balanced on one thigh. "That wasn't the worst of it. I soon realized it was just a matter of time before Breeson would get sick of me and start looking for a replacement from the ranks of the new talent. And as far as losing the star of the stage show, hell, nobody knows better than me that I'm only an average singer, at best. Any shapely gal willing to parade out there on stage showing her legs and wearing gowns barely covering her breasts would sound just as good or better to that rowdy saloon crowd."

"I think you're sellin' yourself a mite short as far as your voice," Lone told her. "But then, most of the singin' I've listened to in my time has either been soldiers warblin' around a campfire or some wrangler who pulled nighthawk duty and was singin' to soothe a cattle herd. So maybe I ain't the best judge."

"Trust me, you're not."

Lone hitched forward a bit on the edge of the bed and leaned forward, resting his forearms on his thighs. "Look," he said, "this is all real interestin' and everything, but so far it ain't moved things very far along as to why you came to see me. If I ain't mistaken, you said something about it bein' beneficial to both of us."

"I did, yes."

"Unless I'm readin' things wrong, I'd say part of what you're wantin' is for me to be the one to help you get away from here—now, while things are in a kind of turmoil followin' Breeson's death and the fire and all."

"You read real good."

"But what was holding you back before this? If you'd wanted out, all you had to do was leave. Just like you left the river. Yeah, you had a contract to perform here, to do a job of work for whoever owned the saloon. But it didn't make you a slave, didn't keep you held back by chains. Contract arrangements get broken all the time. You refuse to perform, the contract is wrecked, you forfeit your pay and it's over."

Jane began shaking her head even while he was still speaking. "Breeson would have never stood still for that.

With me, it was more than just the contract remember. His pride would never have allowed it to be known he got dumped by some cheap saloon floozy. He'd've rather seen me dead first."

"Like what happened to Suzie Belle you mean?"

Jane winced at the question. She squeezed her eyes shut for a moment and then, when she opened them again, they were bright and brittle looking. "I'm sorry for what happened to Suzie Belle. But it doesn't have anything to do with what we're talking about here."

"The hell it don't! Not if Plow killed her to make sure she didn't change the alibi that covered him for the time of the train robbery. If he was going to be your ticket out of here but now you're lookin' for me to take his place, then that pulls me in too close to dealings I don't think I want anything to do with."

"Oh, get off your high horse!" Jane snapped. "I heard the stories making their way around town all morning about you. About how you're some hardcase out for revenge against the whole Scorch Bannon gang on account of a bad wrong they did you in the past."

So, there it was, Lone thought wryly. Sign of Red Trimball's rumors already starting to spread.

"What happened to Suzie Belle was awful and it makes me sick to think that Henry might have had some part in it. Just like I know he played a part in shooting up all those soldiers guarding the payroll," Jane wailed. "But I'd already made my deal with the Devil so there was no backing out. That's how desperate I was ... and how much I still am. Desperate enough to want to try and make a deal with you."

"What if I'm just a different version of the Devil?"

"I suspect you may very well be. But I can see in your eyes the proof of the stories I've been hearing about you—

how frustrated you are that you missed Henry and how bad you want to get your hands on Scorch and the rest. In order to do that, you have to go to Deadwood. So, I'm asking you to take me with you."

"What's waiting for you in Deadwood?"

"Old friends who'll take me in and protect me until I can get back on my feet. Once I do, then I'll continue on with my dream of some day making it to California."

Lone frowned. "With Breeson now bein' dead, why do you still need somebody's assistance rather than just leaving on your own?"

"Because there's every reason to believe Cal Drummond wouldn't look any more favorably on that than Breeson did. He might be bed-ridden from his burns, but you can bet he'll still be reaching with both hands to grab hold of complete control over everything where the saloon is concerned. I figure that includes me. Not to paint myself as some kind of siren who drives men wild with desire, but Drummond has been after me for too long to let me slip from his grasp now that Breeson's out of the way."

"Ain't he in pretty poor shape for tryin' to throw his weight around?"

"He's got Orson to do his bidding. Surely you haven't forgotten him. And Drummond and Breeson also have other hardcases they've hired from time to time in order to get their way using force if they had to."

"You ain't makin' any of this sound particularly appealin' to me, I gotta say. But suppose—just suppose—we did strike a deal. What benefit am I supposed to get out of it?"

Jane's dark eyes bored into his. "Simple. When we get to Deadwood, I can tell you where to find Scorch and the others—where they're holed up, waiting for things to cool down and Henry to re-join them."

CHAPTER 16

——

Prodded by a shared eagerness to reach Deadwood as soon as possible while at the same time recognizing that sticking around Crawford only left the door open for more potential complications, Lone and Jane rode out of town that same day, with only about four hours of daylight left.

In as much as Jane had lost everything to the fire that gutted her apartment, a stop at the downtown general store had to be made for the sake of her acquiring some replacement necessities. Luckily, she had the money for these purchases due to possessing the foresight to set aside a modest stash of "emergency funds" over the past months—hidden in a secret place known to no one and left untouched by the fire.

At the store, Lone also stocked up on a few items. From there, he and Jane proceeded to the livery to retrieve Iron-sides and Rascal. Additionally, Lone also bought back one of the ambushers' horses, the pinto filly that its former owner had allegedly put so much stock in, along with the saddle that went with it. The liveryman made a half-hearted attempt to try and negotiate for a profit on the turnaround sale, but one look at Lone's grim expression made him decide to settle on merely recouping what he'd paid to begin with. The saddle went on Rascal, who would become a mount for Jane, while the re-purchased pinto took over pack animal duties. When Lone first asked Jane if she knew how to ride a horse, she'd quipped, "I know which end the hay goes in and where it comes out, if that's what you mean." But they hadn't ridden far before it was evident, she was quite competent in a saddle.

"I figure around three-and-a-half days to Deadwood. If the weather holds and we don't get interfered with, maybe we can shave it to three," Lone had announced at the outset.

"What do you mean by 'interfered with'?" Jane asked.

"I mean somebody tryin' to slow or stop us from finishin' what we've started," he told her. "We weren't exactly invisible while we were makin' our store purchases and claimin' these horses as part of preparin' to head out. Plenty of folks saw us. So, since you're convinced there are those bent on you stayin' put back there, we gotta figure it won't take long for word to reach them about our leavin'. Might that not be enough to nudge 'em into maybe givin' chase and tryin' to take you back?"

Jane made a face. "There's a dismal thought."

"Just sayin' how it might be." Lone gave a shrug. "You're the one who planted the notion by mentionin' how Breeson and Drumond sometimes called on hardcases to do their dirty work. With Drummond bein' the only one left but laid up like he is, if he wants you bad enough then sendin' some hired toughs to force your return seems like something that might at least cross his mind."

"Yes, that's precisely how a snake like him would think," declared Jane. For a moment she seemed more mad than anything else, but then her angry flush faded and was quickly replaced by a look of concern. "Jesus. With my luck, it would be Injun Jack and Hennessy he'd send after me."

"Injun Jack Calico?" Lone asked in response.

"I – I'm not sure about his last name. I don't think I ever heard it. Why, do you know him?"

"If it's who I'm thinkin' of, no I don't actually know him—but I sure as hell know *of* him." Lone scowled. "He's a half breed, not a full-blooded Injun. Made up from the meanest parts of both races. About my age, dark and wiry, not a big man but tough as baked leather. Always wears a necklace of eagle talons around his neck."

"That's him," Jane affirmed, looking even more worried.

"The other name you said—Hennessy—don't ring no bells."

"You'd remember if you ever encountered him. Luther Hennesy is his full name. Shaves his head bald, sports a bushy reddish mustache. A big brute, not quite the size of Orson but close. I heard somewhere they're cousins, but I can't say for certain."

"Sound like a real charmin' pair, no matter who's related to who."

"They're not to be taken lightly. Don't ever think that."

"With Injun Jack in the picture, I ain't likely to."

Jane brooded for a while as they rode along. Then she said, "If they do show up, what will we do?"

Lone pondered for a minute. Then: "For starters, I don't figure we've got to worry about it right away. Us leavin' out in the middle of the afternoon will have caught everybody by surprise. If Drummond gets around to decidin' he's mad enough over you takin' off to send somebody after us, ain't likely they'd get started before tomorrow. Comes to that and somebody eventually shows up … well, then we'll have to do whatever it takes to prevent 'em from gettin' what they came for."

Jane regarded him. "You'd do that? You'd fight for me?"

"I'd fight for the deal we struck," Lone told her. "I agreed to get you to Deadwood, you agreed to tell me where to find Scorch Bannon once we're there. I don't aim to let anything or anybody get in the way of that."

After some consideration, Jane said, "That's about the best answer I could hope for, McGantry. I'm glad you're on my side."

*****

When they reached a suitable spot for night camp, Lone called a halt. While he was stripping down and picketing the horses, Jane began laying out the fixings for their supper meal. After he had the animals taken care of, Lone got a fire going and by the time the flames were licking high Jane had a pot of coffee and a skillet lined with bacon strips ready to place over them.

"Does it surprise you that a girl like me has any cooking skills?" she asked as the bacon started to sizzle.

Lone cocked an eyebrow. "I'll hold final judgment until after I've tasted your coffee. Then again, you've already dealt enough surprises so that more shouldn't really come as anything new."

Jane gave a little laugh and said, "I'm not sure if that was a compliment or not, but I'll take it as one. And after you've tasted my coffee, you'd better be ready to hand out another."

When it was ready, the coffee was as good as promised and Lone praised it accordingly. Served with the bacon and some stewed tomatoes and canned peaches culled from the supply pack, it made quite a satisfying meal. When they were finished eating and clean-up was done, Lone and Jane stretched out on their bedrolls spread close to the dying fire. Each held a final cup of steaming coffee.

Tipping her head back and gazing up at the cloudless, starry sky, Jane said, "It's going to get cold tonight. Especially when that fire dies down."

"Yeah, 'spect it will," allowed Lone. "It's that time of year when the days keep gettin' warmer but the land ain't yet soaked up enough heat to give any back to the night."

Jane snuggled deeper into the bulky, sheepskin-lined coat she had wrapped around her. "Won't matter that much to me. The loan of this coat of yours is going to keep me just fine."

Lone said, "It might smell more like a horse than the powder and perfume scents you're probably used to, but it will for sure hold off the night chill."

"I don't mind the smell of a horse. In fact, I kind of like it. I'd forgotten how much. And as far as perfume, there isn't a scent been invented yet—at least none I ever found—that can counter the stink that builds up in a saloon on crowded, rowdy nights." Jane paused, continuing to gaze up at the sky, then added, "But out here everything is so clean and fresh there's no need to try and counter it with anything. The mix of different smells are like Mother Nature's own perfume, I'd kind of forgotten that, too."

Lone smiled faintly. "Can't say I ever thought about it quite that way. Just sort of took it for granted, I reckon. You make an interestin' point, though."

Jane brought her gaze down from the heavens. "But getting back to the night chill, no matter how nice it smells, how are you going to keep warm enough after giving your coat to me? It was foolish of me not to think about getting a warmer wrap for myself when we were right there at the store. You shouldn't have to suffer on account of my poor planning."

"I'll be okay. I've got a spare blanket I can dig out if need be," Lone assured her. Then, with a sly grin, he added, "Plus, I got a little something more tucked away to help keep a body warm from the inside out."

So saying, he reached into his saddlebags lying close at hand and withdrew a whiskey flask. Holding it up, he said, "Hope you won't take offense if I doctor up the last of this fine coffee a bit. Might you be interested in a touch to doctor up yours as well?"

Jane didn't hesitate to lean forward and extend her cup. "Feel free to doctor it up with a couple touches if you'd like."

They had grown steadily more at ease with one another during the course of the afternoon. Now, with night descended, wrapped in their bedrolls after a good meal and the whiskey-laced coffee relaxing them even a bit more, they went on talking freely for a spell longer.

It came out that Jane's true name was Margaret. Margaret Humboldt. "About as plain as a name could be. You can see why something flashier was necessary for a 'showgirl', right?" she quipped. But then she proceeded to say how she was tired of being Calamity or Jane or Janie or anything else decided on by others.

At that, Lone told her, "I think Margaret is a right fine name. Still, I gotta say that when I look at you, I see more of a 'Maggie'."

This earned him a delighted little laugh and an admission that "Maggie is what my father and brothers called me when I was a little girl." And from there it was determined that's how she would be re-christened. She would again and from then on be Maggie.

Next it turned to her questioning him about his name. "Surely Mama McGantry didn't look down at her little baby boy and decide to call him 'Lone', did she?" Maggie teased.

With a wry smile, Lone told her the story. "Actually, my ma never called me anything. Leastways, not as far as anybody could ever make out."

"You see, my folks were massacred by Indians when I was just an infant. When their homestead was attacked, they had time to hide me in a hollow log before they got wiped out. Apparently, I stayed quiet enough so the redskins never noticed me. Later, after some Army scouts showed up, attracted by the smoke of the burning cabin, I was squallin' loud enough so they couldn't help but notice me. They took me back to Fort McPherson where I ended up bein' raised, sort of collectively, by the wives of the fort officers. They knew my folks were named McGantry, but nobody ever heard what they meant to call me. I'm told that a few different handles were tried, but none ever took and it always went back to explainin' me as 'the lone survivor of the McGantry massacre' or 'the lone McGantry', until it finally became just Lone McGantry, and that's what stuck."

By the time he finished relating this, Maggie was looking at him with a forlorn expression etched deep by the fading glow of the fire. Quietly, she said, "I'm so sorry I asked, and caused you to have to re-live such a sad memory."

Lone made a dismissive gesture. "No need for that. It's really not any kind of memory at all. Just a story told to me over the years."

Maggie continued to regard him. "Yet somehow—like you said you saw me as a 'Maggie'—I sense the name fits you. Lone. Out here in the wild, away from everybody, you're very much at home, aren't you? I mean, under current circumstances, you're stuck with me. But if I wasn't here, you'd be totally at ease and comfortable, on your own. Alone and apart."

Lone rolled his shoulders, feeling awkward under such scrutiny. "Reckon that's how it's been a good chunk of my life," he allowed. "Lot of years scoutin' for the Army. Ridin' dispatch, huntin' meat for railroad crews workin' their way across the plains. Just wanderin' at times. But you're right, mostly on the fringe of other folks and seldom tied to any one place."

He gazed down into his cup for a moment, idly swishing what little remained in the bottom, but not raising it to drink. "Came a time, though," he continued abruptly, "when I was finally ready to settle. Put down roots. Me and an old friend—an ornery one-legged cuss of a former mountain who never had much truck with other folks either—started a little horse ranch north of North Platte. Got off to a decent start, we did. And then, one day near to four months ago, while I was away on a side job to earn us some extra money, a handful of visitors came by the ranch. Five men, likely sayin' they was lookin' to water their horses. Something wranglers from the surroundin' cattle ranches often did when they was passin' by, which is why my partner must not have suspected anything. But it turned out this bunch wanted more than just water. When they rode away some time later, they left my partner for dead, our cabin in flames, and they took our horse herd with 'em. The steeldust you've been ridin' all afternoon was part of that herd—at one time the favorite of my dead partner."

In a barely audible whisper, Maggie said, "The five men … it was Scorch and Henry and the rest?"

Lone's head tipped in a single faint nod. "That's right. They're what's drawin' me to Deadwood. This is one time

I ain't out to steer clear of folks, I'm lookin' to make the acquaintance of four very particular ones. The four who are left." His eyes narrowed yet, even in the murky light, shone with a bright intensity. "I'm puttin' my trust in you steerin' me to 'em, Miss Maggie. For your sake, I hope to God you're not out to swerve me."

The response came, still in a whisper but stronger this time. "I'm not … I swear."

CHAPTER 17

——

The distinctive *clickety-snick* sound of a six-gun being cocked very close to his head brought Lone instantly and fully awake. He remained very still, except for slowly opening his eyes. Without moving his head, his field of vision was limited. He could make out Maggie's bedroll-wrapped form a few feet away and, in between, the smoldering remains of their campfire. Sighting a handful of still-glowing embers told him he couldn't have been asleep for much more than an hour.

But it had been long enough for somebody to ghost silently into the camp.

Lone mentally cursed himself for not somehow, even in slumber, having sensed the intrusion. Nor had Ironsides, who could usually be counted on to raise an alarm when an unknown presence ventured near, given any alert either. Whoever it was on the other end of that cocked gun was damned good at going undetected—until he was ready to be.

"That's right, you murderin' piece of crud … Open those yellow snake eyes so's you can have a good look at who's come to send you to your deserves in the fiery pit of Hell!"

Lone didn't recognize the voice. Nor did the speaker's menacing spiel give any clue to who he was or what this might be about. Lone had undeniably killed in his time; but never without justification and never under circumstances rating a murder accusation. Though he'd made enemies, considerable in number, who likely saw it different. As to the fiery gates of Hell being in his future, that was a matter to be decided by Powers beyond this campsite.

The voice spoke again, though this time not addressing Lone. "You two—one of you stoke up that fire so we can see to enjoy the business we're fixin' to take care of. The other one, grab hold of that floozy. Make sure she don't try to run off and miss out on the fun."

Maggie came awake during this. "McGantry?" she called in a strained voice. "What's happening?"

By now Lone had rolled his eyes far enough to find himself staring up into the gaping muzzle of a heavy caliber revolver. The man holding the gun was featureless, just a looming black shape against the star-shot sky. To either side, other shapes broke into motion as ordered. Their boots scuffed heavily on the ground as they rushed by.

When one of them reached Maggie, she called him a name and there was the muffled sound of a struggle.

"If it's me you want," Lone said through gritted teeth, speaking straight into the gun muzzle just inches from his face, "leave the girl out of it."

"Tell her to behave then, if she knows what's good for her," came the response.

"You heard him, Maggie—don't make it harder on yourself!"

The sounds of struggling ceased. A moment later the cold circle of the gun barrel's mouth pressed just above Lone's left eye and pushed his head back hard against the underside of the upturned saddle he was propped on. "That was real smart advice. Now shut your trap and follow it yourself. Lay still and quiet until I say otherwise—which will come when we got better light for enjoyin' the fun and games."

It didn't take long for the fire to be bought back to life, flames steadily licking higher and brighter. Unable to move his head with the gun jammed tight against his eyebrow, Lone couldn't see much to either side. But the figure looming over him became clearer and clearer as the flickering illumination spread wider. What came into focus was a man of average height, a notably muscular build clad in fringed buckskin, and a face worn older than its years from exposure to the elements, topped by a thatch of wiry copper hair.

The face seemed vaguely familiar to Lone but he couldn't quit place it. It was the broad, muscular shoulders and the fringed buckskin covering them, though, that broke through the vagueness.

Seeing the recognition flare in Lone's eyes, the gunman's mouth spread in a wide grin. "That's right, Mr. Quick Draw Hero," said the shorter, stockier of the two railroad meat hunters whose knife-wielding brawl over a bar maid in Calamity Jane's Place two nights ago had resulted in the deaths of three men, "it's me—the partner of the man you gunned down in cold blood when he was in no way causin' you no bother!"

"Him and that knife of his was a bother, a *threat* to everybody close by—includin' you, only a few seconds earlier," Lone grated in response.

The gun muzzle lifted momentarily from his brow, but only long enough for the barrel to be crashed hard across his temple. Pain and pinwheels exploded inside Lone's skull.

When his vision started to clear, blurred by an involuntary watering of his eyes, the muzzle was jammed into him again, this time right to the middle of his forehead.

"I told you to keep your stinkin' mouth shut! 'Specially don't you speak of Salty. Me and him had plenty of scuffles durin' our time together and, yeah, we even sliced each other up some. But we never woulda kilt each other—not the way you did when you blowed a hole in him the size of a dinner plate!"

"You tell him, Buster!" called one of the other unseen men. "You got him pegged right down to the ground. A trigger happy damn murderer, that's what he is—an ambushin' snake and a horse thief to boot. He did for two good friends of me and Howie and left 'em layin' on some godforsaken stretch of who knows where."

"You've heard the old sayin' about what goes around comin' back around, ain't you, lad?" said the one addressed as Buster. "Well, that's what we're fixin' to be for this sorry heap of trash—the comin'-back-arounders. If accounts owed by him ain't square by the time we're done here, won't be nobody's fault but our own."

The voices and names swam around in Lone's still-rattled brain and he fought to pull them together, to try and make some sense out of whatever the hell ... Buster, yeah okay, that fit with what he'd heard one of the hunters called that night back in the saloon. Buster, who got clubbed down by Orson; and Salty, the one Lone had shot. But who was Howie? And why did the voice saying that name somehow sound familiar too?

"Okay, you got that fire goin' good enough," Buster addressed the other speaker. "Now slip over here—careful-like, while I got him pinned tight—and take away this polecat's gunbelt and whatever else he's got snugged in close. He ain't the type to crawl in his bedroll without havin' a weapon or two close at hand. And that means the Winchester in the scabbard on the back side of that saddle, too."

A third voice called from the other side of the fire, "Don't forget that big-ass Bowie either, Vern—the one he had strapped on his belt when we butted heads with him back in town."

Vern ... Howie ... The names clicked together in Lone's mind, triggering memory and then recognition of who the voices belonged to: The pair of railroad terriers he'd tangled with outside O'Leary's restaurant, accusers of him ambushing their former co-workers who were in truth the attempted bushwhackers that followed Lone from Clement' trading post. It all fit—the identities of Buster, Howie, Vern—yet what unlikely chain of events could have thrown them together and brought them here now, evidently seeking some kind of unified revenge? It was almost enough to make Lone wonder if he was dreaming or if that crack to the side of the head had left him in a half-dazed condition.

But no, the pressure of the gun muzzle against his forehead and the rough pawing of Vern tugging at his clothes and bedroll, jerking away his gunbelt, knife, and rifle, was all too real and bitterly humiliating.

When Vern had completed his task, he pulled back and straightened up. A moment later, Buster finally withdrew the pressure that had been holding Lone frozen. He too stood up and took a step back, but the long-barreled Remington in his fist stayed aimed steady on Lone's face. For the first time, with the crackling fire throwing a wide circle of light, Lone had a full view of the scene. And an unpleasant one it was. Buster and Vern, both heavily armed, loomed directly over him; across the way, a sneering Howie held Maggie firmly in his grasp, her left arm wrenched up high behind her back, her right shoulder gripped by fingers dug in painfully deep.

"Don't look so good, does it, Mr. Quick Draw Hero?" taunted Buster, his grin now smug and lopsided. "Ain't so easy to gun down somebody eyeballin' straight back and ready for you, is it?"

"And last time me and you eyeballed each other," joined in Vern, aiming Lone's own .44 at him, "you made a big joke about bustin' a gut laughin' at the pea shooter I was carryin'. Remember? You got a joke to tell tonight, funny man? Or maybe I should just go ahead and bust your gut open with a slug from this shootin' iron I got my hands on now."

"Not so fast, lad," Buster told him. "We don't want to be in a hurry. There's time for everybody to have a piece of the fun. I mean to hear this hardcase do some squealin' and beggin' before we send him over. Talk around town was that he used to be some hotshot Army scout and Injun fighter. If there's any truth to that, then he knows how Injuns like to test a man before finishin' him. And if he don't know, then I aim to give him a taste."

"You boys take all the time you want," Howie called. "I go me a nice soft armful of woman here to keep me company while I watch and wait."

"Whatever lousy quirk of fate saw fit to plant you three puddles of yellow pus in my path again, I guess I'm stuck with," Lone grated. "But the girl's got nothing to do with any of it. Let her go!"

"Who the hell are you to be makin' any kind of demands?" Vern made a thrusting motion with the .44. "You want to talk about plantin' something—maybe you'd like me to plant one of your own slugs in you? Come on, Buster, how about lettin' me blow away one of his kneecaps or at least maybe take off an ear? I'll leave plenty for you to have your fun with."

"I doubt you even got what it takes to pull the trigger on a real gun," Lone taunted.

"Shut up!" Buster snapped. "And you hold yourself in check, Vernon. I already told you, there'll be a chance for everybody to get their licks in." He paused, fixing a hard glare on Lone. Then, his tone taking on an added somberness, he said, "Fate? You speak loosely and sarcastically of Fate? What about the truth of it—the undeniable fact that we three ended up together and discovered our shared grudges against you? You need for it to be any plainer than that? Maybe it should be looked at like an omen. An omen that your black deeds have finally caught up with you and now the time is righteously at hand for your stain to be wiped from the earth!"

"Yeah," chuckled Howie from across the way, "me and Vern knowin' Buster from him and Salty bein' the meat hunters for our work crew and goin' to make his bail after we heard he got throwed in the clink over the saloon trouble, that was one thing. But your name then comin' up as a murderin' bastard we all wanted to get even with, that meant something bigger. Too big to turn away from. Even when we went lookin' and found out you'd rode off with this floozy, that wasn't enough to make us give up. With Buster's huntin' and trackin' skills, we knowed we could ride you down. So, we pooled our money for some hayburners to climb on and, lo and behold, here we are."

"And you think what you're doin' is righteous?" Lone challenged. "Even if you convinced yourselves in some twisted way that's true for me, it still don't have to include the girl."

"Oh, I don't know about that," leered Howie, roughly nuzzling his face against Maggie's cheek. "I think it'd be plumb *un*-righteous not to include this little sweetie here in our plans."

Lone tasted bile rising in the back of his throat and his lips peeled back in a snarl. But before he could say anything more, it was Maggie who responded.

"If you'd give this sweet little thing a chance to speak for herself," she said calmly, her tone practically dripping with honey, "maybe I could make your decision a whole lot easier."

CHAPTER 18

———

The unexpected statement from Maggie hung in the air and for a long moment there was only the crackling sound of the fire.

Until Howie drew his head back and grunted, "What are you sayin', gal?"

Maggie met his scrutinizing look with a cool, flat gaze. "I could say it a lot plainer if you'd quit twisting me around like some old shirt you're wringing out from the washtub. What are you afraid of—that I'll run off? Where would I go out here in the middle of nowhere in the middle of the night?"

Vern looked around with a sly grin stretching one corner of his mouth. "She's got a point, Howie. Ease up on her some—but not too much—and let's hear what she's got to say."

Buster, neither his eyes nor his Remington wavering off Lone, was quick to add, "But beware. The tongue of a Jezebel can be as sharp and poisonous as that of a viper."

"Don't worry, old man," said Howie, releasing the arm he had wrenched up behind Maggie's back but keeping his grip on her shoulder. "Just remember, there are other things a gal can do with her tongue that ain't near so dreadful."

Maggie moved her freed arm slowly across her waist and began rotating it in partial turns, working out the cramps. Her gaze swung away from Howie and made a pass over Vern and Buster. "The main thing you need to understand," she said, "is that McGantry is telling you straight. I've got nothing to do with any of this—and I don't *want* to have. Above all, you must believe that he means nothing to me."

Where he lay on his bedroll, propped on one elbow but still locked in place by Buster's unswerving Remington aimed at his face, Lone felt the stab of her words. From a strictly practical standpoint—the way Maggie had to look at it, for the sake of her survival—he could understand and even hope that it helped her succeed. But hearing her say it nevertheless caught him off guard and bit deep.

"McGantry," she continued, "was just a way to help me make it to Deadwood. I heard he was headed that way and, after things fell apart for me back in Crawford, I was desperate. I saw a chance to make a deal for him to take me along."

"Desperation can surely lead to folly," declared Buster. "And the foul company you fell in with stands as bitter proof."

"Yes. I – I see that now," Maggie agreed meekly. "I also see that, if what you three are saying about him is true, he most likely would have taken me part way, abused me, then cut my throat and left my remains in a desolate gully somewhere."

Vern's lip curled. "He for sure ain't no stranger to killin' and leavin' his victims behind to the coyotes and vultures."

Maggie's meek expression changed, hardened. "I paid him money. Even then I … well, I figured I'd probably have to … you know, also be nice to him along the way. But, like I said, I was desperate. Enough to do whatever it took."

At this, Howie threw his head back and crowed. "You hear that? She paid him and was still willin' to be *nice* to him! Don't that beat anything you ever saw?"

"Ever saw?" Vern echoed. "It beats anything I ever even *heard* of. It sure beats anything that ever happened on any of the trails I rode."

"Then maybe," Maggie said suggestively, "it's time for that to change."

Once again, her words were followed by a long beat of silence.

Until she spoke again, saying, "Look. Let's stop kidding around. What you three are up to—no matter how justified you think it is by whatever McGantry did to you in the past—ain't exactly on the up and up. And it ought to be clear by now that neither am I a girl who's always operated on the up and up herself. It's just a matter of degrees."

"Whatever you intend to do to him, I don't necessarily want a part of. But neither will I get in your way. All I want is to get out of this alive. And if that means … well, travelin' with you hombres and bein' *nice* along the way, then I figure I'm woman enough to handle it."

By this point Howie's mouth was stretched in a grin so wide it looked ready to split his face in two. "Oh, fellas," he said through the display of teeth, "this gal is talkin' my kind of language. And I can tell you for a fact" —his free hand moved slowly up over Maggie's stomach and started to cup one of her generous breasts— "that there is plenty of woman here to go around."

"Easy, boy," said Maggie, smiling but still taking a firm hold of his hand and pushing it down. "Don't you have some work to take care of first?"

Howie's grin diminished only slightly. "You know what they say about all work and no play, don't you?"

"I know what *I* say about it!" Vern barked. "You hold you damn horses, Howie! We got shit to take care of here before it's time to worry about that kind of business."

Very demurely, Maggie said, "Can Howie at least take time to get me one of my cigarillos before he finishes ruining the pack he's standing on?"

Without waiting for sanction from Vern, Howie leaned over and retrieved the pack from the folds of Maggie's bedroll. He extracted one, handed it to her, produced a match that he snapped to life with his thumbnail.

"If you're done messin' with that," Buster said over his shoulder, never taking his eyes off Lone, "continue to keep a close watch on the girl, Howie. But that's all—just *watch* her!" Now his eyes bored harder into the man under his gun. "You. On your feet. The sideshow is over, it's time to get on with our purpose for bein' here."

Lone rose slowly, somewhat stiffly to his feet. Buster and Vern had each backed a couple steps farther away and were spread apart. Both their eyes and guns were trained on him with steely intensity. Any attempt to try and rush them would get him riddled with bullets before he could reach even one.

"By the way," Vern sneered, "we'll be takin' back Everertt's prize pinto that you turned into a damned pack animal. And you know what else? After we're done with you, I'm gonna make myself a present of that big, fine gray of yours."

Lone smiled a cold smile. "Good. I hope you do. First chance he gets, he'll kick your stinkin' head off and stomp you into dog meat."

The sneer faded. "We'll see who ends up dog meat

before this night is over. Buster, while this smart-mouthed bastard still has some screams left in him, I want you to let me have a turn with some of that Injun torture stuff you know about."

Now it was Buster who showed a thin smile. "Don't worry, I'm thinkin' this boy-o is gonna entertain us with a lot of screamin'. These tough talkers usually end up bein' like that—they wail and carry on the best."

Lone finally cut his gaze over and took a long look at Maggie. She averted her eyes and just puffed on her cigarillo. But, beside her, Howie was gazing back with rapt attention, obviously eager not to miss whatever Buster and Vern had in store.

Lone almost missed it.

He was starting to turn back to the pair of men in front of him when Maggie suddenly whirled into motion. She'd just taken a couple hard drags on the cigarillo, turning the ash at its tip a bright, cherry red. Then, thrusting her arm out straight and fast with the slender cylinder of tobacco gripped tightly between thumb and forefinger, she stabbed the glowing end hard into Howie's right eye!

The stricken man's bloodcurdling screech of pain cut through the night like the razored edge of a giant sword.

It was too much for Vern—or even the intensely focused Buster—to ignore. Their heads swiveled around in reflexive unison to see what had caused such a terrible sound.

And that was all the opening Lone needed.

He instantly hurled himself forward, springing to a spot directly between his two captors. There, planting his feet, he swung his right fist in a slashing backhand that crashed solidly to the hinge of Buster's jaw, nearly knocking him off his feet and sending him staggering to one side. Immediately twisting at the waist, Lone next swung his left fist in the same manner, slamming it square to the center of Vern's face as the latter was beginning to turn back around.

The impact pulverized Vern's nose and buckled his knees. Hot blood gushing from the ruined beak flooded over the back of Lone's hand and wrist as he continued to pivot and then rushed ahead, bulling into Vern and pounding his right forearm to the man's throat. As Vern made a choking sound and began sagging the rest of the way down, Lone reached with both hands and grabbed the Colt he still gripped in his right fist. Twisting savagely, he yanked the gun free. Cartilage popped and bones splintered loudly as the forefinger inside the trigger guard was bent unnaturally before releasing.

Shoving Vern away, letting him topple loosely to the ground, Lone dropped into a crouch and spun a hundred and eighty degrees to face back in the direction of Buster. The muscular hunter was just getting himself righted after being knocked into a drunken stagger by Lone's first punch. The Remington was still in his fist and he was bringing it level once more on Lone. But the former scout was faster. His Colt roared twice in quick succession. Both times a .44 slug punched deep into Buster's heart. He was sent staggering again, this time for only a couple of steps before his legs gave way and he was dumped into a lifeless heap, the unfired Remington still in his claw-like grasp.

Without hesitation, Lone swung back to Vern. The man lay sprawled where he had fallen, pushed up on his right elbow, left hand reaching over to tenderly hold the mangled right. His battered, bloody face lifted, and he looked up at Lone with eyes brimming full of hate and rage. Through bubbles forming at the corners of his mouth from the blood pouring down out of his destroyed nose, he said thickly, "Go ahead and do what you do, you murderous bastard—kill me, too!"

And so Lone accommodated him. He extended his Colt and fired a round to the center of Vern's forehead, knocking him flat and still.

Stepping over the dead man and skirting the edge of the fire, Lone advanced on Howie, who lay on the ground with both hands clasped to his face, cursing and writhing in pain. Sensing someone standing over him, he wailed, "Oh God, fellas, I'm in a bad way. That rotten bitch burned my eye out!"

Lone looked over at Maggie. She stood staring down at Howie, arms crossed over her breasts, expression tight-lipped, grim.

Lone said quietly, "You okay?"

Continuing to look down at the writhing man, she answered, "I am … now." Then, after a beat, her face lifted and her eyes swung to Lone. They seemed to soften for a moment, but then became edged with anguish. "Those things I said, I hope you understood."

A faint but reassuring smile touched Lone's lips. "You had me goin' for a minute there, I gotta admit. But it's okay. Yeah, I understand."

Hearing this exchange was enough to make Howie stop his writhing and moaning. He slowly parted the hands he was holding to his face and peeked out and up with his good eye. The sight of Lone standing over him brought forth another tortured groan. "Oh Sweet Jesus, it's *you*! I – I heard the shootin', b-but I figured …"

"Yeah, I know what you figured. But you were wrong," Lone said in an icy tone. Then, raising the Colt he'd been holding down at his side, he rasped, "Now you've got one second to figure what comes next."

PART TWO

CHAPTER 19

——

"I don't know which is worse, the eye-stinging, antiseptic smell of the doctor's office, the putrid reek of that salve he's got smeared all over my legs, or the stink of smoke and burnt canvas filling the goddamned air in here!"

Cal Drummond issued this latest lament as Orson pushed him slowly, carefully through the opening to Drummond's private quarters at the rear of the massive tent housing Calamity Jane's Place. The wooden wheels of the rolling chair in which Drumond sat were stiff and jerky from lack of use to begin with; combined with the unevenness of the ground they were passing over, it was nearly impossible to move the patient along without jarring him to some degree.

Getting him transferred from the doctor's office to a wagon for the trip to Tent Row and then from the wagon to the wheelchair—all accomplished more smoothly and with greater ease than would have otherwise been possible if not for Orson's impressive strength when called upon to lift and carry—had involved added pain at every stage due to the extreme tenderness of Drummond's injured legs. Throughout, he had never hesitated to react with curses and admonishments. And now he was cussing the smell in the air.

"Maybe you should've let the doctor put you up for a few days in that room at his place, like he offered," suggested Orson as he moved to light a lantern just inside the doorway, crowding out the evening gloom with a soft glow of illumination.

But Drummond wasn't so inclined, saying, "I already told you—I found the stink there to be just as bad. In a way even worse. Here, at least, I'm home. I'll just have to get used to the smell."

"Once we open up the saloon again and it starts filling with good-sized crowds like we're used to, that oughta help soak up the smoke stink too. Don't you think?" asked Orson hopefully.

"I don't know about that. But it will surely address part of my suffering." From under the lapel of his jacket, Drummond withdrew a brown bottle with a cork in it. Holding it up, he said, "This horrid tasting laudanum helps dull the pain from my burns, but it does nothing for the pain the businessman in me feels at the thought of a closed-up establishment with no money coming in. There's only one medicine for that, and it is to re-open again as soon as possible. Meaning tomorrow afternoon."

Orson looked dubious. "Jeez, Mr. Drummond, are you sure you're gonna be up to it?"

"I'll have to be. I'll force myself to be." Drummond held the bottle of laudanum a little higher and with his opposite hand removed the cork. "With my new partner at my side, we'll see it through together."

Orson watched his boss tip up the concoction and gulp down a big swallow, then another. When he lowered the bottle his face immediately twisted into an expression of great distaste.

His own expression remaining somewhat dubious, Orson said, "Well, you know you can count on me, Mr. Drummond. I'll be on hand to help however I can."

"Yes, I do know that, Orson. And I greatly appreciate it." Drummond regarded the big man. "The most immediate task I'm going to be counting on you for, however, doesn't involve helping with tomorrow's re-opening. It's going to start well ahead of that."

"What have you got in mind?" Orson wanted to know.

"What I've got in mind," Drummond said through clenched teeth, "is you bringing back that ungrateful little rip we've come to call Calamity Jane Jr.! If she thinks she can be the catalyst for all this damage and pain and then fly away free as a bird, she has another think coming. She has a contract she honored for the real Calamity Jane and then for Breeson—now that I've taken over, she will by-God do no less for me!"

"Can you force her to do that ... er, in a legal way, I mean?"

"As far as I'm concerned, I can." Drummond scowled fiercely. "At the very least, I can sue her for breach of contract and force her to stick around until a trial can be arranged. Hell, if that's not enough I'll charge her and her gun-toting new boyfriend with assault and arson, maybe even attempted murder for all the trouble they caused last night! By the time I'm done, that little ingrate will beg for her job back and a place to stay and whatever else she can do to appease me."

"Guess I never knew Janie was so important to rate all that attention," Orson remarked.

"Under different circumstances, she might not be," Drummond replied, his scowl still fixed in place. "But with too much happening too fast—Breeson getting killed, the fire, Jane taking off, me suddenly being the face of the operation where before I was mostly in the background. Those kinds of things occurring in rapid order can wreck the momentum and the success of an operation like this, Orson.

"What do you think gives Calamity Jane's Place the edge over the dozen or more other saloons and booze joints on Tent Row? It starts with the name and the legitimate connection to Calamity Jane herself, of course. But, even with her gone, there remains the connection of the dancing girls she originally brought with her. Breeson could also claim a direct link, having been her partner for a while. And as soon as she was gone he added the singer and the Calamity Jr. gimmick. Not to mention his own flamboyance and the way he would often sit in on high stakes games to add excitement." Drummond paused for a moment, his expression turning sober and grimly determined before he continued. "I don't know if I can maintain or recapture all of that, Orson. But I've been handed the chance and I sure as hell mean to make the most I can out of it. And I'm damn well not going to start by letting some no-name, high-minded songbird who truth be told has more talent for showing her tits than hitting the right note, walk out on me! Little Miss Janie treated me like dirt when she was strutting around under Breeson's wing. Now we'll see who has the last strut!"

Hearing this, Orson winced a little and suspected that, for all of Drummond's rambling, the last part had revealed his strongest motivation. Choosing his words carefully, the big bouncer said, "So what you're wantin' is for me to take after her and bring her back, no matter what. That it?"

Drummond gave him a sharp look. "Yes, that's exactly what I want. I thought I'd already made it plain. You have a problem with carrying it out?"

"No, I said you can count on me and I meant it. But …"

"But what?" Drummond demanded irritably.

"That fella Miss Janie took off with, that McGantry—"

"What about him? You're not afraid of him, are you? I should have thought you'd look forward to a chance to get your hands on him again."

"Damn right I would," Orson declared. "Ain't a man around I'm afraid to go up against when they're standin' in front of me. But that's the thing about this McGantry character, talk spreadin' around town all day has it that he's got quite a reputation as a former Army scout and Indian fighter. That wouldn't mean a lick, like I said, if I had him standin' in front of me. But the fact of the matter is, I've made my way workin' minin' camps and boom towns. Bustin' skulls and beatin' down rowdies in saloons, whorehouses, and the like."

Orson paused, his broad face scrunching into a sheepish look before he went on. "But in open country, tryin' to chase down an hombre like McGantry who's had a half day's start and knows his way around out there in the wild like I know the layout of our saloon. Hell, Mr. Drummond, I may not be able to even *find* him and Miss Janie!"

For a long moment, Drummond just stared blank-faced at the big man. Then, suddenly, surprisingly, he threw back his head and brayed with laughter. Orson looked on, by turns appearing relieved, then uncertain, and all the while quite puzzled.

When Drummond's laughter subsided and he'd caught his breath, he wagged his head and said, "Trust me, my large friend, especially in my current condition I am keenly aware of the limitations one has to take into consideration. Even though I hadn't heard about McGantry's alleged frontier prowess, I nevertheless did recognize your lack of skill in such matters. In my haste to set you after him and our runaway songstress, however, I failed to mention this and to add the rather important detail that I want you to secure the assistance of someone better suited for that kind of work—find Injun Jack before the night is out."

A flood of relief passed over Orson's face. "What about Hennessy, my cousin? They're probably together."

"Yes, and they're likely both drunk. Very well. Roust them both. Get their drunken asses sobered up and ready to ride first thing in the morning. Tell them I'll pay a bonus—and that goes for you too—if the girl is back in time for the weekend shows."

Orson nodded eagerly. "Like I keep sayin', boss, you can—"

"Count on you," Drummond finished for him. "I know. And I'm doing just that. I want you back because I need you around here. But first, more importantly, I need you overseeing the return of Jane in one piece. She can be as angry and upset as she wants, but I don't want her hurt. That's why I'm sending you along, Orson. Injun Jack may be necessary for his tracking skills, but I've also heard stories about how he treats women. It's up to you to make sure he doesn't lay one dirty red finger on Jane."

"He won't," Orson said, his tone turning grim. "How about McGantry?"

Drummond made a dismissive gesture with one hand. "Do with him as you like. But I don't judge him as somebody who'd accept well having something taken from him … Was me, I'd make sure there wasn't anything left to come back for more."

"Yeah. I think the same."

Drummond pulled the cork on his laudanum bottle and

tipped it up for another big gulp. Lowering it, he said, "You'd better get a move on. Find Injun Jack and Hennessy and start sobering them up for an early start in the morning. Whatever supplies you need, charge it to me. Just make sure to put them to good use."

"Consider it done."

Drummond grimaced as he gently lifted the light blanket that covered his salve-smeared, gauze-wrapped legs. "Before you leave, though, go fetch a couple of our bar maids. The two prettiest ones—Esmeralda and Francine, I think are their names. If they're with somebody, get rid of whoever it is."

"Those little doves don't know it yet but they're going to be learning some new tricks, as my nurses, while you're away. The doctor will be here tomorrow to instruct them on applying fresh salve and changing my bandages. Before you go, I want you to show them a little about moving me in and out of this damnable chair. I know any moving about is going to hurt like hell, but I mean to try sleeping in my own bed tonight. And while I can't do a blessed thing else while there, I can at least find some comfort by filling my arms with warm female flesh."

CHAPTER 20

———

"Scorch! Wake up! … Wake up, you're havin' a bad dream!"

Scorch Bannon struggled from the grip of tormented slumber only to find himself in the grip of two strong hands, blunt fingers digging hard into his shoulders as they gently but firmly shook him. Waking fully, he found he was gasping hard for breath and his face was drenched by cold, clammy sweat. When he opened his eyes, he was looking up at a large, coarsely-featured face looming at arms' length directly over him.

"Jesus!" Bannon exclaimed.

Barge Kanelly let go of the gang leader's shoulders and leaned back. Receding in this manner caused his black moon of a face to lose most of its distinction and be all but swallowed by the murky shadows that filled the rustic pinewood cabin.

"No, I ain't Jesus. Not hardly," said Kanelly. "Though, on second thought, maybe I did just chase away some demons that was tormentin' you in your sleep."

Bannon pushed to a sitting position on the straw-filled sleeping pallet that was placed against the back wall of the cabin. Other such pallets were also positioned along the wall. Bannon pulled up an edge of the blanket spread over him and used it to mop sweat from his face. Then, his breathing having begun to level off, he said, "Was it the same dream again? Could you tell?"

Kanelly had by now settled onto one of the wooden chairs pushed in around a sturdy, rough-hewn table in the middle of the room. "Sounded like," he answered. "You was tossin' and mumblin' some of the usual stuff. Cussin' your pap. Then beggin' him and startin' to scream from the pain. That's why I came over and shooked you 'wake. Figured you wouldn't want the others to hear you carryin' on like that."

"No. You're right, I'd as soon they didn't. Thanks for pullin' me out of it, Barge." Bannon mopped his face one more time with the blanket and then cast it away and rose from the pallet. At forty-five, he was a man of slightly above average height, lean and solid, his bare torso and arms displaying hard, ropey muscles that would have been the envy of someone half his age. His movements were smooth and catlike and his thick sandy hair showed not a trace of gray. In contrast to these impressive physical traits, the puckered, pale pink scar that ravaged most of the left side of an otherwise handsome face seemed all the more a cruel reminder of some past misfortune.

Shuffling over to take a seat opposite Kanelly, carrying his shirt and boots with him, Bannon said, "What time is it? Where's everybody else?"

"Sun just broke a few minutes ago," Kanelly answered. "Elroy and his brother are out fetchin' more wood for a breakfast fire. The kid wandered off with a fishin' pole, said he was gonna bring back some brook trout to fry."

Bannon frowned as he leaned forward to pull on his boots. "What the hell gave him the idea to go fishing all of a sudden?"

"How do I know?" Kanelly shrugged. "He got voices inside his head talkin' to him all the time. You know that. Reckon one of 'em musta told him it was time to go fishin'.'"

Bannon shrugged into his shirt and began buttoning it. "Well, I guess some fried trout wouldn't be such a bad idea, would it? Be a welcome change from bacon and beef all the time."

"If you say so," allowed Kanelly. "For me, when I was a child 'bout the onliest meat we had was fish. Bullheads and mudcats, and my mama never could seem to get that muddy taste cooked out. I was happy to get my belly filled, don't get me wrong. But, still and all, ever since then I ain't ever had much of a cravin' for fish. Nossir, I'll take beef or bacon every chance I get."

So declaring, the big man leaned back in his chair, causing it to creak under his bulk. At six-and-a-half feet tall and a frame packed with a thick layer of fat over even thicker layers of muscle, he looked like there wasn't much in the way of food that he ever objected to. Topping this mass, resting on a bull neck, was a face carrying its own share of scars. Most of these came from his time in the fighting pit of a Georgia plantation, back before the war, when he was a slave of above average size and strength who was matched against other young bucks from surrounding plantations in brutal, bare-knuckle slug fests staged for the entertainment of their jaded owners and select guests. The backs of Kanelly's knuckles were also heavily scarred, attesting to the broken bones and teeth of all the opponents who fell before him.

"No matter what gets cooked in the way of grub," said Bannon as he dug the makings from his shirt pocket and started fashioning a cigarette, "what I'm craving the most as soon as they get that stove fired up is some strong, hot coffee."

"Yeah, coffee's allus good," agreed Kanelly.

Blowing a cloud of smoke, Bannon grimaced and said, "I remember the dream now, Barge. The same old nightmare. My damned pap. Drunk, beating on my ma. Kicking me out of the way. And then, when I kept running back against him, trying to get him to stop, him swinging around with that skillet of hot bacon grease and slamming it against the side of my face. The dirty old bastard. Even while I was laying there screaming in agony, he kept beating Ma, wouldn't let her come to try and comfort me."

"Best not to keep re-livin' it. Put it out of your mind as much as you can, Scorch," advised Kanelly. In the beginning, after he started being referred to more and more frequently as "Scorch" on wanted posters and by victims and lawmen, Bannon hated it and only somebody tired of living dared call him that to his face. But over time he had grown to embrace it as both a personal distinction and as fuel for his rage against the world.

"Don't you think I'd like to?" Bannon scowled. "How do you control what comes in your sleep? Why can't I dream instead about the day I went back and killed the old sonofabitch? Then it wouldn't be a nightmare no more!"

Before Kanelly could respond, the front door opened and two men came tromping in carrying armloads of split wood which they took over an dumped on the floor beside the cook stove. Both of the new entrants were getting up in years, each with scraggly gray hair and similar stoop-shouldered builds. But it was the close resemblance of their faces that would have led even a stranger to correctly guess they were brothers.

Elroy "Pops" MacArthur had been riding with Bannon

and Kanelly for more than a half dozen years. His brother Darwin, older by eighteen months, had been manning this cabin in Wolverine Wash for nearly as long, eking out a living by scraping gold out of these lonely hills above Deadwood. Though Darwin had never gone over to the owlhoot side himself, he had no qualms about harboring his kid brother's outlaw gang when they came seeking a place to lay low from the law for a while. A belief in blood being thicker than water was the decider for him and the irony of having under his roof the gold they'd acquired in only a few bloody minutes being worth many times more than the total of what he'd strained his back and muscles for years to dig out of the ground never seemed to occur to him. It did occur to him, though, that getting paid a slice of those ill-gotten gains for his "hospitality" would only be reasonable when the time came.

"I'll have the top of this stove cherry red in just a handful of minutes, boys," he announced as he began feeding in some fuel. "Then I'll cook us up some breakfast."

"And coffee," Bannon reminded him.

"Coffee. You bet."

While his brother got a fire going in the stove's belly, Elroy sat down at the table with Bannon and Kanelly. Rubbing his hands together, he said, "Brisk morning out there. But the day's looking like it's gonna be another fine sunny one."

"Pretty much like most days have been lately," remarked Kanelly.

Elroy nodded. "Exactly my point. Means any and all passes or rugged country between here and Montana high country have got to be plenty clear by now. Don't you think, fellas?"

"I expect that's the case, yeah." Bannon eyed him

somewhat suspiciously. "Is that your whole point, Pops?"

The old man met his gaze without flinching. "You know what my point is, Scorch. And don't tell me you ain't feelin' it just like the rest of us. The itch to get a move on, get away from here. I hear you tossin' and turnin' more each night. That's the demons in you gettin' restless, too."

"How about you let me worry about my demons, old man," growled Bannon. "They ain't ever got in the way of me or this gang doing what needed to be done, have they?"

Although Barge Kanelly was the only one who knew the full story behind Scorch's night terrors, the other gang members had heard him crying out in his sleep often enough to know he had deeper scars than just what showed on the outside.

"I'm just sayin', that's all," Elroy protested, still not withering under Bannon's glare. "Apart from all of us feelin' the move-on itch, there's a fine line between hidin' out and hangin' in one spot too long."

"What's that supposed to mean? You saying your brother is getting sick of having us underfoot?" Bannon wanted to know.

Turning from where he had just placed a large coffee pot atop the cook stove, Darwin said, "Nobody heard that from me. I got no problem with you fellas stayin' as long as you need. You been real good about payin' for the extra supplies I have to stock and, truth to tell, I kinda like havin' somebody to talk to after all the lonely time I been up here by myself. Just me and my old hound Rufus."

"Hear that? So what bug is up your ass?" Bannon demanded of Elroy.

"Yeah, I heard that," the old man came back. "And part of what I heard was one of the things I've started worryin' about."

Bannon said, "So spit it out plain. What big worry am I missing?"

Elroy half turned in his chair and aimed a question at his brother. "Those extra supplies you've had to stock, Darwin … how often have you gone down into town to keep 'em up?"

Darwin looked thoughtful for a moment. Then: "Make it three times so far. But, before we turned in last night, I got to checkin' what's left on hand and it looks like I'll need to make another run in the next day or so. Can't quite get the hang of keepin' ahead of five instead of only one."

"Uh-huh. And how often do you go when you're on your own?"

"Oh, shucks. Not near as much. My needs are pretty simple. Probably go down every nine or ten weeks. That partly depends on the luck I have turnin' up color. If I hit a good streak and fill a pouch of dust sooner than usual, then I'm apt to go down quicker and splurge a little." Darwin paused and gave an exaggerated wink. "And by splurge, I mean a couple hours spent at Madam Lucy's where a body can also find a way to get his loneliness took care of for a while."

A deep chuckle rumbled out of Kanelly. "You randy old goat. Probably a good thing your luck don't run good enough to take you to Madam Lucy's more often—you'd give yourself a heart stroke!"

"I can think of worse ways to go," declared Darwin with a smug smile.

"Doggone it, I'm tryin' to make a serious point here," Elroy said sternly.

"And you succeeded. I see exactly what you're driving at and it's a damned good observation. I hate admitting I didn't think of it myself." Bannon's tone and the matching somberness of his expression quickly wiped the grins off Kanelly and Darwin.

"Admittin' what? What in blazes are you talkin' 'bout?" Kanelly said. "I wish everybody would quit speakin' in riddles and start sayin' their piece straight out!"

Bannon responded, "The straight of it is this: We've been sending Darwin to town too much. We know Deadwood is crawling with soldiers and army investigators not necessarily in uniform, all looking to get a line on us. We made our first mistake by being too cocky about announcing we were headed here in the first place. We figured it would be just a quick stopover to split the haul and then scatter, each with his share, until we met up again later in Montana high country. But that was before we saw all the newly minted coins that we have to hold off spending because there's too many eyes watching for them to turn up."

"Yeah, we know all that. You ain't said nothing new." Kanelly frowned. "That's why we're layin' low, waitin' for things to cool down and for Henry to come 'round before we slip away. Even then, we all agreed not to spend any of those shiny new coins until we're way off in Montana. And we been careful as can be to pick only old coins for Darwin to use when he goes for supplies. So, what's the big problem you and Elroy can all of a sudden see that nobody did before?"

"It ain't the money Darwin is spending," Bannon replied. "Like I already said, it's the fact he's spending it too damn often. You still not see? All those federal hounds swarming throughout Deadwood ain't just looking for new-minted gold coins. They're looking for *anything* out of the ordinary—an anomaly, would be the fancy word—that might be a hint that could be traced to us."

Darwin's brow puckered. "Jeez. Now that you mention

it, a couple of the store clerks where I usually get stuff even commented on that the last time I went. They joshed me about maybe movin' in a new Injun squaw and a passel of hungry papooses along with her, the way I was goin' through vittles."

Elroy frowned at his brother. "What do you mean 'new Injun squaw'—you had on before? I never knew that."

Darwin shrugged. "Never came up I guess. But yeah, I had me a plump little Arapaho gal for near two years when I first settled here. She caught pewmonie and died on me one winter, though, damn shame. She was about the perfect wife. Didn't talk much, leastways not that I could understand, was a great belly warmer on cold nights, and could cook and sew to beat the band. Look around" —the old prospector waved his hand— "a lot of what you see me still usin' today, from the britches I'm wearin' to the blankets and leather workin's, she made for me while she was here."

"I'll be damned. I never knew," said Elroy.

"Well we're all real happy for you and your short-lived domestic bliss, Darwin," growled Kanelly, his dark face clouding even darker. "But what about this other business of makin' too many trips for supplies—what does that mean for us goin' forward?"

Bannon rose from his chair and began pacing, trailing a plume of smoke from his cigarette. "The first thing it means is we sure as hell don't send Darwin to town again anytime soon."

"Comes down to it, I could stretch what supplies we got for quite a spell," said Darwin. "Wouldn't be a lot of variety, though. Got plenty of coffee. Beans and sowbelly, flour for biscuits. That sort of thing. But all good belly fillers."

"Another option, if we're gonna stick for a while longer, is that me and the kid could probably get away with makin' a trip," suggested Elroy. "Where you and Barge would get spotted in no time, we don't look that different than dozens of other fellas, not even with wanted dodgers on us. Hit it at a busy time, maybe around dusk, I bet we could go in and out without anybody ever battin' an eye."

Bannon stopped pacing and stood over by the front door, facing away from everybody for a long count, streaming more smoke. When he turned back around, his jaw was set, his mouth a tight line. "I think you're right, Pops. It wouldn't be totally without risk, but a slim enough one to take if you and young Tom are willing."

"You know the kid will do anything you ask."

"And I'd be asking only for the sake of more than fetching supplies. If it was just that, I'd say we tighten our belts, learn to love sowbelly, and sit tight for a while longer. But I think there's too many signs pointing to it being time for us to move on."

"You really mean it?" Kanelly and Elroy said the words in near perfect unison, their expressions openly eager.

"Said so, didn't I?"

Kanelly's eager look fell quickly. "But what about Henry?"

Bannon's mouth tightened again. "That's what I meant when I said Elroy and Tom would be taking the risk for more than just supplies. It's been near two weeks since Darwin went to town and heard the news that Henry had wangled himself an alibi so the army hounds couldn't touch him back in Crawford, even though they had suspicions he was in on the robbery. That explained why he hadn't made it here to join us yet, he couldn't get away for fear some of those hounds might follow him and bring the heat down on us. He was riding it out there extra long, until he was sure of getting away clean."

"You think that's why he still ain't showed up?" asked Kanelly. ˉ

"That's what I'd like to get some idea of." Bannon cut his eyes over to Darwin. "You said the stage from down Sydney way rolls in every Wednesday, right?"

"Regular as can be."

"And last time you were in town you said the stage had brought in fresh newspaper accounts of the Fort Robinson payroll robbery, including the mention of Henry, that had folks to buzzing about it pretty good."

"Buzzin' like bees they was."

Bannon nodded. "By my reckoning, tomorrow is Wednesday. Means the Sydney stage is due in. That should make tomorrow evening a prime time for Elroy and young Tom to go in for supplies and also try to get an earful of the latest buzz about things in general and the train robbery in particular. That might include another mention of Henry."

"Good or bad?"

"I'd say no mention would be the best news. It would mean they still hadn't been able to make any charges stick and he'd be that much closer to lighting a shuck out of there."

Elroy frowned. "So in that case we'd hang back a while longer to wait for him?"

"No. Long as we know things haven't turned any worse for Henry and he won't need our help slipping out of a noose or something, it'll still be time for us to move on." Bannon paused to flash a rare grin. "Hell, everybody knows Henry can talk the varnish off a cigar store Indian. If those army boys in Crawford haven't nailed him yet, they ain't going to. When the time is right, he'll make his getaway and catch back up with us like he always does and this time it looks like that's going to be in the Montana high country."

CHAPTER 21

—

"Way I had in mind," Lone was saying, "we'd ride due west until we hit the stagecoach road that runs from Sydney to Deadwood, and then follow it the rest of the way on up. Be a sight longer that way, but enough easier goin' so as to make it up time-wise."

Maggie eyed him from where she sat astride Rascal, reined up alongside Lone and Ironsides. "Somewhere in there I heard '*had* in mind', do I take that to mean you're considering something different?"

A corner of Lone's mouth quirked up. "You don't miss much, do you?"

"When you've had the wool pulled over your eyes as many times as I have," Maggie replied, a trace of bitterness unmistakable in her tone, "only a complete dullard would fail to start being more alert."

"I don't make you for a dullard. Not by a long shot," Lone told her earnestly. "As far as the route we take to Deadwood, yeah, I'm figurin' now we maybe oughta go about it a mite different."

"How come?"

"Because if we figure there's a chance Drummond might send somebody to try and take you back where he reckons you belong, then us strikin' out the easiest way also makes it easier for anybody comin' after us to follow our trail. We already had an unexpected taste of that. Seein's how we more or less *do* expect another batch of visitors, I'm thinkin' we oughta accommodate 'em the least amount we can."

"That sounds reasonable," said Maggie. "But if Drummond sends Injun Jack, he's supposed to be a top notch tracker. Doesn't that mean he'll be able to follow our trail anyway?"

"Probably," Lone allowed. "If it's Jack, yeah, by all reports he's mighty good. But if you'll pardon me a little braggin', I happen to know a thing or three about trails and trackin', too. It galls the beejesus out of me that I let that ratty old buff hunter and his pals slip up on us as easy as they did back yonder, and I aim to do my damnedest not to allow any kind of repeat." He paused, scowling. Then: "If we light out across rough country, I ain't claimin' I can lay sign Jack won't be able to follow at all—but I bet I can cause that heathen to stop and do some head scratchin' along the way. And every time he stops to ponder, that's time we can be stretchin' our lead."

"You've got me convinced," Maggie told him. "You set the course, I'll follow."

In the early light of a new day, minus the makeup and smoky saloon shadows, Lone was suddenly struck by just how pretty Maggie truly was. This realization unexpectedly brought on thoughts of Tru Min Chang, the Oriental beauty he had recently parted ways with back in Colorado. While there'd been no promises or commitments between him and Tru other than an acknowledgment of their shared feelings for one another and a hope that the future might hold a chance for them to reunite, Lone nevertheless felt a pang of guilt for taking notice of Maggie the way he caught himself doing in this moment.

As a result, something must have shown on his face that caused Maggie to abruptly ask, "What's the matter? Is something wrong?"

Lone quickly shook his head. "No. Not a thing. Nothing, that is, except palaverin' about what we're *gonna* do ain't accomplishin' much except burnin' daylight."

After the shooting in their camp last night, Maggie had been too unnerved to want to remain there for the sake of trying to get any more rest. So, they packed up their gear, saddled the horses, and by moonlight had ridden a far enough distance to put Maggie more at ease. Stopping again, they spread their bedrolls a second time and were able (Lone at least) to catch a few additional hours of shut-eye ahead of dawn. Breakfast was a simple, rather hurried affair of biscuits and coffee before they were back in the saddle and ready to head out.

Although agreeing to the proposed change in the route they would take, Maggie still appeared somewhat pensive about something. When Lone pinned her with a questioning look, she admitted somewhat sheepishly, "I know I was the one in a big hurry to get away from that camp last night. But now, in the light of day, I ... well, I can't keep from thinking about those men we left back there, just sprawled where they fell."

"If it makes it easier, consider me as the one who left 'em," Lone countered.

Maggie shook he head. "No, I was part of it. I hadn't the slightest qualm at the time. But later, during the night, is when I – I started thinking about it. I heard some coyotes howling in the distance."

"Coyotes howl. It's what they do." Lone took a breath, let it out raggedly. Then: "Look, Maggie, I'm gonna say this as gentle but plain as can be, if you're tryin' to sug-gest we should go back and bury those critters, that ain't gonna happen. In the first place, I ain't inclined to break a sweat over three sonsabitches who came lookin' to kill me. Especially when I went easy on two of 'em I tangled with earlier and look what it almost got me. In the second place, the time we'd waste with them would amount to time that anybody else comin' on our trail would gain. Is that what you want?"

"No. Of course not," Maggie responded.

"Then keep in mind what I said, and let's get a move on."

Maggie regarded him. "You work awful hard at that hard act, don't you, McGantry?"

Lone met her eyes with a flat, emotionless gaze. "If Injun Jack catches up with us, you'd better hope it's more than just an act."

*****

"Come on, Orson," groaned Luther Hennessy. "You got a bottle on you somewhere, I know you do. In your coat pocket, in your saddlebags—some damn where. Spare me just a swallow or two. I need it bad, I tell you. Hair of the dog, man, come on … I feel like elsewise I might die."

Riding along with the early morning sun on his broad back and his derby hat perched atop his head at a jaunty angle that did nothing to shade the fat rolls on the back of his neck, Orson responded over his shoulder to the laments of his cousin riding in line behind him. "You've survived hangovers before, Luther. If you was gonna die from such, you'd've been dead a hell of a long time ago."

"I know. That's what makes me a kind of expert on hangovers," declared Luther. "That's how I know this one truly might kill me, especially bouncin' along on this blasted horse, churnin' up my gut and splittin' my skull all the worse. A little hair of the dog, I tell you is the only—"

He was cut short by a growl from Injun Jack Calico, sitting on a gleaming black gelding at the head of the trio of riders. "Shut up your damn wailin' like a squaw givin' birth! I got a bustin' head, too, and you carryin' on ain't helpin' a bit! You want the hair of something to chaw on, Luther—how about I wheel around and stuff some of my horse's tail down your gullet!"

The reaction of Luther, as well as Orson—two grown men of such intimidating bulk so promptly squaring their shoulders and obediently clapping their mouths shut—would have made a curious sight in most any setting except perhaps within military ranks. In as much as this setting had nothing to do with the military and the one growling the command was scarcely more than half the size of the responding pair, the sight was not only curious but might even have appeared amusing to some.

But only to someone who wasn't familiar with Injun Jack or didn't take time to give him a very close looking over. At fifty years of age, slight of build but propelled by hard, stringy muscles under a leathery hide, Jack moved with the deceptively unhurried grace of a puma who knows it has its prey cornered within easy striking distance. This quiet, subtle sense of menace was amplified more openly by the soulless depth of Jack's coal black eyes and the hard, humorless features of his narrow, copper-hued, deeply seamed face. Around his scrawny neck hung a necklace of eagle talons and around his bony waist hung a U.S. Cavalry gunbelt with a long-bladed, bone-handled hunting knife in a beaded sheath on his right hip and a Walker Colt revolver worn for the cross draw on his left.

There was little doubt that the half breed's reputation and aura had him poised as the dominant member of this group, despite Orson being the one who'd formed it under the direction and finance of Drummond. The tenuous balance was that Injun Jack would take orders—as long as it suited him. Luther, who hung around with him on a regular basis, had grown used to following his lead. For Orson, who was carrying orders from Drummond to make sure Jack didn't "lay one dirty red finger on Jane", the shadow of potential conflict loomed. But for now, he was dependent on the man to find the fleeing girl. If that meant allowing him a bit of dominant swagger in the meantime, he could live with it. Should it be necessary, however, the bouncer was prepared to put his foot down.

For now, Luther, who'd weathered angry outbursts from his drinking pal before, helped deflect this latest one by saying, "Jesus Christ, Jack. 'Hair of the dog' is just an expression. Been around for ages. It don't really mean—"

"I know what it don't mean," Jack cut him off again. "It don't mean what it says. Like so many of the dumb sayings you White Eyes have!"

Luther grunted. "Ha! Us White Eyes have dumb sayings? If all redskins have a sense of humor like you—which is *none*—then no wonder you think our age-old sayings are dumb. I hope to hell you don't think 'hair of the horse's tail' is ever gonna catch on and be around for generations."

"I didn't say it to be an expression for the ages. I said it because I meant it," Jack told him, but sounding more exasperated now than truly angry. Then he added, "Yet you're still wailin' like a squaw!"

Sensing not to push it too far, Luther said, "All right, I'll ease up then, if your eyes are as bloodshot as mine, I reckon you need to concentrate with everything you got to keep spottin' the trail we're followin'."

"I don't allow my eyes to get bloodshot," Jack insisted. "And even if they was actually bleedin', I'd never fail to cut the sign of a trail I was on!"

CHAPTER 22

———

As Lone and Maggie angled northwest away from the Pine Ridge region and beyond the sprawl of the Sandhills, the landscape they rode over began to change. It was still primarily an expanse of grassy hills, but the grass was a shorter, coarser variety and the hills were choppier, more sharply crested, cut frequently by twisty, washed-out gullies. Sandstone ridges like ragged yellow teeth ran along many of the crests and here and there a low, lonely butte could be seen poking up. From higher points, the dense, dark greenery of the Black Hills could be seen due north and, away to the west and a bit south, the uneven peaks of the Laramie Mountains.

Also visible in the distance, directly on course for where they were headed, an increasingly darkening wall of storm clouds was lifting slowly above the horizon. While the sun had been shining down on them all morning from a mostly clear sky, it appeared inevitable that a storm would be greeting them by or before nightfall.

Seeing this and recognizing they had made good progress through the first half of the day, when noon arrived

Lone announced they would make a somewhat extended halt and cook up an extra hearty meal. "By the look of those clouds ahead," he said, "we're in for a wet, unpleasant night and stokin' up a good cookin' fire come supper time might be a bit of a challenge. Given that, I recommend we rest a spell here and fill our bellies with a nice hot noon meal while we got the chance. Later on, I expect it's likely gonna be beef jerky and leftover cold coffee."

Maggie scowled in the direction of the distant clouds. "You don't think there's any chance of that storm breaking up before it gets here?"

"Reckon there's always a chance," Lone allowed. "Storms out here on the plains sometimes take odd notions all their own. But I wouldn't count on it too much, not by the look of that one."

Maggie sighed. "Well, storm or no storm, being out of the saddle and resting here for a while sure isn't a notion I have trouble accepting."

So, while Lone tended the horses, Maggie got a fire going and set a pot of coffee brewing over it. Together they worked up a double batch of pan biscuits and opened airtights of canned beef and stewed tomatoes to go with them. When all was laid out, it made a fine meal. Afterwards, when Lone got ready to wrap the leftover biscuits in oilcloth to have later, Maggie suggested an alternative.

"Do you have another tin of canned beef?" she asked. Getting an affirmative answer, she then said, "What if we opened it up, split the biscuits, and made sandwiches to wrap in the oilcloth for later? We may still have to settle for cold coffee, but wouldn't sandwiches go better with it than just jerky?"

Lone cocked an eyebrow. "A body can go a long way on jerky and hardtack, let alone fresh biscuits. I've done it but comin' up with something a little more creative ain't a bad thing neither."

Once the sandwiches were made and wrapped and their cooking gear cleaned and packed back up, they sat on the soft grass a while longer each with a final cup of coffee.

"This is nice," Maggie said, rocking her head back and slowly tilting it from side to side. "A hot bath right about now would be even better. Not only to get clean but to soothe my aching ... well, never mind that part, with all this grass in every direction you look, it's amazing how much dust the horses still find to kick up."

"That storm hits tonight," Lone drawled, "you can stand out in it and get yourself rinsed off to a fair-thee-well."

"I said a *hot* bath," she reminded him. "And not just to wash off the dust and soothe my aches either. But also to try and scrub away the dirty feel of Howie's ... well, never mind that part, too."

Lone looked over at her. "That'd be the best thing for you to do. Never mind it, put it out of your thoughts like it never happened. Don't let it have any control over you."

"If it's so easy to do," Maggie responded, "why are you on your way to Deadwood? Are you putting what Scorch's bunch did to your friend out of your thoughts like it never happened? Or are you being controlled by the revenge you're hell bent on delivering to them?"

Lone's mouth pressed into a straight, thin line but he made no reply.

Maggie sat up straighter, her brows pinching together. "Aw, damn it, McGantry. I had no call saying that. I'm sorry."

Lone took a sip of his coffee. "It's okay. I asked for it, stickin' my nose in to try and tell you how to feel about something personal."

"But you were trying to comfort me. I snapped back purely out of peevishness," Maggie said. "That's been the story for too much of my life—lashing out at the wrong time or at the wrong person. Sometimes both at once."

Lone gave it a beat before saying, "I can think of one case where your lashin' out wasn't such a bad thing. Fact is, I'm mighty grateful on account of it. If you'll pardon me bringin' up Howie again, the way I saw it there wasn't a blame thing wrong with neither your timin' nor your target when you took a notion to lash out at him last night."

Maggie paused with her coffee cup raised part way to her mouth. She held it there, her eyes seeming to gaze off at something for a long moment. Then she said, "No, I guess there wasn't, was there? That was one time I was—"

When she stopped abruptly, Lone's eyes held on her but again he said nothing, just waited.

Maggie turned her head and met his gaze. Her expression appeared unsettled. "I was about to say, 'That was one time I was dead on'. How dreadfully ironic would that have been as a choice of words?"

"Because Howie actually *did* end up dead, you mean?" Lone frowned. "But you're not the one who killed him—I did."

"But as the result of my action. I – I practically set him up for it," Maggie lamented.

His tone growing annoyed, Lone said, "Yeah, and if you hadn't, where would we be now? Those skunks had me cold. If not for your action, I'd be dead and you probably would be too. Or maybe just wishin' you were. Damn it, Maggie, those were bad men with bad intentions and the ones we expect yet to show—Injun Jack, at least—are worse. Now you can call me hard or harsh or vengeful, or whatever you want. But I call it bein' a survivor, and that means doin' whatever it takes to remain one. And, unless I read you wrong from the start, I make you for bein' cut from the same bolt."

Maggie slowly finished raising her coffee cup to her lips and took a drink. Lowering it again, she said, "You're right, I am a survivor. And, like you said, that means having done some things, whatever it took. Even having Howie's dirty hands pawing me wasn't—"

Quietly but firmly, Lone stopped her. "Don't go there. There's no need."

Maggie drank some more coffee and then went on. "But the thing I always managed to mostly stay away from was violence. Oh I knew, in the places I ended up, that it was taking place *around* me. But I seldom saw it first hand, and even just the knowing bothered me more than … I already told you how it was with Henry, after he took up with Scorch and Kanelly and I started hearing the reports about the shootings and killings they became involved in. I ran away from that and then, when I found myself anywhere that turned too rough and rowdy, I moved on some more."

"The place I worked in Deadwood when I was there before, and then the move to Crawford with Calamity Jane's troupe worked out pretty well in that regard. Despite her reputation, Jane ran a very strict operation. And, I've got to say, so did Breeson after he took over. While shootings and knifings were common in other places all up and down Tent Row, that kind of trouble was rare in our place."

"Until the night before last," Lone remarked. "When things took a mighty drastic turn."

"Boy did they ever," Maggie said wryly. "Two men killed right before my eyes. And a third mortally wounded. I can still picture that knife sticking out of Breeson's stomach and all the gushing blood. Then the fight and the fire only a few hours later. And then, again last night, more killing with me even more directly involved." She paused to take a breath and then exhale it raggedly. "So here I am, on the move again, but the steering clear of violence part doesn't seem to be working out so hot."

Lone lifted his eyebrows. "In case you didn't notice, hangin' around with me ain't a particularly good way to achieve that goal."

"I didn't mean to sound like I was blaming you."

"Not sayin' you was. But the fact remains." Lone drained his cup and then turned it upside down and tapped it against the side of his leg to knock the dregs out of the bottom. "Never seemed like I went lookin' for trouble … except for this current business of huntin' down Bannon and his pack of vermin, but plenty has set itself in my path for about as far back as I can remember. For reasons I already explained, you could almost say I was born to it. Since then well, I ain't one to be Calamity pushed or treated low. I push back. And I can't stomach abuse of the weak or vulnerable. That's the long and short of it. When there's trouble that can't be rode around, I deal with it the best I can and hope each time is the last."

"But it never is."

"Seems like."

"And now, by throwing in with me and being warned that Drummond may be sending some very unpleasant men to try and take me back, you're setting yourself up for still another round." Maggie arched a single brow. "Sounds like it's hardly a one-way street as far as who hanging around with who adds up to courting trouble."

"Reckon you could look at it that way," Lone allowed. "But it's for certain us tarryin' here continuin' to jaw about it is only gonna shorten the street between us and any trouble comin' from behind. So" —as he extended his hand to assist Maggie to her feet— "let's get a move on and try to keep it stretched as far in back of us as we can."

*****

"Whoooee!" Luther Hennessy leaned back in his saddle and wrinkled his nose with exaggerated disgust. "It is a plumb fright, ain't it, how such an awful stink can work its way out of anything human?"

Reined up alongside Luther, Orson looked over at his cousin and said, "In the first place, those three poor wretches ain't human no more—they're the carcasses of what used to be human. In the second place, it's mighty rich hearin' you complain about the smell of somebody else, considerin' how ripe you are all the time without even bein' dead."

Luther's face bunched up and he looked genuinely pained. "Now that's a cruel and uncalled thing for you to say to me," he wailed. "You know durn well us Hennessy boys all got a problem with smellin' sour, no matter how much we scrub or what we try to do to fix it. Mama says it's on account of the hairy backs we inherited from Pa, that it must be in the roots or some such. Whatever it is, we can't help it."

"I don't know about all that. But I'll allow I'm sorry if I hurt your feelin's and you truly can't help it," said Orson, looking marginally contrite. Then he frowned and added, "But, come to think on it, if your pa had a hairy back and a sour smell too, it sure must not have bothered your ma much—not the way the two of 'em pumped out such a passel of kids. What are there, like nine of you and your brothers?"

"That's right. Nine boys and one sister, Mary Beth.

And before you make a smart remark, no, she don't have a hairy back and she smells sweet as a prairie flower." Luther paused to challenge Orson with his eyes before continuing. "As far as my folks makin' babies, well, I guess Mama loved Pa in spite of his smell and hairy hide and so they did what came natural."

"What comes natural to me," chimed in Injun Jack, who was dismounted and prowling among the sprawled remains of Howie, Vern, and Buster, "is scalpin' palefaces. If I'd've run into you Hennessy boys when I was a young buck out on raids, think of the field day I could have had liftin' the crop off all those hairy backs. Trouble is, it would have took the longest war lance in the world to hang 'em all from." Then Jack did what he rarely did, he laughed. It was a sound like two rocks scraping together deep in his throat. It was unpleasant and thankfully only lasted a few seconds.

Once again, Luther looked crestfallen. "That ain't funny. That ain't funny at all," he muttered.

"Something that for sure ain't funny is whatever happened here," said Orson, waving his hand to indicate the carnage before them. "What do you make of it, Jack—did that McGantry fella ambush this bunch?"

Injun Jack shook his head. "McGantry killed 'em, if that's what you mean. But no, he didn't ambush 'em. In fact, it was the other way around. This was the camp of McGantry and the girl. These three are the ones who tried to get the jump on *them*."

"How long ago, you figure?"

"Sometime before midnight."

Luther issued a low whistle. "So these three came a-sneakin', in the dark, and McGantry still got the best of 'em?"

"That's the way it reads."

"Any sign McGantry or the girl got hurt out of the deal?" Orson wanted to know.

Another head shake from Jack. "Nothing that says so. No blood except what came from the dead. You two climb down, come see if you recognize any of the fallen."

Orson and Luther exchanged reluctant looks but then slid ponderously out of their saddles. While they shuffled from body to body, grimacing as they swatted away flies and leaned closer to examine the bloated, scavenger-ravaged carcasses, Injun Jack roamed the perimeter of the campsite, eyes sweeping the ground.

As he and Orson went about their distasteful task, Luther murmured, "I've done some lowdown things in my time, cuz. But something like this, killin' a body and then just leavin' it to rot and get pecked apart by buzzards and the like, that's just deep wrong."

"I ain't sayin' I disagree," Orson responded. "But the main thing for us to keep in mind is makin' sure *we* don't end up like this."

"Good lord, lookit this one," Luther groaned, staring down at the body of Howie (though he knew not his identity). "He's been shot in the head and his eyeball appears *burned out*! Jesus, what kind of devils are we chasin' anyway?"

"Like I said, the kind we don't want to fall victim to," Orson told him.

When Injun Jack returned to the cousins, he asked, "Well?"

"Nobody I know or knew," answered Luther.

"These two" —Orson indicated Howie and Vern— "look vaguely familiar, but I can't say for sure. Probably some miners or railroad workers who came in Calamity's Place a time or two. But the fella in buckskins, oh yeah, I know him. He was one of the railroad meat hunters who started that big brawl in the saloon a couple nights ago, the one where three other men ended up gettin' killed. His partner, the fella he was fightin' with, was the skunk who stuck his knife in Mr. Breeson and mortally wounded him. That was before McGantry shot him dead, but a whisker too late."

"You're sayin' *our* McGantry—the one we're followin'—is who shot this jasper's partner? So, you think he might have come lookin' for revenge?" Luther asked.

Orson scowled. "Could be. But seein's how him and his partner were fightin' at the time—with knives—I don't know how it makes sense for this one to feel any need for revenge. The only thing I know for sure is that the last time I saw him, after I clubbed him down to help end the brawl, he was on his way to the hoosegow."

"For his own good, he should have stayed there longer," grunted Injun Jack. "Okay, we've seen all here that matters. What we want is still on the move out ahead of us. But, since they didn't bother to, the one thing else we're gonna take time for is strippin' what got left behind so's we can sell it off up the trail for a nice added bonus. Belts, boots, hats, guns, the saddles and gear off those nags we found hobbled back a ways, grab it all. We'll set two of those nags free and make a pack animal out of one of 'em to haul the goods until we run across a buyer."

"But won't a pack animal slow us down?" questioned Orson.

"McGantry is travelin' with a pack animal—*and* a damn woman" Jack snarled. "You don't think we're good enough to equal them?"

"I didn't mean it that way."

"All right then."

Luther cleared his throat and then small in a small voice, "Once we've stripped away all their valuables, are we gonna leave these men and not bury 'em either?"

Injun Jack's face turned stonier than usual. His black eyes snapped back and forth between Luther and Orson. After a long, tense beat, he rasped, "If either of you lard asses ever asks me anything that stupid again, I'll leave you where you stand and ride off to collect Drummond's money all on my own. What's more, on the way back—since I figure you two clueless slobs won't make it more than a few miles on your own—if I run across your carcasses lyin' beside the trail, I'll leave 'em just the same as the ones here. *Now get to goddamned work and help me strip these bodies so we can hit the trail and cover some ground ahead of that storm movin' in from the west!*"

CHAPTER 23

The storm rolled in on Lone and Maggie right at dusk. The bloated, sooty black clouds blotted out the last brightness of day. A wind rushing ahead of the rain dropped the temperature several degrees. But then it grew relatively calm again and when the downpour came it was steady, cold, straight strings of water.

Lone spotted a concave windscourn worn in the rocky face of a hill and chose that for their shelter. They made it in time to scrape together enough kindling for a small, quick fire to cook some coffee over. Then, wrapped in slickers that Lone dug from his gear and with his big waterproof soogan draped over their shoulders, they drank hot coffee and ate the biscuit and beef sandwiches they'd packed earlier in reasonable comfort.

"Boy, I could sure go for one of my cigarillos right about now," stated Maggie after she was finished eating. "That blasted Howie crushed both of the packs I had with me when he was thrashing around on the round the other night. You never smoked, McGantry?"

"Nope. Never got caught up by it."

"Smart. Unfortunately, I allowed myself to get caught by the nicotine trap and now I'm suffering the consequences."

"You're a survivor, remember? You'll be able to tough it out."

"Thanks for the vote of confidence but I still wish I had something to smoke."

Both were quiet for a while. Until Lone said, "The good thing about a hard, steady downpour like this is that it will mask our trail even better than the little tricks I've been pullin' as we went along. Injun Jack has already seen the angle we're on for Deadwood, so it ain't gonna throw him off too much. But every little bit helps. He can't afford to just bull ahead and risk over-shootin' us in case we juke off course or double back."

Maggie eyed him over the rim of her cup. "You think about the men on our trail all the time, don't you?"

"Quite a bit, yeah," Lone admitted. "It's an important thing to keep in mind, don't you think?"

"Yes, I suppose. But we're not even positive there's anybody back there."

"Not positive maybe. Not in the way you mean." Lone glared out at the rain. "But they're out there, I can feel 'em."

"Seriously?"

"Uh-huh. It's a kind of sense you develop—leastways you'd better, if you want to stay alive—when you spend enough time out in the wild where there are other critters who don't necessarily mean you well. I learned it when I was scoutin' for the army back when there was still plenty of Indian trouble. Unfortunately, it ain't something you can count on a hundred percent of the time. I guess that got proven the other night when those three polecats slipped up on us so unexpected. Damn, the thought of me lettin' that happen still smarts!"

Maggie said, "Like you would tell me, put it behind you."

A corner of Lone's mouth tugged back. "Guess I had that comin'. But gettin' back to my point. In this case, I *do* have a feelin'—a sense or warnin', whatever you want to call it—that somebody's on our tail. It's strong enough that I ain't gonna ignore it, so we'll keep takin' every precaution we can."

"I got no problem with that. I never meant to be argumentative," Maggie said.

They sat and just listened to the rain for a while.

Until Maggie spoke again. "Back when you were scouting for the army and fighting Indians, was that a personal thing for you? The fighting Indians part, I mean, considering what happened to your parents and all."

It wasn't the first time Lone had faced this question. Often from himself. "Yeah, in the beginnin', it was," he answered. "As soon as I was big enough and old enough to pack a gun, I wanted to ride out and kill every Indian I saw. And I did kill a whole bunch. Sometimes I was fightin' for my life, but other times I killed just because there was a redskin in front of me."

Lone drank some of his coffee and then went on. "Until one day, after a particularly bloody skirmish, the realization hit me. No matter how many Indians I killed, it was never gonna bring my parents back. And the ones directly responsible for what happened to them twenty-odd years prior were probably long dead and gone themselves. So I couldn't even rightfully claim to be an avenger. There was still more fights after that, ones that couldn't be avoided. Yet I started to look at the red man a little different. He'd been pushed and suffered massacres too. Don't mean I all the way forgave what happened to me and mine, but I at least saw that, as is often the case, there are two sides to most stories."

Maggie didn't say anything but Lone could feel her eyes on him in the darkness. "Dang it, Maggie, you're a witch," he growled. "I ain't spoke about any of that to anybody in years."

"I'm sorry if I made you uncomfortable," Maggie said. "But, at the same time, I'm glad you told me. It's not really a surprise, though—you're too decent a person to let your whole life be driven by hate."

"Decent? You've already seen me kill four men and I'm on my way to do more of the same. Not sure many folks would see that as the actions of a decent person."

"Trust me, I've known enough of the other kind. Decency is something that comes from the inside." A bitterness edged into Maggie's voice when she then asked, "For instance, do you know the story behind Scorch Bannon?"

"Can't say as I do."

"Okay, here's the way he told it to Henry: He grew up with a father who regularly beat him and his mother. One day, when Scorch was still pretty little, the old man was beating the ma and the boy tried to stop him. So, his father swatted him away by grabbing a skillet of hot bacon grease off the stove and walloping him alongside the head with it. Knocked him cold and the burning hot grease scarred his face for life."

"Mighty rough treatment for anybody, especially a kid," Lone muttered, though still not sure why he was being told any of this.

"No doubt," Maggie concurred. "When he was a little older, if what he said can be believed, Scorch went back and used a frying pan to beat his old man to death. He caught him pounding on his ma again. She thanked him by turning on him and sending for the local sheriff. So, Scorch went on the run as an outlaw and never looked back or saw his ma again."

"If that's all on the level, then it's a tale with some hard edges," Lone allowed in a measured tone. "But every varmint on the owlhoot trail has his own sad claim for why he does what he does. Somewhere along the way, though, continuin' on is a choice that each makes for himself."

"That's exactly my point about decency being inside a person," Maggie said. "You have it or you would have gone on hating and killing, seeing it as a right owed you for what happened to your parents. Men like Scorch lack it or they, too, would grow *out* of their tragic experiences instead of using them as an excuse to keep visiting tragedy and pain on others."

Neither of them spoke further for a minute or so. The only sound was the steady hiss of the falling rain.

Until Lone said, "I like it that you think I'm decent, Maggie. The rest of what you said was sorta over the head of this simple drifter. But the bottom line on men like Bannon—and Injun Jack, too—is that they're plumb dangerous, no matter what made 'em that way. That's the main thing to never to lose sight of."

Although Lone couldn't see it in the dark, Maggie smiled. "Don't worry, I'm not likely to forget that. But neither will I forget my good fortune to have at my side somebody who is 'plumb dangerous' as well."

Lone chuffed. "You bet. Decent yet dangerous, that's me."

CHAPTER 24

—

It had begun raining in Deadwood shortly past noon and by evening showed no sign of letting up. So it was that when Elroy "Pops" MacArthur and Tom "the kid" List returned to the remote cabin above Wolverine Wash they were mud-spattered and drenched to the skin. Elroy was the first one through the door and all it took was one look for Scorch Bannon to see there was something wrong.

"Bad news?" he immediately asked, his words coming out wrapped in smoke from the drag he'd just taken off his cigarette.

"It ain't good," the old man reported, shrugging out of the colorfully beaded leather pack on his back and thumping it down on top of the table top where Scorch, Kanelly, and Darwin were seated.

Heeling the door shut behind him and bringing his own pack of supplies over to the table, young Tom said, "It ain't good nohow." In his middle twenties, narrow-shouldered and pale and stringy-haired, he seemed an odd fit to the older, more hard-bitten men who surrounded him. He was a former Confederate soldier who had joined the cause as an eager, wide-eyed, ideologue of fifteen and had emerged from the horrors of battle with a haunted, perpetually far-away look in his eyes and the screams of the fallen and dying echoing distantly inside his head. In Scorch and the scars he carried on the outside, Tom had felt an instant kinship for himself and the scars he carried on the inside. His one-time devotion to the Confederacy, as evidenced by the battered, faded kepi hat he still wore, was replaced by a fierce new loyalty to Scorch and wherever he led.

The gang leader rose now, his eyes raking the two new arrivals. "Well? Are you gonna keep holding it in like a couple of impacted mares, or are you gonna spit out what the bad news is? Are the investigators back in Crawford clamping down harder on Henry?"

Elroy stepped over to the cook stove and held his damp, cold hands out over the hot surface to warm them. Over his shoulder, he said, "No, ain't nobody clampin' down on Henry no more." Turning his head, a deep sadness pinching his face, he then added, "Ain't no way to say this gentle, Scorch … Henry is dead."

"He got gunned down in a lousy saloon brawl!" Tom added bitterly. Next to Scorch, Henry Plow had been the other gang member the kid most admired.

A low groan actually escaped Bannon's lips as he took the cigarette butt from the corner of his mouth, slammed it to the dirt floor and crushed it underfoot. "Is that the news that came in on the stage?" he asked, his voice barely above a harsh whisper.

"It came in before that," Elroy answered. "On account of the suspicion Henry was under back in Crawford and with part of the same bunch of army investigators swarm-in' all over Deadwood sniffin' after us, telegraph reports commenced clackin' back and forth right after it happened.

Naturally, word leaked out wider than just the investigators. Folks in the stores and saloons were yappin' about it
a-plenty. Me and Tom started hearin' it as soon as we hit
town, wherever we went. The newspapers that came in on
the stage just added more detail."

Kanelly, who remained seated at the table, his mel-
on-sized fists balled in front of him, wanted to know,
"When did it happen?"

"Two nights ago."

Darwin stood up from the table and moved toward the
stove, saying, "I've got some hot coffee ready, brother.
I expect you and young Tom could use some to counter
being cold and wet."

"You expect right," said Elroy. "If our slickers and
wraps were as watertight as those packs made by your
late squaw wife, we'd be snug enough. But that ain't the
case so, yeah, some hot brew would be good. And it'd
be better yet if you poured in a little something extra to
help it along."

"Bring the bottle when you do," Bannon told Darwin.
His tone was flat and the expression on his face was hol-
low-eyed and still somewhat stunned looking.

While Darwin poured cups of coffee and added a generous splash of whiskey to each, Elroy and Tom shucked
their sodden outer wear and the kid took them to hang on
pegs over beside the door. Darwin handed out the steaming
mugs and then extended the whiskey bottle to Bannon.

Before taking a slug, the gang leader said, "So what
are the details?"

Blowing across the mug he now held before his face,
Elroy replied, "Like the kid said, it all stemmed from
a saloon brawl. Sounds like Henry wasn't actually a
part of that, but it spilled over to a table where he was

involved in a big poker game. The original brawlers were swingin' knives at one another and then somebody—not necessarily one of them by the sound of it—hauled out some heavier hardware and started blastin'. Henry caught one of the slugs."

Kanelly's scowl grew fiercer. "You mean he got killed by accident?"

"Maybe, maybe not."

"Goddamnit, Pops, don't start with the riddles again," warned Bannon.

"I'm tellin' you how it was put to us. Just listen," snapped Elroy. "The newspapers called it 'conflictin' reports'. Some witnesses said Henry got hit by a stray round, others claim he got shot a-purpose by some hombre named McGantry."

"I'm puttin' my money on that yellow dog McGantry!" exclaimed Tom. "He let it be known he was out to get Henry and all the rest of us too, it turns out and I say he took the chickenshit opportunity of that brawl to blindside Henry. He was askin' about us all up and down Tent Row and some say they saw him talkin' one on one to Henry not long before the brawl broke out. That sounds plain enough to me what he was workin' up to."

"Who the hell is McGantry?" Bannon demanded. "And what do you mean he's out to get all of us?"

Elroy sighed. "Just bear with us, will you? It gets a little convoluted."

Bannon took a swig of the whiskey and then, lowering the bottle, he said through clenched teeth, "Henry's dead! I ain't having no trouble following that."

As patiently and plainly as he could, Elroy proceeded to lay out the things he and Tom had heard. "This McGantry showed up in Crawford a couple days ago, lookin' to catch up with our gang. He had the names and descriptions of

Henry and you, Scorch, and he knew there was three more of us. He claimed we killed a man and stole a couple dozen horses from a ranch down in Nebraska."

"What is he? Some kind of law dog?" said Kanelly.

Elroy shook his head. "No. He says he was the partner of the fella we killed. You all remember what he's talkin' about, right? That pissant little spread with the sod hut and the one-legged old goat we left layin'?"

Bannon frowned. "Hell, that was months ago. The only reason we messed with that puny string of hayburners was on account of we needed some quick travelin' money after that bank job down in Benkelman washed out. I don't remember that old goat even havin' a partner."

"He wasn't there that day," Elroy explained. "But from all reports he's lookin' to make up for it by comin' after us out of revenge for his partner and his stole horses."

"One man comin' after the whole bunch of us? Who the hell does he think he is?" boomed Kanelly. "I'm insulted!"

"Never mind bein' insulted," said Tom. "How about bein' pissed off? He killed one of ours, I say he don't have to come *lookin'* for revenge. I say we make it easy for him to find us, only then it'll be us who feeds the revenge back at him for what he did to Henry!"

Bannon held up a hand. "Whoa, kid. Hold on a minute. That's a real swell notion, getting revenge for Henry and wiping this McGantry off our back trail all in one swipe. Under most circumstances and maybe still now I'd definitely be for it. But there's the little matter of a whole bunch of soldier boys and undercover snakes crawling all over these parts already looking for us. We pop out to go gunning after McGantry, what about them? You figure they're going to take time out from their hunt and stand idly by to let us tend to a piece of personal business?"

"To hell with them," Tom sneered. "I'm always up for the chance to kill me some more Yankee soldier boys. I got a fresh taste when we hit that payroll train, but it only whetted my appetite. Seein' all them blue-bellied bastards marchin' around town when me and Pops went in earlier, it was all I could do to hold myself back from mowin' down another heap of 'em. So, if they want to try and get in the way of us deliverin' payback to McGantry, then feedin' 'em some lead right along with him would be frostin' on the cake!"

Elroy scowled. "That's crazy talk. Crazy and wild."

The fire in Tom's eyes flared bright and intense. "You know I don't cotton to bein' called crazy. Not even by you, Pops."

"Now just calm down. Everybody!" Bannon's voice cracked as loud and sharp as a whip. "This is a hard blow and a big change, and we need to think about how best to react. But we're going to by-God do it with clear heads, you hear?"

"What's there to think about?" Tom said stubbornly. "We owe it to Henry to cut down the mangy dog who gunned him. How much clearer can it be?"

Elroy spoke in a low, weary voice. "I been ridin' the owlhoot trail longer than you been alive, son. I never once did a pard false or left one in a tight. Don't ever intend to. But this situation ain't like that. Henry's gone. Ain't nothing in our power that can change that or do him a lick of good. Anything we try will only put the rest of us at high risk for what gain?"

"I can't believe I'm hearin' this!" wailed Tom.

Bannon frowned thoughtfully. "What else do you know about this McGantry? What does he look like? When is he due in?"

"Only thing we heard directly about him," Elroy answered, "was that he used to be a long-time Indian scout with plenty of bark on him. Seems fairly well known through these parts—Nebraska, Colorado, the Dakotas."

"Goin' gunnin' for somebody we don't know the look or whereabouts of while all those army hounds are pantin' just outside the door, waitin' for us to step out, that's got the sound of a mighty risky proposition," pointed out Kanelly. Then he motioned for Bannon to hand him the whiskey.

Bannon took another pull for himself before holding out the bottle. He passed the back of one hand slowly across his mouth, brow remaining puckered in thought. "Nobody was closer to Henry than me," he stated. "We rode together for a long time and knowing I'm never going to see that cocky damn grin again or hear another tale of some gal he lifted the skirt of, is a tough thing. But, as the leader of this outfit, it's my job to think about the good of all over just one. No matter who the 'just one' might be. Henry would have understood that. Especially in this cockeyed situation where, like Pops said—"

"No!" Tom cut him off. "Don't say it, Scorch. Please don't. Don't say you want us to ride away and not try to get even for Henry."

"Damn it, kid, there's nothing we can do for him." Bannon said these words almost like he was trying to convince himself as much as Tom or anybody else hearing them. "We were getting ready to light out for Montana anyway. Remember? I think this is a sign that, more than ever, it's time to go ahead with that move. The longer we stick around here, the greater the risk of more things falling apart and more of us never making it to the high country in order to start living it up and spending all those shiny new gold pieces."

Tom's lip curled disdainfully. "Yeah, us livin' it up while Henry lays dead in some pauper's grave, if they even had the decency to bury him instead of just chuckin' him in a gully somewhere for coyote pickin's." His blazing eyes raked all those before him. "And what about McGantry, even if we do take off? If he's some kind of hotshot scout trained at trackin' and he's so hellbent on gettin' revenge—like we *ought to be*—who's to say he won't continue after us? Do we want to spend our days in Montana always lookin' over our shoulders, waitin' for a bullet to the spines we ain't doin' a very good of showin' if we run?"

Kanelly lowered the whiskey bottle after gulping down a sizable amount. "By damn, Scorch, the kid makes a mighty powerful point," he declared. "If we're gonna have to face that hellbent McGantry anyway, I'd sooner we did it and got it over with."

Elroy scowled at him. "Just a minute ago you said—"

"I know what I said. I'm changin' my mind, okay?" Kanelly worked up a scowl that caused the old man's to wither. "Happens I *don't* like the thought of lookin' over my shoulder for the weeks and months ahead. What's more, after doin' some added ponderin' on the whole thing, no matter how hard we tell ourselves it's the smartest and the least risky and whatever else, lightin' a shuck at this particular time feels more and more to me like runnin' away from a fight. And I don't like the thought of that a damn bit, neither."

All eyes now swung to Bannon. Unhurriedly, the gang leader reached in his pocket for the makings and built a cigarette. After striking a match to it and taking a long drag, he exhaled a cloud of smoke. Through the haze, his mouth could be seen pulling into a grimace. Then he said, "You know what … kid, Kanelly … I don't think I feel much like running and looking over my shoulder either."

CHAPTER 25

—

The storm rolled away in the wee hours before dawn. When daybreak came, it was to a bright, clear-skyed, fresh-smelling morning. The surrounding grassy hills, greening early this spring, were still beaded with droplets of rainwater and the effect of the sunlight hitting them was like mounds of glittering emeralds.

Emerging from their cramped, shallow burrow, Lone and Maggie shook out their slickers and the big soogan and spread them out to dry while they made a quick breakfast of leftover cold coffee and the last of the biscuits. Lone explained that, since it currently would be difficult and time-consuming to find dry fuel for a decent cook fire, they should settle for this meager fare and then later stop for a bigger, better noon meal as they had done the previous day. He further speculated that, if they pushed steady throughout the day, they stood a chance of reaching Deadwood by nightfall.

This was all Maggie needed to hear to willingly forego a breakfast of any greater substance and to urge hitting the trail as soon as possible. Together she and Lone grained the horses and give them a good rubdown after their cold, wet night before saddling up and getting underway. The sun warming their backs as they rode off felt good, the prospect of reaching their destination by the end of the day felt even better.

*****

Half a day's ride behind Lone and Maggie, their three pursuers out of Crawford also settled for a quick, cold breakfast and got an early start. This came at the constant harsh, impatient prodding of Injun Jack. Recognizing that the rain had blurred the trail of their quarry, even to his well-honed tracking skills, Jack knew he had to push harder than before in order to compensate for any added time it might take to cut sign. He had a pretty good idea of the course McGantry was set on but didn't want to risk forging ahead too impulsively without taking measures to make sure there wasn't a sudden, unexpected change.

The softness and incompetence of his two companions was already holding the half breed back from the greater speed he could have all along been achieving without them. But, despite his threats to rid himself of the pair, he knew that realistically he was stuck with them, Orson a least; for the sake of securing final payment from Drummond. Not that it made the chore of putting up with them any easier or certainly not to Jack's liking.

The storm last night, for instance, had caught them out in the open. Meaning the only shelter they had was their slickers and their bedroll wraps spread over their heads as they huddled together. Jack had endured it stoically, since there was no better option. But Orson and Luther,who in their whole lives had never spent a night without a roof over their heads, let alone in a downpour, had shivered and whimpered the whole time. This morning had been more of the same until Jack threatened to cut their tongues out and have them for his lunch if they didn't shut up. And so that's how they'd ridden out of camp, the two cousins hungry and still shivering, but silent.

*****

In Darwin MacArthur's cabin on Wolverine Wash in the hills above Deadwood, Scorch Bannon and the remaining three members of his gang were seated around the sturdy table in the middle of the room, enjoying a breakfast prepared by Darwin. The feed consisted of oatmeal, fresh cornbread, and plenty of hot coffee. In spite of the good food and the relative comfort their host's warm, dry shelter had provided against the storm, all present wore grim, brooding expressions.

The subject under discussion that warranted so much somber focus was the same as it had been before they'd turned in the previous night: How to identify the former scout McGantry, intercept him, kill him to get even for what he'd done to Henry and to eliminate any future threat he might be to the rest of them. Leaving only the added detail of then making it out of the territory without falling prey themselves to the soldiers and investigators swarming all over, already on the lookout for them.

At one point, Bannon muttered, "You know the irony of this? The bitter irony?" Recognizing this as a rhetorical question, none of the others attempted to respond. They just waited. After a sufficient pause, Bannon answered himself, saying, "It's that Henry is the one best suited to put together a plan for making this work. Ain't that the shits?"

Frowning, young Tom said, "But if Henry was here, we wouldn't have to be doin' none of this."

Bannon wagged his head. "That's what irony is, kid. But the fact remains that Henry had the doggonedest knack for looking at something—a job I wanted to pull, like the layout of a bank ripe for plucking or a certain stretch of track if it was a train robbery—and after just a minute or so he'd see, like a picture in his head, the slickest way to make it work with the least risk."

"Yeah, he had that knack alright," agreed Kanelly. "Sometimes it was even kinda spooky the way he'd spit out a plan."

"In that case, we could sure use him now," Elroy muttered glumly. Then he was quick to add, "Not to say I don't want Henry back for a whole lot of other reasons, too. But what we're fixin' to do here … well, nobody can say it ain't mighty complicated. Especially if we aim to make it out with our hides intact."

"Don't worry," Tom said with a sudden surge of confidence. "We're doin' this for our own hides and we're doin' it to square things for Henry. With all that ridin' on it, not to mention the haul of gold we'll be takin' to Montana, Scorch'll see to it we don't come up short. Won't you, Scorch?"

For just a moment, the steeliness in Bannon's eyes seemed to falter ever so slightly at the show of faith behind the question. Then it was back strong again and he responded, "You damn right we're not going to come up short, kid. We owe better than that to Henry and ourselves and to all that gold that's itching to start buying fine things like it was meant for!"

*****

At nine o'clock that morning, a train running on the Fremont, Elkhorn, and Missouri Valley tracks that reached north up through Fort Robinson came hissing and clanging into the Deadwood station. One of the last passengers to step out onto the platform was Capt. Alan "Red" Trimball, this morning in full military uniform. The death of Henry Plow down in Crawford had naturally ended the covert surveillance of him in regard to the payroll robbery and therefore had relieved Trimball of his associated under- cover duties. Back in uniform now, he was reporting to Deadwood to take charge of the ongoing efforts here to locate and pin down the other members of the Bannon gang.

Lt. Gregory Reeves, who up to this point had been the on-site commander of the Deadwood operation, was waiting to greet him. Reeves was five inches taller and as many years younger than Trimball, a trim, square-jawed specimen whose picture could have been featured in the Army manual for what a U.S. Cavalry officer was supposed to look like. But as the two men came together on the platform, the shorter, somewhat weary-looking Trimball had about him an intangible aura conveying a sense of authority that was singular and quite unmistakable.

Reeves snapped a salute. "Good morning, sir. Glad to have you here."

Trimball returned the salute and then one corner of his mouth lifted a bit ruefully. "I hope you mean that, Greg. I hope you don't feel I'm horning in now after you and your men have laid all the groundwork."

"Not at all," Reeves replied earnestly. "To tell the truth, I'm feeling more than a little frazzled and am looking for- ward to somebody like you bringing in a fresh perspective. When I kept having to report we had nothing new, I was afraid ol' Hassett himself might … well, like I said, I'm glad to see *you*."

"I understand all too well what you mean," Trimball

told him. "I had the colonel right next door to me down in Crawford, remember, and things weren't popping very fast down there either. Certainly not fast enough to suit the higher brass. They'd ride Hasset and then guess who he'd ride? So, you're lucky for having this much distance between you and him."

"I guess," the lieutenant allowed. "But he doesn't hesitate to use the telegraph lines, let me assure you. And I can further assure you that he is mighty good at using them to still ride you and chew you out pretty effectively, even over long distance."

"Well," said Trimball, "let's hope that together we can shake something loose that will give everybody a reason to quit riding everybody else. At least until the next crisis comes along."

"I'm all for that. Now, as to accommodations for you, Captain. We've got an encampment set up north of town where myself and the uniformed men are quartered. The handful of undercover men I'm using have found their own places to stay at various spots around town," Reeves explained. "We can make you reasonably comfortable out at the encampment, or would you rather take a room at one of the hotels in town?"

"The encampment will do. We can talk and plan more freely there. And I am, after all, just a soldier too, right, Greg? You think this captain's rank has turned me into some kind of prima donna or something? Damn it, you know better than that."

Reeves grinned. "Just making sure, sir." He led the way to the outer edge of the platform where he waved one arm to indicate the sprawl of the town, stretching away at a northwesterly angle, saying, "As you can see, last night's prolonged downpour has turned the streets of our fair city—indeed the floor of the whole gulch—into a quagmire. I hope you don't think it too prima donna-ish to accept a wagon ride out to the encampment rather than slog through that muck on foot or horseback?"

Trimball took one look up Deadwood's main street, a twisting ribbon of brown-black mud and horse droppings worked into a thick soup by the steady churn of hooves and wagon wheels passing back and forth between the crooked rows of buildings and half-submerged board-walks. "No," he said. "I have no objection to a wagon, unless a boat is available."

The lieutenant tipped his head to indicate a conveyance parked close to the edge of the platform. "I'm afraid a wagon is the best I have to offer. And I can't promise that conditions are totally dry out at the camp, but I've had a tent prepared for you with a floor elevated up out of the mud."

Trimball nodded. "Sounds like it will do fine. Lead on, Lieutenant."

One of the two troopers manning the wagon hopped down and came over to help with Trimball's grip. A couple minutes later the passengers were aboard and the trooper was back up on the seat beside the driver. Slapping the reins and bawling out commands, the driver swung his team in a wide turn out onto the gouged, sloppy street and then they were rolling amidst the rest of the northbound traffic passing between rows of buildings containing businesses that ranged from bawdy houses to clothing and hardware stores to a red brick opera house.

Trimball's eyes took all of this in but, at the same time, he made it clear his mind was strictly on the business that had brought him here. "I trust the news of Henry Plow's demise arrived and has been widely circulated by now?" he asked.

"Yes. Widely," Reeves affirmed.

"And, in conjunction with that, how about the name McGantry as the man who shot him and also as someone who has a personal score to settle with the rest of the Bannon gang?"

"Oh, yeah. That really has the tongues wagging." Reeves turned his head and regarded the captain closely. "Am I correct in having a hunch there's a little more behind that and you might've had a hand in helping it get placed there?"

Trimball smiled. "I'm glad to see your knack for having hunches hasn't dulled, Greg. So, let me tell you what we're hoping the angle with McGantry might gain us …"

CHAPTER 26

———

They came to the river about an hour before noon, a rushing, swirling snarl of brown, foamy water and bits of jagged debris tearing down between the hills on an east to west course. It had overflowed both banks of its usual channel, presently spreading to a width of nearly fifty yards.

"My God," said Maggie, gazing in dismay at the sight. "What is this?"

"A problem," Lone answered tersely.

"I can see that. I meant what river is it?"

"The Elk. Leastways, that's what it used to be. But I never saw it rippin' and snortin' like this before." Lone frowned. "All that rain last night and run-off from higher ground has really got it riled up. Normally it's barely half this wide and runs at a fairly mild current."

They sat their horses a few feet back from the south bank. A flat, basin-like expanse of flat ground lay ahead, on the other side of the river, with more of the same stretching for quite a ways to the west. High, choppy hills rose and fell off to the east. The morning remained sunny and calm. The only sound was the rush of the tumbling, boiling water.

"So what are we going to do?" asked Maggie. "We can't cross this, can we?"

"Not here. Not the way it is now."

"How long before it will tame back down?"

"Hard to say. Hours, at best. Maybe clean into tomorrow." Lone glared off toward the choppy hills. "All depends how many washes and gullies keep pourin' in upstream before they get themselves emptied out."

Maggie's brow puckered. "We can't afford to just sit and wait, can we? Not considering what we figure is coming up behind."

"No. We'd risk losin' the distance gap we've been maintaining, plus anything we gained from the rain slowin' down Injun Jack's ability to cut our sign." Lone set his teeth on edge. "We need to think of something a hell of a lot better than just waitin' on the river. We get caught out on this flat when they show up, we'll be sittin' ducks."

"What then? Maybe we could go up into those hills, find a place to hide, then wait to ambush those rats if they come after us."

Lone gave her a surprised look. "I thought you're the gal who hates violence?"

"I hate being a sitting duck even worse," Maggie shot back. "I'm also a survivor, remember? Besides, look at the company I keep, you and your dangerous decency must be rubbing off on me."

"Could be at that," Lone allowed. "Whatever's behind it, your idea about settin' an ambush up in those hills ain't half bad. The trouble, though, is that we don't know the lay of the land up there, the pattern of gullies and washes we might find once we're in among 'em. There'd be the risk of possibly gettin' ourselves cornered up against some watercourse still runnin' too hot for any chance to get away in case the ambush don't work. Never a good idea not to have a back door."

Maggie waited, sensing he had an alternative to offer.

Proving that he did, Lone said, "I'd sooner follow the river west, stick with the flatter ground. At worst, we'll still be on the move, still be keepin' a gap between us and the bunch on our heels. With luck, we might reach a spot—one with a back door—where we could still try an ambush. With even better luck, we might find a point that provides a chance for crossin' over."

"How can that be, as long as the river is still running so high?"

"It's a long shot, true," Lone admitted. "But you never know. A narrowing, a rocky point on the other side I might be able to get a rope around to help pull us over to it. No way of findin' out until we see. Like I said, at worst we'll still be on the move."

"I can't deny that part sounds good. Okay," said Maggie, "let's go find out."

*****

An hour and a half later, they came to a change in the river that presented the kind of feature Lone had been hoping for. They'd nearly reached the western edge of the basin, its floor sloping upward gradually, when the Elk made a long, wide, swooping curve southward before bending back west after a couple hundred yards and then narrowing and continuing on more or less straight. At the point of the bend, the water scouring steadily against the north bank for countless years, even during times of a gentler flow, had worn the bank away and flattened it so that the river here was always widened out to a sort of broad pool until it was captured once more back into the straightened channel. This morning, the "pool" was of course broader still due to the increased amount of water feeding in. But its loose containment nevertheless made it, as always, a relatively calm interruption to the torrents leading to and away from it.

Lone and Maggie once again sat their saddles and gazed out at the interruption.

"Did you expect this?" asked Maggie.

"Not exactly," Lone told her. "But I'm willin' to take it."

"You really think we could make it across?"

"I think it's worth considerin'."

"It's awfully wide."

"True. But as you can see, it's a whole lot calmer until it swoops back into that west channel again." Lone shifted in his saddle. "There's bound to be an undercurrent stronger than what's showin' on the surface. But it's got to be dulled some by the flarin' out of the water all around, so it likely ain't the same force as in the main channel."

Maggie studied him. "If it wasn't for me, you wouldn't hesitate to try it. Would you?"

Lone let a beat go by before responding. "All things considered, if I knew I had trouble ridin' up behind me. No, I don't reckon I would."

Maggie scowled. "I just wish I was a better swimmer."

"Leave that to Rascal. He knows what to do," Lone told her. "Let your feet float free of the stirrups, hang on to the saddle horn, and lay out on his back. Give him his head, he'll get you across."

Maggie aimed her scowl at him. "You've got an answer for everything, don't you?"

Lone felt the weight of her eyes on him. "Comin' up with answers is the easy part. But havin' 'em turn out right is never a sure bet."

"That's not exactly a confidence-builder."

"I'm just tellin' it to you straight."

"Yes, of course you are. I wouldn't expect anything less." Maggie exhaled a breath she hadn't been aware she was holding. "I've trusted you this far, I guess now is no time to change. In for a penny, in for a pound, as my old granny used to say. Come on, let's go get wet before I come to my senses and remember how granny was always a little touched in the head."

And so they gigged the horses forward and got ready to cross. Lone directed Maggie to stay to the right of him, the upstream side, so in case she got into any trouble the current would carry her to him and give him a better chance to aid her. The pack horse he kept to his left and back away, on the end of a tether. Since he had no idea how good a swimmer the animal was or how it might react to the conditions, he wanted the option to be able to cut it free, sacrifice it if necessary, rather than have it panic and adversely affect the performances he knew he could count on from the other two horses.

Into the water they went. Ironsides and Rascal, immediately sensing what was being asked of them and what they were faced with, quickly began lunging on a straight course for the opposite side, fighting not to let the current carry them. The pack animal followed their lead, appearing to recognize they knew what they were doing.

There came a somewhat jarring moment when the horses stepped off the lip of the near bank, submerged and unseen due to the expanded width of the "pool" and dropped into the deeper, faster-moving main channel. They quickly righted themselves, however, digging in, maintaining their balance, and once again forged straight ahead, not allowing themselves to be pushed sideways by the current.

The deeper water was now suddenly up to mid-thigh on the riders, icy cold and hitting with surprising force. And the rushing sound of the current pouring against them seemed much louder here than it had up on the bank.

"Hold on tight!" Lone hollered over to Maggie. "If it gets much deeper, do like I told you, lay out on his back. Get a good grip on the saddle horn, never mind the reins. He knows where he has to go!"

Maggie glanced his way, trying hard to look brave in spite of her anxiety. .

On the other side of Lone, the pack horse began showing signs of struggle and panic. A shorter-legged animal to begin with and loaded down with the supply bundles, experiencing the drop-off into deeper water and the stronger undercurrent was not setting well with the pinto.

Lone gave a sharp jerk on the tether. "Straighten up there, you little cuss! Come on, you can make it okay."

They were only about a quarter of the way across. Lone knew conditions would worsen, as far as depth and the force of the only partially subdued central current, before they started to come out of it. Lone didn't want the animal to fall to harm and he certainly didn't want to lose the supplies but was prepared to cut the tether if the pinto foundered too badly.

But then, suddenly, there was a greater concern than the struggling pack horse.

"Lone!" Maggie's voice rang out sharply above the roar of churning water.

Looking around, Lone immediately saw the reason for the alarm in her tone. Rushing toward them, just starting the first sweep of the river's curve, came a fallen tree caught in the flooded current. The trunk looked to be more than a foot in diameter, a white birch not fully mature but certainly more than a sapling, its multi-pronged snarl of torn-loose roots thrusting in the fore with the remainder of its bole and then the tangle of branches and leaves following behind.

A curse ripped from Lone's lips. Ever since arriving at the river they had been seeing bits of jagged debris swept along in the flooded water. Some branches, a few tangles of brush. But nothing this big or menacing. And yet here it was, deciding to show up now.

Lone cursed again. Watching, he saw the tree coming on around the bend of the river and start to swing end for end as it entered the widening "pool". The top swept out wide, extending toward the opposite bank, but the ball of twisted, clawing roots was headed straight for Maggie!

"Rein back hard! Hard as you can!" Lone shouted to her. "Wheel him around, back out of the way, back to this side!"

At the same time Lone was unable to follow his own advice because the pack horse was faltering, unsuccess-fully fighting the current, and thereby not only preventing Lone from wheeling Ironsides but also threatening to pull both of them off course and farther into the undertow. A slashing swipe of Lone's Bowie severed the tether line and freed him and Ironsides from the pull of the frantically fighting pack horse.

All the while, the menacing tree was hurtling closer.

Released from the counter-tug of the pinto, Lone succeeded in getting Ironsides quickly reined up short and swung around back toward the bank they'd left only moments ago. Mere few feet away, Maggie was flaring having trouble doing the same. She'd made the mistake of bringing Rascal around to his right so that he couldn't help but see the grotesque mass of tree roots bearing down on him. He instantly jerked back, throwing his head high and issuing a frightened shriek. Then he twisted his body so suddenly and unexpectedly that it threw Maggie off balance and pitched her from the saddle.

Luckily, this threw her directly toward Lone and Ironsides. She went under for a moment before bobbing back up, coughing and flailing desperately. Lone leaned out from his own saddle and extended an arm for her to grab. As soon as he felt her fingers digging in and her hands grasping firmly, he crooked the arm and pulled her in close. At the same time, turned almost completely around now, Ironsides dug his front hooves deep and lunged hard to regain the southern edge of the pool. Once he'd clambered up over the submerged embankment he broke into long strides across the shallows. Water streamed from him and his passengers, catching glints of sunlight like a rain of sparks.

Out in the pool, Rascal was struggling valiantly but not faring as well. With Maggie gone from his back and Ironsides no longer on his downstream side, instead of making his own break for the edge of the pool he had continued all the way around in a hundred and eighty degree turn and was now swimming with the current instead of crossways to it, allowing it to pull him out into the faster undertow where all he could do from there was kick as hard as he could to try and stay ahead of the relentlessly onrushing tree.

Lone caught a couple glimpses of him but was too busy maintaining his hold on Maggie and staying astride Ironsides as the big gray carried them the rest of the way to safety and dry ground. When the latter had been achieved, he and Maggie slipped off onto the soft, warm, welcoming grass and just lay there, exhausted, gasping to catch their breath. When Lone lifted his head to look again, both Rascal and the uprooted tree were gone around the second bend of the river and could no longer be seen.

CHAPTER 27

——

Maggie was shivering and still coughing up occasional spatters of river water. Lone had scrounged enough sufficiently dry fuel from a nearby cluster of cottonwood trees to build a good fire. From his saddlebags he'd taken a small sack of "emergency" coffee beans and a tin cup. After crushing a few of the beans between two flat rocks, he dumped them into a cup of water and boiled up a crude serving of coffee that he laced with a generous splash from his whiskey flask. Stripped of most of her clothes, which were spread out on the grass to dry in the sun, Maggie sat close to the fire with Lone's relatively dry bedroll blanket draped over her and the cup of coffee pressed between her palms.

"As long as you understand that don't represent the best coffee I'm capable of making," Lone was saying. "But it's hot and it's got some prime 'adder' mixed in, so it should help fetch you 'round."

"It's fine. It beats the heck out of river water, I'll guarantee you that," Maggie replied. "I'm very grateful and I do believe it's doing some fetching 'round already."

Lone frowned. "I hope so. Bad enough I dang near drowned you, I don't want you to think I'm tryin' to finish the job by poisonin' you."

"You just helped me get that bath I was pining for the other night. If that stupid tree hadn't come along, I could have got my bath *and* we would have made it across. And if I'd managed to handle my horse properly, I wouldn't have had to drink so much of Mother Nature's bath water."

"You did fine. I'm surprised and disappointed Rascal spooked on you the way he did." Lone grimaced. "I thought he had more sand than that."

Maggie took a drink of the coffee. Her shivering seemed to be somewhat diminished. Her eyes following the way Lone's gaze had drifted off toward the second bend of the river and beyond, she said, "You can hardly blame Rascal. What animal wouldn't have spooked at the sight of that tree rushing straight at him?"

"Ironsides wouldn't have," Lone answered with quiet confidence. "He'd've stuck to the point of gettin' crushed before he ever quit on me."

Maggie's gaze swung to where the big gray, stripped of his saddle now, stood grazing nearby as calmly and contentedly as if he'd done nothing more strenuous all day than chew grass and swat flies with his tail. The bond between this animal and Lone, she realized, was something quite special.

Returning her focus to the former scout, she asked, "Do you think there's any chance Rascal might have somehow made it to safety?"

Continuing to look downstream, Lone said, "I've been wonderin' the same thing. If that tree swung around straight and he let it get past without snaggin' him. Yeah, I guess there's a chance he could've then managed to find a spot where he'd be able to clamber back up on the bank."

"I'd like to think he did," Maggie said. "How about the pack horse?"

Long wagged his head. "No, I don't have much hope he made it. He was too panicked and too weighed down by the supply packs. I cuss myself for not takin' time to re-distribute part of his load. It would have been easier on him and I could have made sure I kept some of the essentials on Ironsides, knowin' he'd make it if any of us did."

Maggie held up her cup. "You managed to save this essential. And I bet you've also got some jerky somewhere in your saddlebags."

"You're right. Hardtack, too," Lone affirmed. "But that adds up to a lot poorer lunch than what I promised when we made do with a cold breakfast this mornin'."

"You once told me a person could go a long way on jerky and hardtack."

"Yeah, and I told you we could make it across this river too." Lone frowned. "Maybe it's time for you to start questioning my judgment a little more."

"Now's a fine time for you to tell me that," Maggie said sarcastically. "In case you haven't noticed, my options for somebody else to trust are sort of scarce right at the moment. So, I'm stuck with you and your lousy skill at picking river crossings and you're stuck with me not being able to control my horse. Now that that's settled, what's your plan from here?"

Lone held out his hand. When Maggie placed her cup in it, he tipped it up for a big swallow. Handing the cup back, he said, "We've already lost a lot of time. Those comin' up behind, if they're pushin' hard, are probably nearin' the river about now. When they reach it, they'll see it's too high for us to have crossed and they'll find our tracks showin' we came this way. They'll come after us. They may be as close as three hours, not much more."

"Three hours?" Maggie echoed dismally.

"We could double up on Ironsides and stay on the move," Lone went on. "He's strong enough to carry the both of us at a pretty good clip and for quite a spell. But he's bound to start tirin' sooner or later and, unless we can find a way to cross that river, they'll keep comin' and narrowin' the gap. Plus, even if we stay ahead of 'em, we'll be movin' farther and farther away from Deadwood."

Maggie's brows knitted. "What other choice do we have?"

Lone turned his head and looked at her. One corner of his mouth quirked upward slightly. "You happen to recall, from a while back, somebody bringin' up the notion of an ambush?"

CHAPTER 28

———

The shimmering orange ball that was the sun had descended to just above the rim of the western horizon when they came in sight. Three riders and one pack horse; Orson, Injun Jack, and Luther leading the pack animal. They were following the edge of the river, fanned out wide and approaching at a cautious trot. Orson was nearest the water, Jack rode in the middle and slightly ahead.

Lone and Maggie had erased all sign of Lone's original campfire and had built a new one a ways further on, down nearer to where the river made its second bend and went rushing full force again. Maggie once more sat before it, alone. She was fully dressed now in the sun dried and retrieved articles of clothing that had previously been spread out on the grass. She was once more wrapped in a bedroll blanket, though spasms of shivering still gripped her from time to time. Ironsides' saddle and gear lay on the grass beside her. The big gray stood close by, returned to grazing after giving some warning chuffs about the approaching riders.

Fifteen feet away from where Maggie sat, concealed

behind a hump of grass-fringed ground on the edge of where the churning current began picking up steam again after coming out of the "pool", Lone lay totally silent and motionless. His legs extended back into the water, partially sunk into the muck underneath to hold him fixed against the force wanting to sweep him away. He would have been cold and uncomfortable if he'd allowed himself to think about it too much. But his encounters with the Apaches and Comanches had taught him well about enduring discomfort for the sake of achieving what had to be done. Right now what had to be done was to wait. Wait and be ready to strike only when the moment and opening were right.

Injun Jack reined up ten yards short of Maggie. He immediately waved a hand, motioning for Orson and Luther to stay wide and stay back. In his concealment, Lone grimaced. The half breed bastard was shrewd. He sensed this might be a trick and knew that, if it was, one of the surest ways to fall prey to it would be for him and the other two to bunch close together and expose themselves to a tight grouping of shots.

Jack barely skimmed a glance over Maggie but slowly, intently scanned the lay of the land all around and especially the stand of cottonwoods a short ways to the south, the most logical place for someone planning an ambush to be hiding. Lone stayed calm, willed his breathing even slower. His Apache and Comanche encounters had taught him not only about enduring discomfort, but also about finding cover where none seemed to exist. He'd never quite mastered their skill for hiding behind a mere pebble, but he could come damn close. He was confident Injun Jack was unable to spot him, certainly not from where he presently sat his horse.

Maggie broke the tension by saying, "I've been wondering when you would come along."

Jack's black eyes bored into her. "Why would we be along at all?"

Maggie ignored him and focused instead on Orson. "Because I know Drummond. Know that he wouldn't easily let me, what he considers to be his *property*, get away."

"Well now. I guess us bein' here shows you were right about that much, don't it? But what about the rest of your little plan to get away anyhow?" Orson sneered. "Where's the boyfriend you hightailed out of town with?"

"Isn't it obvious?" Maggie snapped back. "He let me down. Look around. The damn fool thought we'd be able to get across the river here. He was about as wrong as wrong could be. We lost everything. All our supplies and two horses, plus he got swept away and drowned to boot. I only managed to still be here thanks to that big gray just barely dragging me out."

Orson chuckled nastily. "Now that's a real sad tale. It purely is. I'm sure I will bring a tear to Mr. Drummond's eye and maybe it will even help gain you some forgiveness from him for your ungrateful behavior."

With that, Orson started to gig his horse forward. But he was brought to a quick halt by Jack swinging out an arm and saying sharply, "Hold it! Everybody just stay where you are for a minute!"

"What for? What the hell's wrong with you, Jack?" Orson demanded.

"Something about this don't smell right to me," the half breed answered. "I don't trust this woman. I think she's lyin'."

"Lyin' about what? You can see the fix she's in, can't you?"

"I can see what she *wants* us to see. The fix we're meant

to believe she's in," argued Jack. "But I can't help thinkin' it might be a trick. This McGantry we've been followin', nothing about the things he's done so far says he's the kind who'd be foolish enough to let himself get drowned in a swollen river."

"That's what I thought, too," Maggie said wryly. "As you can see, I was wrong."

Orson said, "Everybody, including this hotshot McGantry, is capable of makin' a mistake some time or other."

"All I'm sayin'," snarled Jack, "is let's not be in a big damn hurry to make a bad mistake of our own."

Luther piped up for the first time, saying, "Jack has good instincts about this kind of stuff, Orson. That's why we brung him along, remember?"

Orson heaved an exasperated sigh. "Okay, okay. For Chrissakes. What do you want us to do, Jack? How should we go about this?"

"That's better," Jack grunted. "The main thing is to stay spread out, so we don't make a bunched-together target in case McGantry is lookin' to pick us of from somewhere. For starters, Orson you swing out wide around to the other side of that campfire. Take a position over there, pull out your rifle, keep it trained in the general direction of those trees. So much as a grasshopper flutters in there, be ready to blast the hell out of it."

"What do you want me to do, Jack?" asked Luther.

"When Orson gets over where I told him, I want you to climb down and walk up to the girl." As he issued these instructions, Jack pulled his own handgun and aim it casually at Maggie. "Stand right beside her. Take out your pistol, cock it, hold it to her head."

"Come on!" wailed Orson. "Any harm comes to that girl, Drummond won't pay out shit. More like he'd send somebody to hunt *us*."

"The girl will only get hurt if McGantry is lurkin' somewhere, plannin' to make trouble. Luther doin' like I told him is to show we mean business," Jack explained through clenched teeth. "McGantry will quick see that if he opens the ball, she's bound to be sorry for it. Even if he plants a pill in Luther, there'd be the risk his body jerk would cause the pistol to go off and blow her brains out." Suddenly Jack threw his head back and shouted out, "You hear that, McGantry? I'm on to you, you yellow bush-whackin' dog! I know every dirty trick in the book and you ain't pullin' one over on me!"

In his concealment, Lone winced and swore under his breath. Infuriating as they were to hear, it was hard to dispute Jack's words. His innate suspicion and refusal to accept things at face value were traits Lone hadn't counted on, at least not to such a strong degree. That meant, for the moment, the 'breed might have him outfoxed.

But that only mattered if Lone lost his cool and tipped his hand out of desperation before the right opening presented itself. Patience and confidence were great equalizers. Lone had the patience and the confidence to believe a chance would still come to turn the tables on these three hired hounds. Conversely, he knew that Jack couldn't be totally confident of Lone's presence, that he might still be alive. It was only a gut instinct on his part. But without some solid evidence to back up this hunch, Lone sensed that his two reluctant, impatient partners would start to pull against him. That might be what provided Lone the opening he needed.

The other factor that had to hold up was Maggie. From his vantage point, Lone couldn't tell for sure what her face was showing. He could see her shiver occasionally, but that was from the dunk in the river. She was a tough gal, she'd already proven that. A survivor. But she'd been through a lot in the past couple of days. Having nearly drowned just hours ago and now getting a cocked gun held to her head, hearing talk of blowing her brains out at the slightest hint of trouble, everybody had a breaking point.

In his mind, Lone kept urging her: *Hang in there, Maggie gal.Hang in there."*

With the two cousins positioned as he'd directed them, it was Maggie who Jack now turned his attention to. He dismounted and walked toward her, but then hung back to maintain a distance from Luther. Addressing Maggie, he said, "You sure called it right about your brave friend and protector, girl, when you said McGantry let you down. Either he let you down when he damn near got you drowned, which I don't buy for a second or he's sure as hell lettin' you down now by leavin' you out here like a staked goat while he's off hidin' somewhere, tryin' to be clever."

"I told you what happened to him," Maggie responded. "What more do you want me to say?"

"I want you to say the truth, you lyin' bitch!"

"You go to hell."

Injun Jack bared his teeth in a sneer. "All right then. If McGantry is already among the dear departed, then it shouldn't bother you if I had Orson cut loose with a few rounds into those cottonwoods over there, should it?"

"You want to shoot a bunch of trees, be my guest," Maggie told him.

"Do it, Orson." Jack abruptly ordered the big bouncer. "Pour some lead into those trees, half a dozen rounds all along the base!"

After looking momentarily bewildered, Orson went ahead and did as told. He raised his Winchester and swept a line of six slugs crashing into the underbrush and fallen branches just above ground level.

As the shots began booming out, Jack was closely watching Maggie's face for a reaction, expecting (*hoping?*) she would suddenly protest as a sign of trying to protect McGantry's presence in that undergrowth. But the exercise came up empty. The hail of bullets raised nothing, but some puffs of dirt and splintered twigs and Maggie's expression remained flat, unresponsive.

But while the ploy fell short for Jack, it was a different story from Lone's perspective. It suddenly gave him, he realized, the best opening he might get from the way things were laid out. While Orson was concentrating on firing into the trees and Jack was focused on Maggie's reaction, Luther had allowed himself to be distracted from his assigned task of holding a gun on Maggie. His gaze followed the sweep of Orson's rifle fire to see what it might hammer loose and this caused his gun hand to involuntarily drift away from Maggie's head.

It was risky but recognizing it as the best and maybe only chance that would present itself, Lone had to seize it!

CHAPTER 29

——

Up out of the muck and onto the grass-fringed hump Lone shoved himself. Extending his already cocked Colt, he squeezed the trigger and drilled a .44 slug straight into the side of Luther's head, just ahead of his ear. The big man stiffened then pitched straight out and down, toppling like a tree. A splatter of gore erupted out the opposite side of his head and his gun arm flopped loosely at his side, the pistol in his grasp never discharging.

The roar of Lone's Colt came so quickly on the end of Orson' rifle fire that that it almost sounded like part of the same volley. But there was no mistaking it to Jack's ears, especially not given the way Luther went down before his very eyes. And while he might have tried using his own drawn handgun to make good on the threat to Maggie, his sense of self-preservation, knowing he was sure to be Lone's next target, made him react defensively instead. Dropping first to a crouch and then instantly throwing himself into a rolling dive, the wiry 'breed escaped the next two rounds coming from Lone, chasing him, gouging up the ground mere inches from his heels.

At the end of his roll, Jack sprang to his feet behind the horse he'd dismounted from only minutes earlier. Grabbing the bridle to hold the animal steady, he then ducked under its belly and snapped two fast return rounds in Lone's direction.

But those shots were hurriedly aimed and went way wide, causing Lone no immediate concern. A concern the former scout *did* have, though before he spent any more of the three remaining cartridges left in his wheel on the temporarily missed opportunity Jack now represented, was taking care of Orson before he loomed as an added threat.

The big bouncer was a little slow on catching up with the sudden turn of events taking place around him. He'd been turned partly away from everybody, aiming into the trees, and wasn't the greatest horseman in the world to begin with. Getting his mount somewhat awkwardly wheeled about, his gaze swept in horror over his fallen kin and then saw the desperate efforts of Injun Jack scrambling to escape the gunfire chasing him. By the time his wide-with-shock eyes fell on Lone, the former scout was already re-adjusting his sights away from Jack. It was entirely possible that what was about to befall him never fully registered with Orson before Lone's Colt spoke again and the bullet exploding from its muzzle went in at an angle just under the big man's nose and up and out through his brain. Orson seemed to crumple in the saddle, his broad shoulders sagging, and then he slowly tipped to one side and dropped to the ground.

Immediately after making this shot, Lone threw himself into motion. While Injun Jack's first try at him had been hurried and McGantry's sloppily aimed, Lone knew that in the intervening seconds the 'breed would have had time to get better situated and there wouldn't be anything sloppy about any more lead he threw. He was proven right when two rapid-fire rounds punched into the grassy hump Lone had been steadying his arm on, hitting an eyeblink after he lifted said arm and dragged it with him as he rolled away just above the water's edge. Then it was Lone's turn to thrust his arm back up and trigger a couple of blind shots in Jack's general direction, just to give him momentary pause.

Dropping back lower, slipping on the grassy, muddy incline, digging in his heels to keep from sliding all the way into the water, Lone twisted onto his back. With fingers that were usually very fast and nimble when it came to performing the act, but now were slowed some by a bit of stiffness from being wet and cold, Lone pulled a full, freshly-loaded cylinder of cartridges from his shirt pocket and slammed it into place in exchange for the wheel of spent shells he'd just burned through. Though it seemed agonizingly slow, the whole thing took no more than a couple clock ticks. And when Lone rolled onto his stomach once again and got ready to ease up for another try a Jack, it was with his Colt comfortably heavy and full in his fist.

Later, Lone would blame the dull roar of the tumbling, churning river for being so caught off guard by the sight that greeted him when he rose up over the top of the slope. Bearing down on him at a hard gallop, the hammering of hooves indeed muffled by the rush of the floodwater, came Injun Jack astride his gleaming black horse!

Jack had drawn a Henry repeating rifle from his saddle scabbard and was waving it wildly, though making no attempt to take aim with it, as he shouted at the top of his lungs, "You sonofabitch! You never fooled me. I knew you were alive out here somewhere!"

For one of the few times in his life, Lone McGantry was momentarily frozen to inaction. So startled was he at finding the thundering horse and rider practically on top of him that he failed to get his Colt raised for a single shot. And then it was too late. The black's front hooves lashed out, rising and then stomping down. And an instant later came its broad, ramming chest.

Lone spun away to avoid being struck, staggered off balance and went sprawling on the greasy, wet grass. He went into a roll and stopped again on his stomach, digging hard with the toes of his boots and with his hands, trying to keep from sliding down into the water. The Colt slipped from his grasp.

The black's hooves pounded down between his outstretched arms. He jerked his head back, cursing. Above him, leaning out and down from his saddle, Injun Jack swung his rifle and slammed it across Lone's shoulders. Lone's curse turned into a cry of pain.

Jack swung the rifle again. This time Lone got his left arm up and blocked some of the force with his forearm. He tried to grab the rifle but missed. Twisting onto his right hip, still fighting to maintain purchase on the slope, he ducked another swing of the Henry.

In desperation, bending his knees upon finally feeling some solidness under his feet, Lone thrust upward hard and fast, reaching with both hands. He got his right arm in between Jack's leg and the saddle fender and hooked it tight. At the same time, he snaked higher with his left hand and got hold of the breed's belt. Jack cursed and slammed his rifle down across Lone's shoulders again. But the former scout refused to let go. When he felt Jack's torso stretch back, getting ready to club some more with the Henry, Lone abandoned all caution and heaved outward as hard as he could, dragging Jack after him. The black, feeling this sudden shift of weight pulling him toward the rushing water, swerved the opposite direction and finished the job of spilling his rider from the saddle.

Lone and Jack, tangled together now, pitched out and down, plunging into the roiling river.

The current immediately grabbed them and sucked them into the strongest part of the flow, spinning and tumbling them like bundles of rags. For several frantic moments, the two men ignored each other and struggled, kicking and clawing, only to keep their faces bobbing above the rising and falling swells of water. It was inevitable, though, that when they collided back together they immediately began throwing punches and underwater kicks at one another.

All the while they were being hurtled along by the raging torrent as it alternately tried to suck them under and then fling them up and forward in sudden surges. The water was cold and muddy-tasting. Periodically they were slammed against submerged, out-thrusting sections of the former bank that battered their bodies before bouncing them back out into the central flow.

Attempting to make use of his superior strength, Lone clamped his hands around Jack's throat and tried to hold him under. This worked intermittently, but every time Lone had the 'breed under long enough to start to weaken him, the river would send them into a whirl and Jack's grimacing face would bob above the waves again.

Vaguely, Lone was aware that in the distance of the western direction they were being swept, the sun was nearly gone from behind the jagged horizon. This awareness was suddenly increased when one of its final brilliant rays caught and glinted off something very near to Lone's head. At the last instant, giving the former scout barely enough time twist his face away, he realized Injun Jack was thrusting a knife at the side of his throat! Lone's maneuver resulted in only taking a slice to his earlobe.

But Jack still had the knife in his grasp and was far from finished trying to use it. He did so without hesitation, immediately stabbing down again. This time Lone countered by craning his neck forward and slamming his head as fast and hard as he could toward Jack's face, managing to partially duck under the knife. He felt his forehead successfully mashing nose cartilage and teeth but he also simultaneously felt the edge of Jack's blade scraping across the top of his head, laying open flesh. Lone slammed his head again and even though the cold, churning water he could feel the warmth of smeared blood.

Jack twisted away from the second blow, partly of his own volition and partly because the current spun him half around. Lone twisted too, getting his shoulders and torso turned so that now his back was pressed against Jack. From this position, with both of them continuing to be rushed along by the current, he reached up and seized the forearm and wrist of Jack's knife hand, wrenching it savagely downward like a pump handle. His shoulder was too far back toward the breed's armpit to get the full wrong-way torque he wanted on the elbow joint, but it was enough to make Jack howl with pain.

Lone wrenched harder and Jack screamed and cursed in his bloody ear.

The river kept them whirling and hurtling and along.

And then—suddenly, jarringly—they slammed to a stop.

They had been pushed up against some sort of blockage extending out from the south side of the river. Whatever it was, was large and solid but didn't feel like a shelf of rock or some other natural feature. It was lumpy and seemed to have a certain amount of give, yet not enough to indicate it was ready to tear loose, not even under the relentless hammering of floodwater or the two struggling men now pinned against it.

Lone refused to release his hold on Jack's arm, continuing to pull down, continuing to bend it the way it didn't belong with the aim of either breaking the damn thing or ripping it from its socket. Having Jack positioned on the outside and continually driven against him by the force of the water helped some, but Lone still couldn't get his shoulder shifted to the optimum fulcrum point under the elbow joint. And all the while Jack was twisting and thrashing desperately, kicking his heels against Lone's shins underwater and reaching back with his free hand, throwing awkward, largely ineffective punches and trying to gouge the former scout's eyes.

Swiveling his head from side to side to avoid these tactics, Lone was able to catch brief glimpses and finally figure out what they were jammed against—it was the supply bundle tied to the back of the pack animal that had been swept away earlier during his and Maggie's attempted crossing. An ancient, gnarled old tree, at one time growing close on the edge of the bank before its current flooded condition widened the river, had snagged the bundle as well as the hapless pinto it was attached to. The carcass of the latter, unable to kick loose and therefore eventually drowning, was a bobbing, frothy, hairy mass trailing out toward the middle of the main current.

For some reason, the sight of the dead pinto sent a jolt of rage and adrenaline through Lone. An inner voice rang out from deep in his survivor's core: *I am not going to die in this rush of muddy water like that poor, dumb beast!*

Propelled by this, Lone lunged forward against the force of the onrushing river and of Jack's squirming, struggling form being driven into him. Turning partly to one side, rolling his shoulder, he finally got it where he'd been trying for, directly under Jack's elbow joint. Instantly, he hauled down on the end of the extended arm with all his might, wrenching it savagely the opposite way from which the elbow was meant to bend. There came the satisfying crack of bones and pop of tendons, those sounds quickly overwhelmed by Jack's piercing, agonized scream as his entire body convulsed in pain.

From there, it was almost too easy. Lone had little trouble prying the half breed's knife from his trembling, nerve-numb fingers. Then, taking possession of it and gripping the bone handle tight in his right fist while his left reached around to clutch a handful of Jack's hair, jerking his head back, a single swipe of the blade across the exposed, bulging throat laid open a ghastly second mouth grinning from just below one jaw hinge to the other.

After making a final thrust with the knife, leaving sunk to its hilt in the side of Jack's neck, Lone twisted hard to one side and shoved and kicked repeatedly until he managed to push what was now a corpse far enough off him so that the rushing current once again caught hold and swept it the rest of the way clear. For a bizarre moment it got hung up on the carcass of the drowned pinto, the dead riding the dead but then it abruptly slipped free and disappeared for good in the swirling water.

But Lone still wasn't completely out of danger. He remained largely pinned to the blockage caused by the snagged supply bundle, held there by the flood torrent relentless pounding against him. As he'd just proven, however, he wasn't unable to move his body parts, even though they were growing stiff and numb from the cold water and weary from constant struggle. So, with great effort, he fought to get himself turned the rest of the way around in order to now be facing the supply bundle. Reaching up with first one hand and then the other, grabbing the tie ropes that held the canvas-shrouded collection of smaller, individual packs together, he began pulling himself up out of the pummeling pressure of the onrushing river.

With each increment he lifted himself above the water, he felt more invigorated, more determined. And then, when he was high enough to reach out and grab one of the gnarled branches of the old tree, he was able to not only pull himself higher but also farther out toward the edge of the water, away from the raging current. He crawled out farther, shifting from the supply bundle onto the tree itself. From there, coiling his knees underneath him, he took a deep breath and kicked off as hard as he could.

He ended up on a flat, grassy surface. Grassy and solid, but still wet from the closeness of the splashing, churning river. Lone rolled away from this. He rolled over and over several times until he came to rest on soft, welcoming, grass that was not only dry but still retained some of the day's heat even though the sun was now set. He lay flat on his back, aching arms and legs spread wide, and sucked in great mouthfuls of fresh air that never tasted sweeter.

Before too long, aware of warm blood dripping down the side of his face from the gash atop his head and beginning to wonder how far the river had actually carried him, how far from Maggie, Lone pushed to a sitting position. Although the sun was gone, there was still plenty of light remaining in the orange-tinted sky.

Despite his overall exhaustion and the dozen or so aches and bruises that riddled him, Lone knew that if he hoped to make it back to camp before nightfall, he'd better set to it. But then, after pushing to his feet with a well-earned groan, he gazed in the direction he meant to head and there, in the distance, something was approaching.

The something was a large shape and it was growing nearer at a steady, fairly rapid pace. The shape began to take on definition, familiarity. Lone's breathing quickened again and his heart began pounding in kind. Until there was no longer any doubt it was Ironsides galloping toward him. And on his back, bathed in twilight's orange glow like a radiant angel of mercy, was Maggie!

CHAPTER 30

———

Back at the stand of cottonwoods, by the glow of a big, blazing campfire and the remnants of twilight, Maggie stitched up the knife cut on the top of Lone's head. That done, while Lone with the aid of Ironsides dragged away the bodies of Orson and Luther and pushed them out into the river, Maggie started supper from the provisions of their former pursuers. By the time Lone had the horses staked for the night, the meal was ready. Nothing special, just heaping helpings of bacon, beans, and fresh biscuits that seemed as succulent under the circumstances as the finest cuisine imaginable. All washed down by cups of hot coffee generously laced with splashes of whiskey from Lone's flask as well as from a bottle found among the confiscated supplies.

Much as the meal hit the spot, so too did these servings of strong brew strengthened even more with copious amounts of "adder". For the sake of Lone's bone-deep chill and various aches from his prolonged tumble in the river and also for Maggie's continuing bouts of the shivers as well as a nagging cough that seemed to be developing from her own time in the water and the amount of it she had swallowed, the often lauded medicinal value of alcohol was well put to the test.

Curiously, even though the pair grew rosy-cheeked and quite relaxed during the course of the evening, the kind of small talk and easy banter that had become common between them over the past couple of days, tonight seemed somewhat strained. In fact, they talked very little.

Lone was occupied for much of the time with his Colt, which Maggie had retrieved from where he'd dropped it at the start of his fight with Injun Jack. After breaking the piece down, he used a patch of flannel and a tin of gun oil from his saddlebags to carefully clean and lightly lubricate every part, right down to the cartridges he reloaded into the cylinder. He did the same for the spare wheel and its loads, as well as all the cartridges from his gunbelt.

"You treat that as tenderly as a mother cares for an infant," Maggie observed.

"Kinda the same thing. Only in reverse," Lone replied. "An infant needs its mother to survive. For me, the proper care and handling of this baby" —a flourish of the Colt— "can be what keeps *me* alive."

Later, when it was time to turn in, Maggie walked purposefully over to where Lone was spreading his blankets. Standing over him, she announced, "I don't want to be alone in my bedroll tonight, McGantry. I want to lay with you. I want you to hold me and warm me and comfort me. I want you to tell me we'll reach Deadwood tomorrow and, even if it's not true, there'll be no more trouble or killing along the way."

Lone gazed up at her and said softly, earnestly, "I'll do anything you want except lie to you, Maggie. Several weeks ago, I set out to hunt down and kill five men who murdered my partner. So far I haven't laid a finger on a single one of 'em. In the course of my hunt, though, I've so far had to kill nine others. Trust me when I say nobody wants more than me to avoid further trouble along the way. But as far as reachin' Deadwood tomorrow, which I do believe we will. Then there'll be more killin' left to do."

That said, he lifted his blankets. Without hesitation, Maggie slipped in beside him.

*****

The river settled down during the night. The flooded sides receded back from the banks and the swift current calmed to its normal gentle flow.

In the morning, Lone and Maggie crossed without incident. Maggie rode Luther's former mount. The other animals, including Injun Jack's gleaming black gelding, they stripped of their gear and turned loose.

Once they were on the other side, Lone told Maggie he reckoned they would make Deadwood by afternoon and she imparted to him everything Henry had shared with her about the Bannon gang and how they were holed up at a place called Wolverine Wash.

CHAPTER 31

—

"Since he didn't make it yesterday," Capt. Trimball was saying, "I fully expect McGanty to show up some time today. I'm guessing all that rain must have slowed him down. But knowing how bad he wants to get here to confront Bannon's bunch, he'll be pushing hard to make up for it."

"The question then," replied Lt. Reeves, "is whether or not Bannon will be as anxious to confront him. You really think there's the chance he will be, even knowing how many eyes are peeled to catch sight of him if he makes any kind of move?"

"Do I think there's a chance?" Trimball echoed. "Yeah, I do, or I wouldn't have dragged McGantry into it. But there's no way to be certain. Let's face it, if I had a clear idea what Bannon's thinking or what his next move might be, we wouldn't be still twisting in the wind like we are."

"Us twisting in the wind is hardly all on you," Reeves pointed out. "Unless that scar-faced devil has already slipped through our fingers and—"

"Whoa! Don't say that out loud and don't even think it," Trimball cut him off. "If it turns out Bannon and the others have already rattled their hocks out of here and we've been sitting on nothing but a pile of empty all this time. Man, I don't want to think what kind of a hellhole outpost the brass would ship us off to as a result. And probably Hassett right along with us."

Reeves made an extremely distasteful face. "You're right. Forgive me for letting even a hint of a thought cross my mind that would conjure up the remotest possibility of such an outcome. I won't let it happen again."

"See to it you don't," said the captain with mock severity.

The two officers were seated on canvas chairs at a folding table in the captain's tent. The table held the remains of the breakfast they had recently taken together. They were down to final cups of coffee and Reeves had lighted a cigar.

Getting back to the heart of their discussion, Trimball stated, "As to the question of how, or if, Bannon will react to this whole McGantry business, all I'm angling for is that it might provide an added jolt to what has become a logjammed situation. The death of Henry Plow should have provided the first jolt. Plow triggering something when he finally thought it was safe to try and make a break from Crawford was a possibility I was counting on all along. Seems reasonable to figure his death should serve the same purpose. And it doesn't seem *un*-reasonable to think that weaving McGantry into it, his presence and questionable role in Plow's shooting, the revenge he's sworn on the rest of the gang, won't help nudge Scorch a little harder."

"It's sure worth a try, especially since you got McGantry to agree to it and it's all set in motion," Reeves allowed. "Bannon and the others can't stay holed up forever. *Something's* got to shake 'em loose."

"Exactly. So now, more than ever, we make need sure

every man under our command keeps their ears and eyes trained all the sharper. And that also means a key, discreet detail focused on McGantry," Trimball stressed. "I've set him up as a stalking horse, hoping to help draw Bannon out, so it's only fitting we keep him safe as part of the bargain."

Reeves frowned. "But if we want Bannon to make a try for him, we can hardly have bodyguards hovering around him, can we?"

"Did you not hear me use the word 'discreet'?" snapped Trimball. "Send out four of your best undercover men. Have them watch the incoming roads and trails and pick up McGantry as soon as he arrives. Then shadow him, close but unseen, ready to intervene if Scorch or his boys try anything. By the way, McGantry has more than a little bark on him. Warn your men not to get sloppy enough to draw his ire."

"How will they know him?"

"He'll be riding a big gray gelding and his shoulders are about as wide as the horse's. Looks like he'd be capable of clearing out any saloon in town without sloshing the foam out of his beer mug."

Reeves lifted his eyebrows. "Should I be sending a second set of men to protect the ones shadowing this friend of yours?"

"Just send the first ones. McGantry is tough, but bullets don't bounce off him. And if Scorch takes the bait, he won't be showing up to trade punches."

"Understood. I've got four good men in mind." The lieutenant rose from his chair. "I'll get them on their way, and then I'll dispatch the regular town patrols with orders to stay extra sharp."

"Sounds good. Report back to me when all that is underway."

As Reeves turned to leave, a private appeared just outside the open doorway of the tent, announcing himself with a clump of heels on the wood planking that stretched out for a ways in front. Snapping a salute, he said, "Begging your pardon, sir. May I collect your breakfast dishes now?"

"By all means. Come and get them," Trimball called from where he remained seated.

The private hesitated. "Also, sirs, I have a fella out here with me. A citizen from town, one of the storekeepers. He showed up first thing this morning wanting to speak with our commander. We made him wait until you finished your meal, but he's awful anxious to have a word."

Reeves looked at the captain questioningly. Trimball hesitated a moment, then nodded. "All right. Show him in, Private. You can still gather up the dishes, I'll speak with the citizen. Lieutenant, go ahead and take care of the matters we discussed."

A handful of minutes later, Trimball and the storekeeper had the tent to themselves. The captain had gestured his visitor into the chair formerly occupied by Reeves. The man was a pudgy, round-faced specimen sporting a goatee to hide his double chin. He was closer to fifty than forty, with thinning hair parted in the middle, combed to either side and slicked down.

"My name's Ross, Captain. Jed Ross," he introduced himself. "I own and run one of the oldest hardware stores in town. I'm here to see you on account of all the posters tacked up everywhere and how your soldiers have been going around asking for information and urging folks to report anything they see or hear that might help lead to that gang of robbers and killers you figure is hid somewhere around these parts."

"It's true that input from the citizens of Deadwood could

prove very crucial to our apprehension of those scoundrels," Trimball replied encouragingly. "Do you have some useful information, Mr. Ross?"

Ross fidgeted. "Well, I – I'm not sure … Perhaps … That is to say, I observed something that seems curious enough to be … No, suspicious is the right word. Not just curious, but suspicious. And that's what it says on those posters—report anything suspicious or out of the ordinary and let the authorities determine if it amounts to something serious."

"That's right, Mr. Ross. The men in question are very dangerous and very skilled at taking precautions. But sooner or later they're going to slip, maybe in just a small way, and that will give us the opening we need. But we don't want citizens like you to endanger yourselves. Just tell us if you spot something odd and let us take it from there."

"Don't worry, I'm not out to be no hero," Ross stated firmly. "I just want to help if I can."

The captain nodded. "That's all we ask. Now what is this suspicious thing you came here to tell me about?"

"Well, it's got to do with a fella named Darwin MacArthur. He's an old trapper and sometimes prospector who lives by himself up in the hills above a place called Wolverine Wash. He comes into town every couple, three months to cash in his pelts and what little bit of dust he scrapes up then uses the money to stock up on supplies. That was the first thing that struck me as unusual, how often he's come to town lately. In the past few weeks, see, he's been in two or three times for supplies."

"Unusual, like I said, but I didn't think too much of it. Only then, a couple days ago—the evening when all that rain was pouring down—those strangers showing up with ol' Dar's packs really struck a wrong chord with me."

"What was so wrong about that?" Trimball asked.

"The packs I'm talking about are kinda special pieces of leatherwork. Finely stitched and treated to be waterproof, designed with some real pretty beads and such. They were made for Darwin by an Indian wife he had for a while. He's mighty proud of 'em. Never shows up without having them along to tote off his supplies."

"But the other night a couple of strangers showed up using those packs instead of him. Is that it?"

Ross's head bobbed. "Uh-huh. The more I've thought about it, the more it bothers me. Something about it just don't feel right. I almost questioned that pair right that evening. But there wasn't nobody else in the store at the time, the rain keeping everybody in their homes I guess, and something about those two well, they looked like they wasn't much for small talk or answering questions. So I let it ride, and have been feeling kind of low and regretful about it ever since."

"What did these two men look like?" Trimball want to know.

"They were covered in rain slickers and other outerwear against the bad weather, so I couldn't tell a lot," Ross answered. "But one was old, well into his fifties I'd say, pretty drenched and scraggly. The other much younger, only about twenty or so, had a kind of wary, haunted look about him. I've seen the posters on Scorch Bannon and Barge Kanelly. These weren't them. I can say that for sure. But they've got others with them who've never been described very clearly, isn't that so?"

Trimball regarded the storekeeper. "Is that that what you suspect? That the Bannon gang might have somehow horned in on this old prospector?"

"I don't know for sure what to think," said Ross, his

face scrunching with anguish. "All I know is, like I keep saying, something feels wrong about those two strangers, no matter who they are, having ol' Dar's special packs. I tried to talk to the marshal about it, but he says Wolverine Wash is too far out of his jurisdiction. That's the other troubling thing, nobody else hardly ever goes up that way no more. So, if Darwin *was* in some kind of trouble, it could go unnoticed for a coon's age."

"Mr. Ross, I appreciate this information. I truly do," Trimball assured him. "I don't know what to make of it, but it's exactly the kind of out-of-the-ordinary thing we can't afford to overlook. I'll send some men up to check on the old prospector, and I'll get word back to you on what we find."

Ross stood up. "I appreciate your time, Captain. I hope it hasn't been a waste. That is to say, not that I *want* anything to be wrong for Darwin."

"I understand what you mean. We'll check and let you know. As you leave, please send in the private posted outside."

Moments later, a young private was standing and saluting before Trimball's table. "You sent for me, sir?"

"Indeed I did. I want you to do two things. First, catch up with Lt. Reeves and tell him I want him to report back here as soon as he can. Second, I want you to round up a good map of the area that shows a spot called Wolverine Wash. Bring it to me. That is all."

CHAPTER 32

———

Darwin MacArthur had once again whipped up a fine breakfast and was being roundly praised for it.

Leaned way back in his chair and rubbing his ample stomach, Barge Kanelly proclaimed, "Man oh man, Darwin. You got a way with vittles that's about as pleasin' as anything I ever wrapped my lips around. If we was to hang around here much longer, I might decide I was so fond of your cookin' I'd have to haul you off to Montana with me so's I wouldn't have to do without it."

Seated across the table from Kanelly, Scorch Bannon said, "Watch out, old man. He lays it on any thicker, he might be asking for your hand in marriage."

From where he stood shuffling pots around atop his cook stove, Darwin grinned and replied, "Hey now. Havin' me a rich husband? Might be I'd have to give that some consideration."

"Well, don't get your hopes up," Kanelly told him. "Been a long time since I had me a woman but the memory is still pretty clear. Your cookin' ain't *that* good, you wrinkle-assed old fossil."

Darwin cackled and even Bannon worked up a wide smile. Near the front of the room, where he'd been standing gazing out the window with a cup of coffee in hand, Elroy MacArthur looked around, frowning. "You're an awful light-hearted bunch, don't you think, considerin' the serious business soon layin' ahead of us?"

Bannon' smile faded. "We always got serious business ahead of us, Pops. Never stopped us from poking a little fun amongst ourselves before. What's got you strung so tight? Soon as we get this McGantry character taken care of, we'll be scattering and make dust out of here. Ain't that what you've been so anxious to do?"

"Yeah, of course. You know it is," Elroy said. "But you also know I ain't crazy about takin' time to even mess with McGantry. That don't mean I won't go along with it, though; and, like always, you can count on me to hold up my end. I'm just antsy to get it done and over with, that's all."

"Well, the time for that is nearer than farther. Just try to keep a lid on your antsyness in the meantime," Bannon advised. "As soon as we get a bead on McGantry, what he looks like, how he's maneuvering about once he makes it to town, then things will pick up momentum. We can decide how we're going to make our move on him, get it done, then be on our way."

"You make it all sound awful easy," Kanelly remarked.

Bannon shrugged. "What's so hard about killing one man? He ain't even a law dog or anything. Just a loudmouth who thinks he can go around blowing about hunting us down and settling some personal score for a handful of scrawny nags and an old cripple who'd lived too long anyway? So now he'll find out he's given *us* a score to settle and, when we do, he can go join his one-legged old friend and they can lament together in the Hereafter about tangling with the wrong crew!"

"I like the sound of that," said Elroy, seeming less agitated. "I just hope me and the kid won't have too much trouble spottin' McGantry when we go back to town."

"The way you described tongues wagging last time you were there about how he'd plugged Henry and was on his way here to hunt us," Bannon pointed out, "the big talker showing up in person ought to cause quite a stir, wouldn't you think? That should make it easy enough to spot him."

"Yeah. I guess it should at that," Elroy agreed. "We just need for me and the kid to be on hand when he shows up. You still think we ought to wait a while longer before we go in?"

"Town won't get stirrin' much before the middle of the day," said Darwin from over by the stove. "You go in too early, you're more apt to draw attention to yourselves. You wait until mid-day you'll be lost in the throng and, even if your man has already arrived, you'll hear talk of it quick enough."

Bannon nodded. "Your brother makes good sense. You and the kid wait a few more hours, then the time will be better for your return trip to town."

Looking around, Kanelly said, "Where is the kid anyway? You see Tom out the window there, Pops?"

"Naw. Hell, he wandered off an hour ago. Him and that damn fishin' pole of his," the old man answered. "He's bound and determined to catch a fish somewhere in one of the creeks around here."

Kanelly grunted. "If there *was* any fish in any of these creeks, all that rain the other night probably washed 'em clean away to Colorado."

Bannon made a dismissive gesture. "No harm in letting him go drown some worms."

"Long as he don't lose track of time and gets back for when we need to head into town," Elroy said.

"Don't worry about that," Bannon replied. "Bad as young Tom wants to get at McGantry for revenge on what he did to Henry, he won't be late."

*****

Capt. Trimball and Lt. Reeves stood hunched over the map spread out on the table in Trimball's tent. "Well?" said Trimball, tapping his forefinger on the spot marked *Wolverine Wash*. "Are you familiar with this area? Did your men check it out at any point?"

Reeves turned his head to look at a stocky sergeant who stood at his left. "Sgt. Jochem? You said you recognized the name Wolverine Wash and I believe you led some men up that way shortly after we arrived in the area. What do you recall about it?"

Thirtyish, plump-faced, clean shaven but with thick, curly blond sideburns, Jochem replied, "Not much to recall, sir. Just a lot of empty rockiness. High cliffs, fringes of fir trees and scrub brush. Some creeks higher up, but the wash that gives it part of its name is mostly always dry, though maybe not right now after the recent rain. The way we heard, there was a patch or two of gold up in there at one time but it's long since been picked clean. Nothing going on up there these days, except for that one old hermit."

"That would be MacArthur?" asked Capt. Trimball.

"Yes, I believe that was his name, sir. I'd have to check my report to say for positive."

"You spoke with him?"

"Yes, sir."

"Nothing about him or anything he said that struck you as suspicious or odd in any way?"

Jochem shook his head. "No, sir. I mean, nothing other than him living off by himself like he does. Him and his old hound dog. That's kind of odd in my book. But that's his business. He was friendly and seemed calm, no sign of anything being wrong."

"Did you search his property? Go inside his cabin?"

Jochem frowned. "No, sir. There wasn't … well, there didn't seem no reason to. He was cooperative. We told him what was going on and he promised if he saw anything suspicious he'd be sure to let somebody know."

"It's all right, Sergeant. You handled it appropriately." Trimball sighed. Straightening up, he swept his gaze over the two officers before him. "But, in view of what the storekeeper told me, what think you, gentlemen? Is it worth another visit to Mr. MacArthur to make sure nothing has changed?"

"I don't see why not," answered Reeves. "It's been a few weeks since the earlier visit. Even if everything was okay back then, that's not saying Bannon's bunch or some other pack of skunks, hasn't moved in on the old hermit in the meantime. And if there's a chance it *is* Bannon—"

"I'll go," the sergeant blurted eagerly. "I'd be happy to go check it out again. I can take a half dozen men and leave right away."

Trimball arched a brow. "Okay, Sergeant. You just got yourself an assignment. Take a ten-man detail, though, not just half a dozen. In case the Bannon gang *is* up there, you'll want to be able to not only defend yourselves but also contain them until back-up can be sent if necessary. But don't let your willingness and eagerness turn into foolish heroics. You know what Bannon is capable of. No matter how friendly it seemed up there before, use caution on your approach the situation over good before you show yourselves."

"Yes, sir!"

"Send a runner back with a report as soon as you determine anything, one way or the other."

"Yes, sir!"

"Quit 'yes, sirring' me and hop to it!"

"Yes, sir!"

*****

After ascending all morning through rocky gorges and up over mounds overgrown with stands of the distinctly dark green pine and spruce trees that gave name to the central Black Hills off to the southeast as well as this region to the north and west, Lone and Maggie came to the southern tip of the great natural gulch in the heart of which lay the town of Deadwood. They reined their mounts and sat for a minute looking down on the destination they had started out for back what seemed like a long time ago.

"Jeez," Maggie marveled. "It looks so small down there. Not to mention so cramped and crowded, all jammed in amongst the hills and trees."

"Your time out on the wide-open plains of Nebraska spoiled you. They'll do that," Lone told her.

"Wide open and empty, that's how I saw them when I first got there. Miles and miles of nothing but miles and miles, as the old saying goes."

Lone grinned. "I never noticed before, but you're startin' to sound like a hard lady to please."

Maggie responded with a long, ragged coughing fit. Something she had been doing with greater frequency and severity all through the morning.

Lone's grin quickly disappeared. He said, "One good thing about all that crowdedness down there is that it's bound to have some doctors somewhere in it. And we're gonna be takin' you to see one just as soon as we hit town."

"Just find me a tobacco store where I can get some cigarillos," Maggie argued, fighting to catch her breath. "Breathing so much fresh air without a whiff of smoke to counteract it is all that's wrong with me."

"Nice try. I'll believe that if I hear it from a doctor, not before."

"You can quit worrying about me now," Maggie said stubbornly. "You held up your end of the bargain by getting me this far. Besides, once you're down there you're going to have plenty else to worry about."

Lone twisted his mouth wryly. "Yeah, and maybe even before then. Which is another worry I got concernin' you."

"What's that supposed to mean?"

"Got to do with a certain agreement I made with an old army friend," Lone explained. "A little something aimed, for the benefit of me and him both, at hopefully helpin' to flush out the Bannon gang. Long story short, it involves spreadin' false word on ahead that I had a direct hand in killin' Henry Plow combined with the truth about me comin' to Deadwood to do the same for Scorch and the rest."

"Jesus Christ, McGantry," Maggie exclaimed, "that amounts to practically having a bull's-eye painted on your back the minute you show up down there!"

"That's the flushin' out part. Bannon's bunch can't make a try for the bull's-eye, see, without steppin' up to the firin' line. Doin' that means exposin' themselves. Not only to me, but also to some back-up that will soon be waitin' in hiding all around me."

Maggie had another coughing spell before she could speak again. As soon as she could, she said, "But I told you last night where you can find Bannon and the others. Wolverine Wash. That was my end of the bargain. Especially if you've got the army siding you in this, why not try for them there instead of taking the risk of setting yourself up as bait?"

"For starters, this thing with the army was already set in motion before you showed up with your offer," Lone told her. "Second, there's no guarantee the gang will take the bait of tryin' for me. They've got to know there are soldiers and army investigators crawlin' all over Deadwood, even if they don't smell me as bein' in cahoots with 'em. It still makes botherin' with me a two-way risk they might be too savvy to take. In that case, your information about Wolverine Wash becomes the basis for a mighty good fallback plan."

"Once you tell your army friend about knowing where Scorch's gang is holed up," Maggie said hopefully, "maybe he'll agree with me and use that as the *first* plan for going after them."

"Except if Bannon has already caught wind of the false information spread about me and is figurin' to do something about it. Then it may already be too late," Lone pointed out. "He may not even be at the Wolverine Wash place any longer, but instead maneuverin' to intercept me when I show up. What's more, I can't tell anybody anything that might cause a change in plans until I'm able to get down there and make contact with somebody."

Maggie's brows pinched together. "Boy, you're a real ray of sunshine, you know that?"

"I'm just tellin' it straight and tryin' to play it safe

for the sake of both our hides. My original idea was for us to go into town separate, so you'd be removed from any harm aimed my way." Lone paused, scowling. "But now I've come to wonder if news I'm travelin' with a woman might not also have spread on ahead. Plus, I don't want to leave you on your own considerin' how sick you've become."

"For crying out loud, it's just a cough!"

"Yeah, but a couple of times I saw it wrack you so hard you nearly fell out of your saddle fightin' for breath," Lone countered. Then, giving a firm shake of his head, he added, "No, I ain't about to leave you on your own."

Looking more relieved than she probably meant to, Maggie said, "So what have you got in mind?"

Lone scowled downward at the town. "There are several roads and trails leadin' *to* Deadwood. But there's only two or three passages commonly followed for gettin' down into the gulch. I'm thinkin' I can find us a not so common passage, a way no one would be lookin' for anybody to use."

"My friends have a boarding house on this near end of town," said Maggie.

"So much the better. If they're true friends they'll see that you need a doctor and they'll agree with me about fetchin' one for you." Lone nodded. "I can settle for that. Then, once you're safe with them, I'll head on out and make myself seen around the town."

Maggie fought hard to suppress a cough and then said, "I'll be safe and you'll stubbornly be looking to make yourself un-safe."

Lone's mouth pulled into a tight, straight line. "Not as un-safe as I'll be lookin' to make Bannon and his pack of vermin."

Maggie gazed at him intently for a long moment before saying, soft and quiet, "You know how much I don't want you to go through with that. Yet I know there's nothing I can say or do to stop you."

Lone was able to hold her gaze for only a short time before he had to look away. "Come on," he said gruffly. "Let's get you to that boardin' house where you'll be took care of."

CHAPTER 33

———

Tom List would have been more disappointed about once again failing to catch any fish if it wasn't for the pending trip to town. The sun overhead, nearing its noon peak, told him it was time to get back to Darwin's cabin where he and Elroy were scheduled to make a return to Deadwood. The team of "Pops" and "the kid" being called upon for the crucial task of identifying that lowdown dog McGantry and setting him up to get what he had coming for killing Henry and then having the gall to boast he was going to take down the whole gang.

The big-feeling, big-mouthed son of a bitch. Tom seethed at the thought of Henry's killer not only still walking around but blowing that kind of talk while doing it. Balancing this simmering rage, just barely was knowing that the time was near for McGantry to pay and pay big. The kid's only worry was if he'd be able to hold back in case he was the one who first laid eyes on the murdering scum.

Having a simmering rage inside was nothing new for Tom. Maybe not one burning quite as hot as this one fueled by Henry's killing, but an ever present ball of churning, boiling hate and resentment for most everything and everybody was always there. Had been ever since enduring the horrors of war, seeing the bloody hell and fury that chewed up comrades all around him, brave men laying down their lives for a cause, just to have it all turn out seemingly without meaning due to a cowardly surrender and the cause being ground to dust under the boots of the defeated and retreating.

Only his chance falling in with Scorch and Henry had helped Tom control the way he felt in the aftermath, keep it channeled into the business of the gang rather than exploding in some wild, reckless manner that surely would have brought about the kid's demise long before this. By robbing and killing alongside Scorch and the others, convincing himself it was Yankee money and dirty, dead Yankee hands he was ripping it from. Tom found a way to keep fighting his war and keep telling himself he was still striking for the cause.

Though the trip into town and subsequent revenge for Henry were foremost on Tom' mind this morning, his ever-present other demons were also there, writhing just below the surface. That was why, when he first saw the line of soldiers, all dressed in hated blue-belly uniforms, making their way up the rocky slopes of Wolverine Wash, he thought he might be seeing things. That happened sometimes, a flashback of blue clad devils rising up out of nowhere and seeming to come at him, only to fade as suddenly as they'd appeared and leave him in a clammy sweat, panting to catch his breath.

But these blue bellies today didn't fade away. They were real, not a flashback vision. And then the sergeant leading them glanced up, catching sight of Tom at the same time he spotted them. The kid was caught flat-footed right out in the open, on his way from a creek off to the north, cutting just above the dry wash and getting ready to start his own ascent up toward Darwin's cabin. For a moment he considered bolting, making a run for it. But something told him that would only make things worse for whatever this was shaping up to be.

The sergeant helped him make up his mind to stay put, at least for the moment, by calling out to him. "Hey, young fella. Hold on, I'd like a word with you."

Tom froze where he was, feet planted wide, fishing pole in his left hand and his Winchester in his right. He felt his pulse quickening and beads of too-familiar clammy sweat threatening to burst out on his forehead. The rifle in his hand felt hot and heavy, like it was tugging on his arm, begging to be raised and used the way it should be against these hated blue bellies. But he willed himself to stay calm, not allow any outward sign of the emotions running through him.

The sergeant made his way closer, his men trailing behind him. Tom resisted the urge to glance around and up toward the cabin to make sure there was nothing showing that might draw added attention from the soldiers in case they weren't already on their way there. None of them could see it from where they were now, he assured himself, they were too far down away. The cabin was another hundred or so yards farther up the slope and tucked back on a ledge against a higher cliff, nestled in brush and trees. They weren't even close enough yet for Darwin's old hound Rufus to have begun raising an alarm.

"That pole looks kind of empty," noted the sergeant as he drew within a few feet of Tom. "Fish ain't biting, eh?"

"No," Tom replied somewhat sullenly. *Dumb bastard. If the pole's empty do you really need to ask about the fish biting?*

"You from around here?" the sergeant asked.

"Hereabouts."

"We're on our way to check on a fella named Darwin MacArthur. We had the impression he's the only one who lives up this way."

"Even folks from town sometimes come to fish the streams. Don't mean they live particularly close."

"I see. Do you know Darwin?"

"Some."

"Have you seen him around lately?"

Tom was liking this less and less. This nosy damn blue-bellied sergeant was getting on his nerves, pecking at his temper. And the rest of his men, even though they stayed in single file, kept edging up closer. "What do you mean by you're aimin' to 'check on' ol' Dar?" he wanted to know. "He in some kind of trouble?"

The sergeant cocked his head and regarded Tom more closely. "Why do you ask that? Do you think he might be?"

Tom didn't like the way he was being looked at and he felt more and more panicky as the other soldiers edged nearer. And at the raw edge of panic was anger, which was never very far away for Tom, certainly not with a pack of blue bellies in front of him. Fighting to keep his voice level, he said, "A whole passel of soldier boys swarmin' in on an old hermit, strikes me a body'd have to be a mite dim to take that for just a social call."

The sergeant's expression pulled tight, clearly not liking Tom's answer. "Soldier boys?" he echoed. "I call that term and your tone pretty damned disrespectful, mister. You and your Johnny Reb cap. Especially when I've been nothing but cordial to you. What's your name and exactly where are you from?"

That was enough for the explosion to go off inside Tom. Whatever had stirred them up, it was clear this pack of blue bellies was here sniffing for trouble and if they reached the cabin there'd be no turning them away, no matter how much smooth talking Darwin tried to do, without it erupting beyond the old man's control. So the way Tom saw it, the best thing he could do was trigger the blast right here, give Scorch and the others as much warning as possible, and take as many of these Yankee peckerwoods he was able to before they got any farther. The kid always knew the war wasn't over for him and he would someday go down still fighting it. It looked like today was the day, and he was pleased it was with a bunch of blue bellies in full uniform. His only regret was that it was coming before he got any chance at that murdering dog McGantry.

Eyes blazing, teeth bared menacingly, Tom threw back his head and let out a rebel yell immediately followed by: "The name's Thomas List, you Yankee scum, and I'm straight out of the undyin' glory of Dixie!"

With that, he whipped his left arm cross-body, slashing the fishing pole across the sergeant's face, laying open a bright red welt and sending the man staggering back, cursing. Dropping the pole and then using the emptied left hand to cup the forestock of his Winchester as he swung it up level, Tom triggered a round to the center of the sergeant's chest. This sent the officer staggering even more wildly, arms windmilling, until he toppled and fell dead, skidding on the rocky slope.

The remaining soldiers, though momentarily stunned by this act, were too well trained not to react promptly and properly. The fact they had remained in single file behind their commanding officer gave them the advantage of not being bunched together for the follow-up barrage of lead

Tom began pouring down on them immediately after killing the sergeant. As the kid cut loose, spitting a string of curses in concert with the slugs sizzling out of his Winchester's muzzle, the soldiers broke from their line, splitting half to either side, and dove for cover behind rocks or into wash-out crevices.

Tom continued firing mercilessly, levering in fresh rounds and then immediately expelling them in a sweeping pattern back and forth over the scattering row of men. Those closest naturally took the worst of it. One private jerked and spun crazily in mid-air as he was diving for cover. Another yelped in pain while toppling back in much the same manner as the sergeant had.

As he continued firing, Tom taunted in a high-pitched screech, "Had your lunch yet, boys? How about a big ol' servin' of hot lead!"

But then, suddenly, the tide started to turn and he was no longer in a position to taunt. Having gained reasonable cover, the remaining eight soldiers began returning fire and Tom was caught largely out in the open. Armed with single-shot Springfield carbines, the soldiers couldn't individually match the kid's rapid fire but they more than made up for it by sheer force of number.

Bullets started gouging into the ground at his feet and spanging and ricocheting off rocks to either side. It was just a matter of time—mere seconds—before the riflemen got sighted in better and the first .45-70 slug tore through the kid's side, splintering ribs and sending a chunk of meat flying in a spray of blood.

Twisted half around by the impact, Tom dropped to one knee and immediately cranked off a response, hollering, "You blue-bellied bastards never could shoot for sour apples!"

But more shots hammered his way. One punched through the meaty part of his right thigh, one chipped away bone from his left shoulder. Pushing jerkily to his feet, Tom fired once more and then turned and began a staggering scramble up the slope. Up above, on the flat that led back to Darwin's cabin, the hound dog Rufus began barking and howling.

The slope up where Tom was, had been worn mostly flat by the elements, providing little in the way concealment or cover such as what was available to the soldiers down lower. All he could do was attempt a zig-zag pattern as he tried to go higher. But his wounds slowed him too much and the hail of bullets chasing him was too intense. More slugs punched into his back and legs. Discarding the Winchester because he couldn't afford to pause and turn back to shoot with it, Tom instead pulled a converted Navy Colt from his waistband and extended his arm backward, firing blindly down the slope as he continued to crawl upward.

His final words, rather than another taunt at the soldiers below, was a shout up ahead. "They're on us, boys! Blue-bellied hell has come a-callin'. Defend yourselves!"

And then a bullet entered the back of the kid's head at an upward angle, lifting the top of his skull like a lid and splattering a pattern of gore ahead onto the slope as his face was simultaneously slammed against it. His body collapsed instantly limp and lifeless. The Navy Colt slipped from his dead fingers and went skidding and clattering down the slope for several feet before thumping to a halt.

CHAPTER 34

————

Maggie's friend turned out to be a handsome middle-aged woman named Bea Forbes. As previously mentioned, she and her husband Frank ran a boarding house near the south end of Deadwood, just off the main drag. Frank, Lone would learn as introductions were made, was currently not there because he also clerked at a dry goods store downtown.

In as much as Maggie hadn't had a chance to send word ahead that she was returning, her arrival came as quite a surprise. But this in no way diminished the warmth of the welcome she received.

After a whoop of joy and a great, whirling hug, Bea held her at arms' length and exclaimed, "My gracious, girl, let me have a look at you. You little brat, you haven't aged a minute! You're as lovely as ever." But then, on closer examination, the smile left Bea's face and her brows pinched warily together. "Hold on, though. Those circles under your eyes certainly aren't very becoming, and" the back of her hand abruptly pressed to Maggie's forehead, "Lord a-mercy, you're burning up with fever! I should have noticed when I first hugged you. Dear, what is ailing you?"

Before Maggie could protest, Lone beat her to it by saying, "We had some misfortune in a flooded river yesterday and she came out of it with a cold and a bad cough that's grown steadily worse all mornin'. I been tellin' her she needs to see a doctor as soon as we can get her to one."

"That's nonsense. All I need is—" In her haste to argue, Maggie brought on a coughing fit that lasted the better part of a minute before she got it under control.

That was more than enough time for Bea to form a very determined scowl and, as soon as the coughing abated, to declare, "You certainly *are* going to see a doctor, young lady. We have a very good one just up the street. Frank will be home for lunch any minute and he goes right by there on his way to and from. When he leaves to return to the store, I'll have him send Dr. Welles straightaway."

"It's just a cough. I've had this before and—"

But Bea was in no mood to be dissuaded. "I'll not have you return after all this time only to cough yourself to death under my roof, and that's final! Now come sit down. I'll fix you a cup of hot tea with whiskey, honey, and lemon. Maybe some broth, to help comfort you until we can get the doctor here."

Maggie rolled her eyes, but at the same time her shoulders sagged resignedly as Bea steered the way through a spacious, well-furnished and fastidiously clean parlor into a plushily cushioned chair. Following, Lone glanced to his left through a wide doorway and saw a rectangular dining room with a long table draped by a checkered cloth and set with a row of plates and silverware on either side.

Over her shoulder, the take-charge Bea said, "You may have a seat at the table in there, Mr. McGantry. I'm about to set out some fresh-baked bread and a big pot of chicken and dumplings for our boarders and for Frank when he gets here. There'll be plenty for you to partake as well."

"That's very kind, ma'am, and the smell of that chicken and dumplings is mighty hard to resist," Lone told her. "But I really need to be on my way. Now that I see Maggie is in good hands, I have some pressin' business I—"

"It's hard to believe you have such pressing business after only just arriving in town," Bea cut him off. "You'll have to eat some time, won't you?"

"Well, uh … Yeah, I guess that's true enough, ma'am," Lone admitted reluctantly, getting his own taste of Bea's determination and trying to think of something more to say to talk his way past it. He could see Maggie's mouth curving into a smug little smile.

Before anything more was said on the subject, the front door suddenly burst open and a sparely built man of fifty or so, wearing spectacles, a bow tie, and sleeve garters, barged eagerly through. "You're not going to believe this, Bea, but—" Whatever he'd been about to so excitedly announce was halted by the unexpected sight of others present before him. And then, after a double take, his expression brightened with recognition and he exclaimed, "Maggie!"

As the man, who was obviously Bea's husband Frank, hurried across the room to embrace Maggie, his wife said, "Isn't wonderful to have her back again?"

"It certainly is," Frank agreed, not seeming to notice Maggie's fever or wan appearance. "This makes the day all the more momentous."

Maggie smiled. "I'm happy you're glad to see me, Frank. But there's hardly anything momentous about me showing up anywhere."

"That's debatable, kiddo," Frank said, smiling and patting her shoulders. Then, jabbing a thumb over his shoulder, he added, "But there's something going on outside that surely rates up there!"

"What are you talking about? What's got you so worked up?" Bea wanted to know.

Frank turned back to her, beaming. "I's not just me who's worked up, darling. The whole town is,they're pouring into the street like it's a Fourth of July celebration. The army finally got 'em, Bea! They got the whole Scorch Bannon gang pinned down and under siege at a place called Wolverine Wash, up in the hills north of town!"

CHAPTER 35

———

Lone bolted from the Forbes boarding house without a word. He trusted Maggie would adequately explain his reaction to the news Frank had delivered, just as he trusted Bea would make good on seeing that Maggie received the attention of a doctor. These concerns flashed through the former scout's mind, but foremost in his thoughts was the resounding echo of what Frank had reported: *"The whole Scorch Bannon gang pinned down and under siege at a place called Wolverine Wash, up north of town!"*

It was at once excitingly welcome news and yet it sent a deep pang of remorse knifing into Lone. The thought of Bannon and his bunch cornered and brought to account *without him* suddenly felt intolerable. It was probably a sorry comment on his value system, he told himself, but it was nevertheless the way he felt. All this time he'd been claiming inwardly and to others the main thing was that the murderers of his friend met proper justice, even if it wasn't directly by him. Now he realized that wasn't true, he wanted the blood of those scurvy bastards very much *on his hands!*

Astride Ironsides, Lone pounded recklessly through the crowded, deeply rutted streets of Deadwood, plowing apart congestion when he came to it, shouting for others to get out of his way and enduring curses and angry glares in return. His reckoning for north came naturally, but even apart from that the course toward Wolverine Wash could hardly be missed due to the stream of townsfolk flowing in that direction. People "worked up" and "pouring into the streets" as Frank had described it, anxious to try and get close enough to see something they'd be able to add to boasts later in their mundane lives about being part of the big event.

A short ways past the northern limits of the town and a slight jog to the northeast, the flow of people had been brought to a halt and were being held in a restlessly shifting throng by a line of soldiers preventing them from going any farther. In the distance, high up in ragged, rocky terrain studded with stands of spruce and thick tanglebrush, the sporadic crack of gunfire could be heard.

On the back of Ironsides, Lone pushed his way, slower now but still steadily, through the packed citizens. There were several unhappy grumbles and even a few men who turned with fire in their eyes, ready to object more strongly; but when they saw the look on his face, the fires cooled and the men went ahead and edged aside wordlessly.

When he got to the front of the citizen pack, Lone found himself facing the line of soldiers.

A young corporal with a defiant thrust to his chin took a step forward and said, "Check down that animal, mister, and hold it right there. You can't come any farther."

Slowly, Lone stepped down from his saddle and also took a step forward. His expression was somber but not belligerent. His eyes flicked in the direction of the distant gunfire and then back to the corporal. "Is Captain Alan Trimball involved in that fracas up there?" he asked.

"Details of this engagement will be made available to the public in good time, sir. Until then we just need everyone to stay back until the matter is resolved."

Now Lone's expression hardened and turned impatient. "I asked you a simple question in a civil tone, Corporal. My name's Lone McGantry. If Captain Trimball *is* up there, which I strongly suspect to be the case then I assure you he'd want to know I'm here and would agree to have me brought forward."

The corporal's chin thrust out more firmly than ever. "I'm sorry, sir. I have my orders and they include no exceptions for anyone by your name or any other. Therefore I must ask you again to—"

A few steps away, back in the line, a walrus-mustached private of considerably more years than usually found in a trooper at the bottom rank, cleared his throat in a way meant to draw attention. The corporal's head snapped around. "You have something to say, O'Doul?"

"Beggin' your pardon, sir … if I could have a quick word," came the reply.

Scowling fiercely, the corporal turned and walked back to the veteran trooper, the latter taking a step to meet him. Their heads tipped together and there was a quickly muttered exchange. When it was done, the corporal came back to stand before Lone. He was still scowling, but it was different, more thoughtful now. He said, "It seems there are some contingencies to this whole matter I wasn't made fully aware of. O'Doul tells me that, until just before the trouble broke out at this end of town, he was part of a special detail earlier assigned to intercept you. Said assignment, he assures me, with the full sanction of Captain Trimball."

The young officer paused, as if not liking the taste of the words he was about to say. But then he went ahead anyway. "O'Doul is notorious for a host of discipline problems that account for his perpetual private status. But his years of service have nevertheless given him certain instincts and a range of wisdom that I, for one, have learned to trust. Therefore, I'm allowing you to proceed with him. He'll take you to Captain Trimball."

*****

Fifteen minutes later, after ascending on the heels of O'Doul up through clumps of tanglebrush and tangle brush in and out of gullies and crevices running between rock outcrops, Lone found himself in a narrow ditch crowded by walls of more jagged, head-high rocks on either side. At the far end of the ditch, peering up and out through a V-shaped gap, crouched Capt. Trimball with a service revolver gripped in one gloved fist. Lone also noted several troopers manning positions of cover on all sides. The shooting seemed to have ceased for the time being.

Moving stooped-over up behind Trimball, O'Doul announced to him, "I brung you a present, Cap'n."

Looking around, Trimball's gaze quickly fell on Lone. Cocking a single brow, he said, "Well. It's about time you showed up."

"If I'd known you were gonna be rude enough to start the party without me," Lone chuffed, "I might've pushed a little harder to get here. But it so happens I ran into considerable interference along the way."

"Since you made it anyway, I guess that means the interference must have got the worst of it."

"Eventually," Lone affirmed. He edged past O'Doul and settled in next to Trimball. "So what's the situation here, Red?"

Before Trimball could answer, O'Doul said, "Beggin' your pardon, Cap'n. But you want I should go back to the line, or can I stay here?"

Looking somewhat bemused, Trimball said, "Do you *want* to go back to the line, Private?"

"Hell … er, I mean, no, not really, sir. I'd rather stay up here where the action is."

"All right, then do so. Pick a spot and keep your head down."

With that settled, the captain returned to Lone's question. "The situation here," he said, "can either be looked at as a siege or a stand-of."

"I'll say right now I don't like thinkin' of it as a 'stand-off'. Not if that's for sure the Bannon gang up there," Lone was quick to respond. "Callin' it a stand-off makes it sound like they got some kind of edge or bargainin' chip on their end."

"Well, that *is* the Bannon gang up there. What's left of 'em," Trimball confirmed. "They tried to make a break for it when the trouble first broke out. But the men I'd sent up here, though only few in number, were sharp enough to split and cover both flanks in order to keep them hemmed in. As part of that exchange there were some who got a good look at scar-faced Bannon as well as the big Negro, Kanelly. There was no mistaking who it was."

Lone swore under his breath.

Trimball pointed. "Look at that slope stretching down out there in the middle, the one that's worn mostly smooth and bare all the way to the rubble near the bottom. See the body sprawled about two-thirds of the way up? That's one of the gang, the younger one nobody ever had a clear description of before. It was him who panicked and set this ruckus suddenly into motion after a detail of our men ran into him inadvertently when they were on their way to check on the old hermit who lives up at the top of the slope.

"You can see his cabin from here, over on that ledge where the slope flattens, about a dozen or so yards back. Back down the slope, below the dead gang member, you can see three more bodies. My men. Caught off guard and mowed down by that little bastard when he went nuts and started shooting without any warning. So far we haven't dared risk trying to pull their bodies away."

Lone set his teeth on edge. "That' rough, Red. But you've got to tell yourself that they themselves are beyond pain or caring, no matter where they're layin' for right now. Not riskin' more lives to try and pull 'em away is the only thing you can do."

Trimball countered, "No. There's more I can do. I can make damn sure the rest of the scum behind those boys ending up that way are made to pay and pay dear."

"I'm all for that," Lone told him. While Trimball had been talking, the former scout was busy scanning the overall scene, taking in more than just the things being directly pointed out. He saw that the captain and men with him here were off to the right of the smooth, open slope and the cabin up at the top. Directly behind the cabin rose a high, flat-faced cliff also weathered bare and smooth. And on the other side, another shoulder of rocky ridges and troughs and tanglebrush angled up toward the cabin, with more soldiers positioned at various points to prevent any flight that way.

Noting Lone making his appraisal, the captain said, "So you can see how it shapes up. They can't get down, we can't get up. At least not in any way we've hit on so far. I've got Lt. Greg Reeves, a good man, in charge on the other side. We've been trading messages back and forth."

"No thought to chargin' in from the flanks and hittin' that cabin from both sides at once?"

"We thought about it, sure," Trimball answered. "But, for one thing, attacking over that flat, open ground on each side would be mighty costly. Secondly, we've got to give some consideration to the hostage they've got in there with them."

"Hostage?" Lone echoed.

"That's right. The old hermit who lives in the cabin," Trimball explained. "The gang must have heard about him right after they hit the area, how he stays up there all alone, except for an old hound dog, and nobody else hardly ever comes up this way anymore due to the ground being long since played out. So, we figure they swept in, overpowered the old bird, and have been using his out-of-the-way shack to hole up in all this time."

"Just a few minutes ago, Bannon called down wanting to make a deal using the old hermit's life as a bargaining chip. Says, him and his bunch will leave the gold behind if we give them passage to get clear of the area. They'll keep MacArthur as their hostage until they're convinced they've made it far enough away without us on their tail, then they'll let him go."

Lone scowled. "I hope you're not swallowin' any of that. Not even for a second."

"Hell no," the captain declared. "I'm just stalling, pretending I'm considering it. That's why there's no shooting currently taking place. I told Bannon I had to get somebody off to the telegraph office and send word back to Fort Robinson to try and get authorization for such an arrangement. I'm not wasting any time actually doing that, of course. What I am doing, is hoping to buy a little time in order to put together a plan."

"How about I toss you a little tidbit for free to help your plannin'?"

"Like what?"

"Like not havin' to worry any more about Bannon's so-called hostage," said Lone. "Yeah, there's an old hermit up there by the name of MacArthur. Darwin MacArthur. And ridin' with Bannon's gang for the past half dozen years, the other hombre nobody ever got a clear description of has been an old timer named Elroy MacArthur, Darwin's brother. So maybe Darwin ain't no ridin', robbin', shootin' member of the gang, but he ain't no overpowered hostage neither. He's been plumb willin' to allow his brother's gang to hole up here all this while."

CHAPTER 36

Captain Trimball's gaze bored intently into Lone. "I've never had cause to doubt your word, old pal. But are you certain of what you're saying? Are you sure Darwin MacArthur is the brother of one of the gang members?"

"I'd stake Ironsides and my favorite saddle on it, Red," replied Lone. "It's a long story, but I got the straight of it from a gal who used to be the girlfriend of Henry Plow. I traded gettin' her out of Crawford for her handin' over what she'd learned from Plow about the rest of the gang. She named the other members and told me about Wolverine Wash bein' where they were holed up before I ever got in this morning and heard how the skirmish had gone ahead and busted out here."

"Damn!" said Trimball, an excited gleam in his eye. "That still doesn't give us an exact way to proceed but taking away worry over the old hermit is nevertheless a big help."

"You've got the polecats pinned down, why not just haul off and blast 'em out?" Lone asked. "You must have some explosives layin' around somewhere, don't you?"

"We've got some dynamite back at the camp. A couple of light mountain howitzers, too, that would do the job." Trimball grimaced. "We actually thought about blasting, a bit earlier. But them having a hostage was one of the reasons that prevented going ahead with it."

"So that's not a reason any longer. What else?"

Trimball pointed. "That high cliff rising up right behind the cabin. What would be the result of an explosion or two at its base? Seems like a chance it could shake loose a good-sized landslide. Not that I'd shed any tears over burying the whole Bannon gang. But it would purely break my heart, not to mention the hearts of the big brass, to see the payroll money get buried with them."

"Everybody knows the big brass don't have any hearts," Lone grunted. "Besides, the gold in those payroll coins got dug out once before, why not again? The army has plenty of picks and shovels and men to swing 'em."

"Maybe so," allowed Trimball. "But I'm guessing, just guessing, mind you that those same big brass types might figure there was a better use for their fighting men. More likely they'd bust me down to private, give me a spoon and a fork if I was lucky, and assign me to the digging. No, we need to come up with some better idea than blasting."

"You could always fall back on the long, drawn-out solution of waitin' 'em out. A siege, like you said at the start. They're bound to run out of food and water eventually, while you can keep a holding force re-supplied all the way to Christmas." But even as he was saying this, it was clear by Lone's tone that he didn't much care for the idea.

"I even thought of trying to put that damn cliff to work in our favor," the captain muttered bitterly. "If I had two or three mountain goats with rifles up there at the top, they could punch .45-70 slugs through the roof of that old shack and raise holy hell with all inside. But the thought of the hostage also being in there largely queered that idea. And then there was the issue of whoever tried to shoot down from the rim up above would have to lean out in order to do so, and after taking a few shots they'd mark themselves as easy targets for somebody positioned to pick them off from below."

Lone hitched forward with the glint of an idea dancing in his eyes. "Wait a minute, though. That cliff, that roof, there might be another way."

"Like what?"

"See the smoke stack pokin' up out of that roof? It's puffin' pretty good, has been right along. What if somebody snuck real quiet-like out onto the roof and plugged that stack? It'd back up on the inside and smoke out whoever was in there plenty quick, I'm thinkin'. Then, if you had forces crowded in tight on either flank, waitin' and ready, a pack of polecats pourin' out with their eyes burnin' and chokin' from smoke oughta be prime for the pluckin' without bein' in any shape to take a heavy toll in return."

Trimball scowled in thought. "By God, that's not a bad idea. But how would we get somebody on the roof?"

"From above. From the top of the cliff." As soon as he said it, Lone could see doubt starting to form in Trimball's eyes. So he quickly added, "I could do it, Red. There's got to be a way up and around to the top. Get me a long enough rope and somebody to anchor it at the top for me, I can make it from the rim down that cliff's flat face and onto the cabin roof. Come on, you know how much it means to me to be in on takin' those bastards!"

Trimball dragged a hand down over his face. "Jeez, Lone, I don't know. The idea has some merit. But it's damned risky. Plus, you're a civilian."

"Then assign me as a volunteer scout for the army," Lone demanded. "It'll hardly be the first time. It won't even be the first time for you to be the one doin' it."

From where he'd positioned himself close by, O'Doul said, "You can count me as volunteerin' to go with him, Cap'n. Everybody knows I ain't no stranger to risk or crazy ideas. And this one sounds crazy enough to me to have 'bout half a chance of workin'!"

*****

After what seemed like a frustratingly long time for some rope to be brought up (the lasso from Ironsides' saddle along with another length secured from somewhere else) Lone and O'Doul, each with a coil slung over one shoulder, promptly set out to find a way around the side of the cliff and to the top. Clawing their way through clumps of tanglebrush turned out to be the hardest part. Otherwise, there were enough outward-jutting rocky knobs and slanted seams to provide decent purchase the whole way. Still, both men were breathing hard and dripping sweat by the time they made it. The sun was half-way descended but still bright in the afternoon sky. The bare rock along the rim of the cliff was hot to the touch.

Lone bellied down and worked his way to the edge of the rim. Shifting slightly to one side, he centered himself over the cabin roof below. Then, lifting his head and shoulders, he waved a signal off to where he reckoned Trimball to be. There was no signal back, of course, for fear of alerting any of the outlaws in the cabin. Before temporarily sliding back from the rim, Lone looked to either side and noted that well-concealed clumps of troopers had crowded up closer on each side of the flat, ledge-like area where the cabin was perched.

Behind him, O'Doul whispered, "Well? What did you see?"

Lone hitched back and rolled up on one elbow. "Saw plenty. Saw out across the whole wash and saw troopers moved up tight on both flanks." Then, pausing to grin ruefully, he added, "Mostly I saw that it looks a helluva lot farther down from up here than it did from down there."

O'Doul peeled down his bottom lip and chuckled. "Ya blamed idjit. You shoulda thought of that before you stepped in it."

"I ain't worried about steppin' in it. I'm worried about *fallin'* in it. A fella could break his neck from up here," Lone said.

O'Doul chuckled some more as he began uncoiling Lone's lasso. "Save the act, sonny. I seen too many of you hell-for-leather types. You ain't gonna turn away now, not with everybody watchin'. Besides, I also seen the fire in your eye for wantin' to take down Bannon's bunch. The captain ain't got enough men to hold you back from bein' in the thick of this. So tell me what it is you want from me, and let's commence gettin' it over with."

CHAPTER 37

———

The purpose for Lone signaling from the top of the cliff had been twofold: One, to let Trimball know he was in place; two, for the captain to then initiate further conversation with Bannon, inside the cabin, in order for their talking to help hide any inadvertent sound Lone might make coming down from above.

Below him now, as he started lowering himself hand-over-hand down the rope he and O'Doul had played out, Lone could hear the words going back and forth. He didn't pay any attention to what was being said. It was all bluster, on both sides. The only thing that counted was that it was noise to help cover any that might result from his efforts.

Down, down the former scout eased himself.

Five feet … Ten …

Up above, back over the rim, the rest of the rope was wrapped securely around a large boulder and O'Doul was gripping it to make extra sure it held fast.

Fifteen feet … Twenty …

Below, the coarse army blanket knotted at the end of the rope swayed ten inches above the inside peak of the cabin roof. Lone kept easing himself down. One hand, then the next, each time letting his clenched knees and stockinged feet relax just enough to allow controlled slippage on the rope.

Twenty-five feet … Thirty … Almost there.

The back end of the cabin was a little over four feet from the face of the cliff, leaving just enough room to exit and make a sharp turn to the rickety outhouse that stood off to one side. This meant that, in order for Lone to come down on the roof, he'd have to swing out away from the cliff and drop the last couple of feet as lightly as he could. When his feet reached the end of the rope where it was knotted around the blanket, he released the squeeze his knees and feet had on the rope and he let his feet dangle free. He was hanging on entirely with his hands now, sweat pouring from his face down on his forearms and the crooks of his elbows.

Planting his bootless feet against the cliff, he pushed out and swung himself over the roof. He swung back and kicked out again, trying to time his drop with some calling out from inside the cabin.

He got what he was hoping for when a voice he reckoned to be that of none other than the hated Scorch Bannon hollered to Trimball: "You go ahead continue stalling the way you are, you're only going to add a dead hostage to all the rest of the bloodshed you seem bent on causing!"

Lone settled silently just back from the inner peak of the cabin roof and locked immediately into a slight crouch. No creaking timbers, no clattering of dislodged shingles, so far, so good. Confirming this all the more was the uninterrupted hollering that continued between Bannon and Capt. Trimball.

Breathing a sigh of relief, Lone sleeved sweat from his face and turned to begin untying the blanket he would soon be stuffing down the stove pipe. When he had the blanket free, he turned back to said pipe and took a careful step toward it. The pipe stuck up from roughly the center of the roof, so he didn't have far to go.

But he never got any closer.

The second step Lone took brought about unthinkably disastrous results. The center beam of the roof—ancient, weathered, possibly dry-rotted or of lousy quality to begin with, who the hell would ever know for sure? decided to suddenly sag and start to break apart with a loud *snap!* that sounded like the crack of an enormous whip. The jolt of the sudden sag under his feet caused Lone to lose his balance and pitch forward onto his face. This sudden deposit of weight, pounding down like a fist on the already partially broken beam, made it break the rest of the way and, as it parted and dropped as two separate ends, also pull down torn-away rafters and a gaping section of shingles, laths, and debris that all poured into the interior of the cabin.

Included in this deluge was a battered and stunned Lone McGantry!

One minute Lone had been right where he wanted to be, the next second he was tumbling through the air, getting clobbered by flying shingles and chunks of wood and choking on gritty dust and dirt. He landed hard from the fall, knocking much of the wind out of him. When he fought to suck some breath back in, he gagged on the swirling wood particles and retched until he nearly blacked out.

No! Must fight, must stay alert! Must make being in the midst of the murderous Bannon scum count for something!

Lone's iron will to survive and to deliver his sworn vengeance forced him to cling to consciousness. He pushed onto his hands and knees and struggled to stand. All around him was chaos. Men were groaning and coughing and cursing. He could make out some movement, some fleeting, murky shapes, but everything was swallowed by churning, blurring clouds of dust and wood particles.

Making it creakily to his feet, Lone's hand went to his hip and he found that his Colt, secured by the keeper thong, was still in its holster. A surge of hope and excitement coursed through him. He was still fighting for breath, carefully sucking each intake through his teeth to try and keep out the crud that would trigger another coughing fit.

He drew the Colt. He was unsteady on his feet, but a ragged thought was forming in his head, propelling him, giving him strength. His vision and breathing and everything else was impaired but he realized he nevertheless still had a big advantage over everybody else in here with him. He knew what had happened, they didn't. Hell, they didn't even know he was here in their midst. And no matter if they did, making a move against him would be inhibited by not knowing whether or not his indistinct shape might be one of their own.

But Lone had no such problem. Any shape he saw was certain to be an enemy. And killing the enemies holed up here, the murderers of the best friend he ever had was precisely why he was present.

As if bidden by these thoughts, this realization, the vague outline of a man shifted behind a billowing brown cloud. Lone didn't hesitate. He extended the Colt and fired a .44 slug straight into the middle of the outline. A man yelped in pain and the outline faded suddenly away.

Lone quickly shifted away from his telltale muzzle flash, reaching out with is free hand to try and avoid bumping into anything.

"What the hell was that shot? Who fired it?" demanded a voice out of the churning fog. It sounded like he same one, the one Lone reckoned to belong to Bannon, that had been calling to Trimball.

"It sure wasn't me. I can't see shit to shoot *at!*" responded a different voice.

The first voice again: "Pops? Was that you? What are you trying to do?"

When there was no response, a third voice said timidly, "Brother? Elroy? Answer somebody, for Heaven's sake!"

Lone couldn't resist. He grated, "I'm thinkin' his answerin' days are past and Heaven didn't have a damn thing to do with it."

"Who said that? Who's out there?" demanded the second voice.

"What did you do with my brother!" wailed the third. A dog barked in support.

Lone didn't answer with words. Instead, when another murky shape showed itself in the gloom, he let the Colt speak for him again. The recipient emitted no sound this time, there was only the sound of his body dropping heavily to the floor. And then, moments later, came the gentle, concerned whimpering of the dog.

"Sonofabitch, now he got Darwin. There's somebody in here with us, Scorch!" exclaimed he second voice which, by virtue of elimination, had to belong to Barge Kanelly.

"No shit," Bannon grumbled sarcastically. Then: "Whoever's out there, you're a dead man, you stinking, back-shooting snake! We know you're in here now and the dust is starting to clear. You'll never make it out past both of us."

He barely got this out before Kanelly said, "Hey Scorch, you better look out the window. We got bigger problems than the snake in here. There's soldiers closin' in on both sides. Dozens of 'em, with rifles aimed and ready."

"They're not going to do a damn thing with those rifles, Barge. Not yet, not while one of their own is in here with us. They won't risk riddling him by accident, especially not when it's pretty clear the jig is up for us anyway."

"Jesus, Scorch. You sayin' it's time to hand ourselves over?"

"You call it for yourself, big man. It's a certainty that what we'd be handing ourselves over to would be a hangman's noose. I don't intend to go that way. I always knew the trail would end violently for me, so I made up my mind a long time ago it would be in a hail of lead, not at the end of a hang rope."

Everything went quiet for a long beat. The dog continued to whimper.

Faintly, Lone could hear the creak of leather straps and boots scuffing on the rocky ground outside as the soldiers drew closer on each flank. But Scorch was right; they'd hold their fire as long as they believed Lone was still alive on the inside.

Scorch was right, too, about the dust hanging in the air starting to disperse. Visibility in the cramped quarters was slowly but surely beginning to improve. While it was still poor, Lone got down on his hands and knees again and made his way under and up behind one of the fallen beams slanting down from the ruptured ceiling. There, he slowly, quietly replaced the spent cartridges in his Colt, then rose to a crouch and held like that, listening and waiting.

"Well, hell," Kanelly abruptly announced. "I stuck with you this long, Scorch, reckon I'll stick all the way. A hang noose don't sound much to my likin' neither. So how we gonna play it. Go blazin' out the front and take as many of the bastards with us as we can?"

"Not quite. First," Scorch said, "I mean to take care of

the sneaky son who tried to play it so cute by dropping in on us like a spider from the ceiling! We mow him down on our way out the back and *then* we circle around to the front and finish off with the soldiers."

"Ready when you are."

"Okay. Use both barrels of your scattergun to clear us a path, then grab a Winchester and follow me!"

The roar of the scattergun came an instant later and shook the already shredded interior of the cabin. The idea of using it as a path clearer might have been a good one except for two things: In the first place, Lone had gotten himself sufficiently out of the way to avoid any damage from the blasts except for one or two stray pellets grazing the top of his head and a few more pecking at his legs underneath the beam. Secondly, the reverberating booms rattled loose more dust and diminished visibility all over again.

But Bannon and Kanelly went ahead with their charge anyway. Through the freshly boiling, brownish clouds they came. The smaller, hazy outline of Bannon leading the way, the hulking shape of Kanelly close on his heels. Wading forward with a pistol in each hand, Bannon threw shots wildly to one side and then the other. "Show yourself, you goddamn yellow spider!" he bellowed.

Lone waited until he was partly past, then rose up behind the beam and triggered a round into his silhouette. But he misjudged. Bannon was moving too fast and the bullet only clipped the back of his left shoulder, spinning him half around. The scarred man cursed and tried to bring up the six-gun in his right. Before he got a shot off with it, though, an over-anxious Kanelly bumped into him and knocked him off balance. The slug sizzled wide of Lone and the round the former scout simultaneously fired plowed into the left forearm of big Kanelly.

Kanelly spun toward Lone with a roar of pain and rage. Brandishing the Winchester he held on his opposite side like it was as light as a willow switch, he swung it in a high arc and then brought it down in a way meant to split Lone's skull wide open. Jerking his head to one side and ducking at the last second, Lone managed to avoid taking the blow where it had been aimed but instead received a clubbing smash across his shoulders and back that turned him numb clear down to his toes.

Intent on following up, Kanelly lunged over the slant-ed beam and grabbed a handful of Lone's hair in his left hand, showing no regard for the bullet hole in his forearm. Yanking Lone up higher, he tried to bring the muzzle of the Winchester to the side of his face but awkwardly clunked it against the side of the beam before he got it how he wanted it. From somewhere past his shoulder, Bannon said, "Save some for me, Barge."

But Lone wasn't about to hold still for that. Nor was he willing to wait for Kanelly to get his Winchester into position. As Kanelly yanked him higher still, Lone slipped his gun hand up between his chest and the inside of the beam he was being pulled against. He kept right on bringing it up until the Colt's snout was jammed into the soft pad of flesh under the big man's chin. The report was only slightly muffled by the gun being held in that manner. Kanelly's eyes bugged, blood squirted out both ears, and a halo of gore and skull bits formed behind his head as he hurtled back into it.

Seeing this seemed to suddenly change Bannon's mind about having any of it "saved" for him. He wheeled and bolted for the back door.

Lone lost precious seconds getting Kanelly's legs kicked out of the way so he could scramble out from behind the fallen beam. As soon as he was clear, he also raced for the back door. He cursed inwardly as he pushed through the remaining swirls of dust, thinking Bannon had gotten too much of a start on him. But then, just before he reached the open doorway, he heard the thud and thump of entangled bodies combined with muttered curses.

Plunging outside, he saw what was happening. Bannon was struggling with a flailing, obviously injured O'Doul (who, it would turn out later, had fallen and broken both legs attempting to shinny down the rope in order to try and help Lone after he saw the roof collapse). The private was clinging desperately to one of the outlaw's ankles in an effort to restrain him but was getting savagely kicked and pummeled in return. He was about to get even worse as Bannon was bringing the pistol in his right hand to bear just inches from the trooper's head. Lone prevented that from turning deadly with a snap-shot that knocked the gun away and shattered Bannon's hand in the process.

The scarred man staggered and half fell against the face of the cliff. He twisted around to face Lone. "Damn you, first you crippled my shoulder, now my hand! Who the hell are you?"

Baring his teeth in a snarl, Lone said, "I'm payment for you past sins, you scurvy dog. One in particular, a one-legged old man you beat down and left for dead. But you didn't get the job done. Not before enough of him stayed alive to send me after you."

"You're McGantry?"

"To you I'm Payback. Death. Take a good look."

Bannon's lips peeled back. "Do it, then. I been waiting for you my whole life. Let's finally get it over with."

Lone's face went cold, emotionless. He could hear the soldiers coming closer. He took a step toward Bannon and as he did so he reached out and wrapped his free hand around the rope dangling down from above. With the blanket untied from the turns formerly wrapped around it, the rope now reached nearly to the ground. Lone pushed it out ahead and said, "Yeah, Scorch, let's do that. Let's get it over with."

Bannon's eyes turned huge. His chin quivered. "No. You can't be serious. Not that!"

Lone let the rope dangle once more, holstered his Colt, and waded into the outlaw with a flurry of fists. Slashing, hammering, beating him until he was limp, barely able to stand. Next, he turned him around and pressed close behind him. Grabbing the rope again, twirling it, he looped it under Bannon's chin then twisted it tight with his right hand at the back of the bastard's neck. He could hear the soldiers getting closer. Raising his left arm, Lone placed the edge of the forearm on the back of Bannon's head, not far above where he continued to twist the knot in his other hand.

Pressing steadily forward and down with the forearm, he leaned his face close to Bannon's ear on the side that bore the scar and said in an icy whisper, "You don't get to choose, you sonofabitch. You die by the rope!"

EPILOGUE

———

First came the sense of personal satisfaction for having ridden the cold trail until it led to final vengeance for Peg. Then came the gratitude of the army (despite a gentle dig from Trimball about failing to "leave alive at least one") for helping to recover the stolen payroll money. And finally there was a general appreciation from the town for being part of removing the shadow of the Bannon gang that had been cast over it too long.

Lone enjoyed all of this for a while. Maybe even basked in it a bit. Until he remembered fairly soon why he was so good at living up to his name. Being around very many people for very long never suited him, especially not when it involved being at least partially the center of attention. By the time he was done answering enough questions to satisfy local authorities and providing sufficient fodder for a stack of army reports, he was more than ready to move on.

That didn't mean there weren't still those he wanted to spend some more time with before he did, though.

At a local saloon, he shared a drink with Trimball, who was scheduled to soon be departing himself, heading back to Fort Robinson. They toasted old times and fallen comrades and reckoned their paths would likely cross again one of these days.

From there, Lone snuck a bottle into Private O'Doul where he was recuperating from the broken legs he'd suffered after falling in his attempt to climb down the rope dangling over the cliff face.

"This is prime stuff," O'Doul declared, smacking his lips after a big gulp from the bottle, "but don't think it earns you full forgiveness or gettin' me into this fix."

"How am I to blame for landin' you here," Lone protested. "All I asked you to do was stay up top and anchor the rope for me. I never told you to climb down yourself, you stubborn old cuss."

"No, but you made it look so easy the way you done it, slitherin' down like a doggone monkey. I figured I could make it, too, when it looked like you was in trouble."

"Well, I appreciate that," Lone said sincerely. "And you did help plenty, by hangin' on to Bannon long enough for me to catch up with him. I'm just sorry you ended up so busted up as a result."

"Aw hell, some broken bones ain't no big deal. They'll heal. And, in the meantime, I'm on light duty with plenty of pain medicine. Plus now I got this" O'Doul brandished the bottle Lone had brought, "so I got it made. The fix I'm talkin' about bein' in is waitin' to find out if the doggone army is gonna just settle for givin' me some kind of medal or if they're gonna try to promote me again. Every time they waste their time doin' that, I find a way to get bused back quicker than before. I'm gettin' plumb wore out tryin' to convince 'em I'm happy bein' a private and to just leave me be that."

Lone chuckled as he stood to leave. "You keep workin' on 'em, old timer. I'm bettin' you're more stubborn than they are, and you'll get it pounded through their heads eventually."

The old private sighed. "I hope so. In the meantime, Hell For Leather, keep your powder dry and stay off of dilapidated old roofs that can't support your monkey-climbin' ass!"

From there it was all downhill. A sharper drop than from the steepest cliff.

Since the skirmish above Wolverine Wash, Lone had stopped by the Forbes boarding house twice to see Maggie. Both times she'd been asleep and he hadn't wanted to disturb her; and each time the report from a sad-faced Bea was that she didn't seem to be getting any better.

This time it was worse. The doctor was just coming out of her room when Lone got there. The look on his face said it all, even before he put it into words. Maggie wasn't expected to be able to hold on much longer. Some childhood disease, likely rheumatic or scarlet fever, the doctor judged, had left her system quite frail, subject to never reaching a ripe old age. Now pneumonia had set in and settled deep. Whether the dunk in the flooded river and swallowing some of it had been the catalyst or it was just time for her system to start breaking down, the doctor couldn't say. The only thing he *could* say was that she was fading fast and there was nothing more he knew to do for her.

Lone didn't ask if it was okay for him to go in, he just did.

Maggie looked chalky, extremely pale. Her breathing was so shallow Lone could barely perceive it.

He sat on the edge of the bed and took one of her hands in his. It was alarmingly cold.

Her eyes opened. "About time you showed up."

Lone grinned. "I been here before. You were just too lazy to wake up and say hi."

Maggie coughed a little and then said, "So … Did you bring me a pack of cigarillos?"

"Reckon I didn't think of it."

"No, I suppose not. Been too busy being the big hero and all. Leading the cavalry charge up Wolverine Wash. Wiping out the bad hombres single-handed. But no time to bring a few smokes to an old friend."

"I'll go out and get you some now if you want. A whole carton," Lone told her.

Maggie's head rolled weakly back and forth on the pillow. "No. Stay. Your hands are so warm. Just keep holding mine."

"Sure."

"Remember that night on the trail? When we lay together and you held me and kept me warm?" Maggie smiled. "That was nice."

"You bet it was."

Her smile took on a devilish twist. "I'm afraid Bea might have a conniption if you crawled in here with me now."

"Let her. I'll get in there if you want."

"No, that's okay. Stay, though. Just keep holding my hand, won't you?"

"You bet," Lone said again.

And so he did. On into the night.

Bea came in from time to time. Brought Lone a glass of buttermilk and some biscuits, got Maggie to take a few sips of water.

In the deep, quiet shadows, Lone sat listening to Maggie's shallow breathing and occasional bouts of coughing. At one point, after her breathing went totally quiet for several beats and then started up again, Lone whispered hoarsely, "Keep it goin', kid. Show that doc he's wrong."

But he wasn't.

A little while before daybreak her breathing went silent again and this time never restarted.

*****

They buried Maggie the next morning. Not many people were there. Lone; Bea and Frank; three women who apparently knew Maggie from before but never bothered to introduce themselves; the undertaker and his crew; a preacher who delivered a simple but nice sermon.

Lone rode out early that afternoon.

On the way, he stopped again at Maggie's grave when no one else was around. He and Bea had made arrangements for a proper stone marker to be prepared and put up but, for now, the undertaker had erected a temporary wooden cross with her name on it.

Lone dismounted, walked over to the mound of fresh earth, knelt beside it. From his pocket he took a pack of cigarillos he bought earlier when purchasing trail supplies. He stood it on end, tipped it back against the base of the cross to steady it. "Hope it's your brand, Margaret," he whispered.

The he swung back into the saddle and wheeled Ironsides around toward, where?

Back to the Busted Spur Ranch?

Back to look up Tru Min in Fort Collins?

Or maybe it was time for some place he'd never been before?

He tipped back his head, breathed deep a gust of fresh air. Then he nudged his heels lightly against Ironsides' ribs. "Pick a direction, big fella. Take us somewhere."

A Look At: The Bodie Kendrick Bounty Hunter Collection

AWARD-WINNING AUTHOR WAYNE D. DUNDEE SPINS ANOTHER EXCITING YARN OF GRIT, GUN-FIRE, AND GALLANTRY IN THE BODIE KENDRICK BOUNTY HUNTER COLLECTION!

Bounty hunter Bodie Kendrick makes a living bringing in wanted men, sometimes face down across a saddle. In this tenacious, hard-edged collection follow Bodie on his countless journeys through the Old West.

The Bodie Kendrick Bounty Hunter Collection includes: Hard Trail to Socorro, Rio Matanza, Diamond in The Rough, Gunfire Ridge and Wanted: Dead.

AVAILABLE NOW ON AMAZON

About the Author

Wayne D. Dundee is an American author of popular genre fiction. His writing has primarily been detective mysteries (the Joe Hannibal PI series) and Western adventures. To date, he has written four dozen novels and forty-plus short stories, also ranging into horror, fantasy, erotica, and several "house name" books under bylines other than his own.

Dundee was born March 24, 1948, in Freeport, Illinois. He graduated from high school in Clinton, Wisconsin, 1966. Later that same year he married Pamela Daum and they had one daughter, Michelle. For the first fifty years of his life, Dundee lived and worked in the state line area of northern Illinois and southern Wisconsin. During most of that time he was employed by Arnold Engineering/Group Arnold out of Marengo, Illinois, where he worked his way up from factory laborer through several managerial positions. In his spare time, starting in high school, he was always writing. He sold his first short story in 1982.

In 1998, Dundee relocated to Ogallala, Nebraska, where he assumed the general manager position for a small Arnold facility there. The setting and rich history of the area inspired him to turn his efforts more toward the Western genre. In 2009, following the passing of his wife a year earlier, Dundee retired from Arnold and began to concentrate full time on his writing.

Dundee was the founder and original editor of Hardboiled Magazine.

His work in the mystery field has been nominated for an Edgar, an Anthony, and six Shamus Awards from the Private Eye Writers of America.